A
Slight
Trick
of the
Mind

ALSO BY MITCH CULLIN

Whompyjawed

Branches

Tideland

The Cosmology of Bing

*From the Place in the Valley
    Deep in the Forest*

UnderSurface

The Post-War Dream

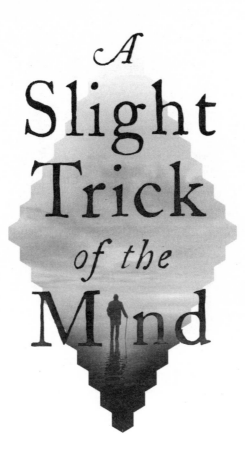

A Slight Trick of the Mind

Mitch Cullin

CANONGATE

Edinburgh · London

Published in Great Britain in 2014 by
Canongate Books Ltd, 14 High Street, Edinburgh EH1 1TE

www.canongate.tv

1

First published in the United States in 2005 by Nan A. Talese,
an imprint of Doubleday, a division of Random House, Inc.

British Library Cataloguing-in-Publication Data
A catalogue record for this book is available on
request from the British Library

ISBN 978 1 78211 330 0

Book design by Caroline Cunningham.

Printed and bound in Great Britain by Clays Ltd, St Ives Plc

For my mother, Charlotte Richardson,

a fan of mysteries and life's scenic routes;

and for the late John Bennett Shaw,

who once left me in charge of his library

I was sure, at least, that I'd finally seen a face which played an essential part in my life, and that it was more human and childlike than in my dream. More than that I didn't know, for it was already gone again.

—Morio Kita, *Ghosts*

What is this strange silent voice that speaks to bees and no one else can hear?

—William Longgood, *The Queen Must Die*

ACKNOWLEDGMENTS

With gratitude to the following for support, information, advice, friendship, and inspiration: Ai, John Barlow, Coates Bateman, Richard E. Bonney, Bradam, Mike and Sarah Brewer, Francine Brody, Joey Burns, Anne Carey and Anthony Bregman and Ted Hope, Neko Case, Peter I. Chang, the Christians (Charise, Craig, Cameron, Caitlin), John Convertino, my father, Charles Cullin, Elise D'Haene, John Dower, Carol Edwards, Demetrios Efstratiou, Todd Field, Mary Gaitskill, Dr. Randy Garland, Howe and Sofie Gelb (www.giantsand.com), Terry Gilliam, Jemma Gomez, the Grandaddy collective, Tony Grisoni, Tom Harmsen, the Haruta family (whose help with this book was most appreciated), lovely Kristin Hersh, Tony Hillerman, Robyn Hitchcock, Sue Hubbell, Michele Hutchison, Reiko Kaigo, Patti Keating, Steve and Jesiah King, Roberto Koshikawa, Ocean Lam, Tom Lavoie, Patty LeMay and Paul Niehaus, Russell Leong, Werner Melzer, John Nichols, Kenzaburo Oe, Hikaru Okuizumi, Dave Oliphant, the Parras (Chay, Mark, Callen), Jill Patterson, Chad and Jodi Piper, Kathy Pories, Andy Quan, Michael Richardson, Charlotte Roybal, Saito Sanki, Daniel Schacter, Marty and Judy Shepard, Peter Steinberg, Nan Talese, Kurt

Wagner and Mary Mancini, Billy Wilder and I. A. L. Diamond, Lulu Wu, and William Wilde Zeitler.

An extra-special nod goes to William S. Baring-Gould and his excellent *Sherlock Holmes of Baker Street* (Bramhall House, 1962), which has been a favorite since childhood and proved invaluable during the writing of this novel. Mycroft's mention of his "old friend Winston" was taken directly from this edition.

PART

I

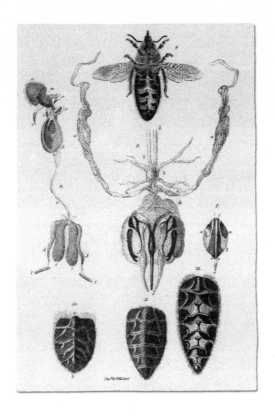

1

U PON ARRIVING from his travels abroad, he entered his stone-built farmhouse on a summer's afternoon, leaving the luggage by the front door for his housekeeper to manage. He then retreated into the library, where he sat quietly, glad to be surrounded by his books and the familiarity of home. For almost two months, he had been away, traveling by military train across India, by Royal Navy ship to Australia, and then finally setting foot on the occupied shores of postwar Japan. Going and returning, the same interminable routes had been taken—usually in the company of rowdy enlisted men, few of whom acknowledged the elderly gentleman dining or sitting beside them (that slow-walking geriatric, searching his pockets for a match he'd never find, chewing relentlessly on an unlit Jamaican cigar). Only on the rare occasions when an informed officer might announce his identity would the ruddy faces gaze with amazement, assessing him in that moment: For while he used two canes, his body remained unbowed, and the passing of years hadn't dimmed his keen gray eyes; his snow-white hair, thick and long, like his beard, was combed straight back in the English fashion.

"Is that true? Are you really him?"

"I am afraid I still hold that distinction."

3

"You are Sherlock Holmes? No, I don't believe it."

"That is quite all right. I scarcely believe it myself."

But at last the journey was completed, though he found it difficult to summon the specifics of his days abroad. Instead, the whole vacation—while filling him like a satisfying meal—felt unfathomable in hindsight, punctuated here and there by brief remembrances that soon became vague impressions and were invariably forgotten again. Even so, he had the immutable rooms of his farmhouse, the rituals of his orderly country life, the reliability of his apiary—these things required no vast, let alone meager, amount of recall; they had simply become ingrained during his decades of isolation. Then there were the bees he tended: The world continued to change, as did he, but they persisted nonetheless. And after his eyes closed and his breaths resonated, it would be a bee that welcomed him home—a worker manifesting in his thoughts, finding him elsewhere, settling on his throat and stinging him.

Of course, when stung by a bee on the throat, he knew it was best to drink salt and water to prevent serious consequences. Naturally, the stinger should be pulled from the skin beforehand, preferably seconds after the poison's instantaneous release. In his forty-four years of beekeeping on the southern slope of the Sussex Downs—living between Seaford and Eastbourne, the closest village being the tiny Cuckmere Haven—he had received exactly 7,816 stings from worker bees (almost always on the hands or face, occasionally on the earlobes or the neck or the throat: the cause and subsequent effects of every single prick dutifully contemplated, and later recorded into one of the many notebook journals he kept in his attic study). These mildly painful experiences, over time, had led him to a variety of remedies, each depending on which parts of his body had been stung and the ultimate depth to which the stinger had gone: salt with cold water, soft soap mixed with salt, then half of a raw onion applied to the irritation; when in extreme discomfort, wet mud or clay sometimes did the trick, as long as it was reapplied hourly, until the swelling was no longer apparent; however, to cure the smart, and also prevent inflammation, dampened tobacco rubbed immediately into the skin seemed the most effective solution.

Yet now—while sitting inside the library and napping in his armchair beside the empty fireplace—he was panicked within his dreaming, unable to recall what needed to be done for this sudden sting upon his Adam's apple. He witnessed himself there, in his dream, standing upright among a stretching field of marigolds and clasping his neck with slender, arthritic fingers. Already the swelling had begun, bulging beneath his hands like a pronounced vein. A paralysis of fear overtook him, and he became stock-still as the swelling grew outward and inward (his fingers parted by the ballooning protuberance, his throat closing in on itself).

And there, too, in that field of marigolds, he saw himself contrasting amid the red and golden yellow beneath him. Naked, with his pale flesh exposed above the flowers, he resembled a brittle skeleton covered by a thin veneer of rice paper. Gone were the vestments of his retirement—the woolens, the tweeds, the reliable clothing he had worn daily since before the Great War, throughout the second Great War, and into his ninety-third year. His flowing hair had been shorn to the scalp, and his beard was reduced to a stubble on his jutting chin and sunken cheeks. The canes that aided his ambling—the very canes placed across his lap inside the library—had vanished as well within his dreaming. But he remained standing, even as his constricting throat blocked passage and his breathing became impossible. Only his lips moved, stammering noiselessly for air. Everything else—his body, the blossoming flowers, the clouds up high—offered no perceptible movement, all of it made static save those quivering lips and a solitary worker bee roaming its busy black legs about a creased forehead.

2

Holmes gasped, waking. His eyelids lifted, and he glanced around the library while clearing his throat. Then he inhaled deeply, noting the slant of waning sunlight coming from a west-facing window: the resulting glow and shadow cast across the polished slats of the floor, creeping like clock hands, just enough to touch the hem of the Persian rug underneath his feet, told him it was precisely 5:18 in the afternoon.

"Have you stirred?" asked Mrs. Munro, his young housekeeper, who stood nearby, her back to him.

"Quite so," he replied, his stare fixing on her slight form—the long hair pushed into a tight bun, the curling dark brown wisps hanging over her slender neck, the straps of her tan apron tied at her rear. From a wicker basket placed on the library table, she took out bundles of correspondence (letters bearing foreign postmarks, small packages, large envelopes), and, as instructed to do once a week, she began sorting them into appropriate stacks based on size.

"You was doing it in your nap, sir. That choking sound—you was doing it, same as before you went. Should I bring water?"

"I don't believe it is required at present," he said, absently clutching both canes.

"Suit yourself, then."

She continued sorting—the letters to the left, the packages in the middle, the larger envelopes on the right. During his absence, the normally sparse table had filled with precarious stacks of communication. He knew there would certainly be gifts, odd items sent from afar. There would be requests for magazine or radio interviews, and there would be pleas for help (a lost pet, a stolen wedding ring, a missing child, an array of other hopeless trifles best left unanswered). Then there were the yet-to-be-published manuscripts: misleading and lurid fictions based on his past exploits, lofty explorations in criminology, galleys of mystery anthologies—along with flattering letters asking for an endorsement, a positive comment for a future dust jacket, or, possibly, an introduction to a text. Rarely did he respond to any of it, and never did he indulge journalists, writers, or publicity seekers.

Still, he usually perused every letter sent, examined the contents of every package delivered. That one day a week—regardless of a season's warmth or chill—he worked at the table while the fireplace blazed, tearing open envelopes, scanning the subject matter before crumpling the paper and throwing it into the flames. The gifts, however, were put aside, set carefully into the wicker basket for Mrs. Munro to give to those who organized charitable works in the town. But if a missive addressed a specific interest, if it avoided servile praise and smartly addressed a mutual fascination with what concerned him most—the undertakings of producing a queen from a worker bee's egg, the health benefits of royal jelly, perhaps a new insight regarding the cultivation of ethnic culinary herbs like prickly ash (nature's far-flung oddities, which, as he believed royal jelly did, could stem the needless atrophy that often beset an elderly body and mind)—then the letter stood a fair chance of being spared incineration; it might find its way into his coat pocket instead, remaining there until he found himself at his attic study desk, his fingers finally retrieving the letter for further consideration. Sometimes these lucky letters beckoned him elsewhere: an herb garden beside a ruined abbey near Worthing, where a strange hybrid of burdock and red dock thrived; a bee farm outside of Dublin, bestowed by chance with a slightly acidic, though not unpalatable, batch of honey as a result of moisture covering the combs one particularly warm season; most recently, Shimonoseki, a Japanese town that offered specialty cuisine made from prickly ash, which, along with a diet of miso paste and fermented soybeans, seemed to afford the locals sustained longevity (the need for documentation and firsthand knowledge of such rare, possibly life-extending nourishment being the chief pursuit of his solitary years).

"You'll live with this mess for an age," said Mrs. Munro, nodding at the mail stacks. After lowering the empty wicker basket to the floor, she turned to him, saying, "There's more, too, you know, out in the front hall closet—them boxes was cluttering up everything."

"Very well, Mrs. Munro," he said sharply, hoping to thwart any elaboration on her part.

"Should I bring the others in? Or should I wait for this bunch to be finished?"

"You can wait."

He glanced at the doorway, indicating with his eyes that he wished for her withdrawal. But she ignored his stare, pausing instead to smooth her apron before continuing: "There's an awful lot—in that hall closet, you know—I can't tell you how much."

"So I have gathered. I think for the moment I will focus on what is here."

"I'd say you've got your hands full, sir. If you're needing help—"

"I can take care of it—thank you."

Intently this time, he gazed at the doorway, inclining his head in its direction.

"Are you hungry?" she asked, tentatively stepping onto the Persian rug and into the sunlight.

A scowl halted her approach, softening a bit as he sighed. "Not in the slightest" was his answer.

"Will you be eating this evening?"

"It is inevitable, I suppose." He briefly envisioned her laboring recklessly in the kitchen, spilling offal on the countertops, or dropping bread crumbs and perfectly good slices of Stilton to the floor. "Are you intent on concocting your unsavory toad-in-the-hole?"

"You told me you didn't like that," she said, sounding surprised.

"I don't, Mrs. Munro, I truly don't—at least not your interpretation of it. Your shepherd's pie, on the other hand, is a rare thing."

Her expression brightened, even as she knitted her brow in contemplation. "Well, let's see, I got leftover beef from the Sunday roast. I could use that—except I know how you prefer the lamb."

"Leftover beef is acceptable."

"Shepherd's pie it is, then," she said, her voice taking on a sudden urgency. "And so you'll know, I've got your bags unpacked. Didn't know what to do with that funny knife you brought, so it's by your pillow. Mind you don't cut yourself."

He sighed with greater effect, shutting his eyes completely, removing her from his sight altogether: "It is called a *kusun-gobu,* my dear, and I appreciate your concern—wouldn't want to be stilettoed in my own bed."

"Who would?"

His right hand fumbled into a coat pocket, his fingers feeling for the remainder of a half-consumed Jamaican. But, to his dismay, he had somehow misplaced the cigar (perhaps lost as he disembarked from the train earlier, as he stooped to retrieve a cane that had slipped from his grasp—possibly the Jamaican had escaped his pocket then, falling to the platform, only to get flattened underfoot). "Maybe," he mumbled, "or maybe—"

He searched another pocket, listening while Mrs. Munro's shoes went from the rug and crossed the slats and moved onward through the doorway (seven steps, enough to take her from the library). His fingers curled around a cylindrical tube (nearly the same length and circumference of the halved Jamaican, although by its weight and firmness, he readily discerned it wasn't the cigar). And when lifting his eyelids, he beheld a clear glass vial sitting upright on his open palm; and peering closer, the sunlight glinting off the metal cap, he studied the two dead honeybees sealed within—one mingling upon the other, their legs intertwined, as if both had succumbed during an intimate embrace.

"Mrs. Munro—"

"Yes?" she replied, about-facing in the corridor and coming back with haste. "What is it?"

"Where is Roger?" he asked, returning the vial to his pocket.

She entered the library, covering the seven steps that had marked her departure. "Beg your pardon?"

"Your boy—Roger—where is he? I haven't seen him about yet."

"But, sir, he carried your bags inside for you, don't you remember? Then you told him to go wait for you at them hives. You said you wanted him there for an inspection."

A confused look spread across his pale, bearded face, and that puzzlement that occupied the moments when he sensed the failing of his own memory also threw its shadow over him (what else was forgotten, what else filtered away like sand seeping between clenched fists, and what exactly was known for sure anymore?), yet he attempted to push his worries aside by inducing a reasonable explanation for what confounded him from time to time.

"Of course, that is right. It was a tiring trip, you see. I haven't slept much. Has he waited long?"

"A good while—didn't take his tea—can't imagine he minds a bit, though. Since you went, he's cared more for them bees than his own mother, I can tell you."

"Is that so?"

"Yes, sadly it is."

"Well, then," he said, situating the canes, "I suppose I won't keep the boy waiting any longer."

Easing from the armchair, the canes bringing him to his feet, he proceeded for the doorway, wordlessly counting each step—one, two, three—while ignoring Mrs. Munro uttering behind him, "Want me at your side, sir? You got it all right, do you?" Four, five, six. He wouldn't conceive of her frowning as he trudged forward, or foresee her spotting his Jamaican seconds after he exited the room (her bending before the armchair, pinching the foul-smelling cigar from the seat cushion, and depositing it in the fireplace). Seven, eight, nine, ten—eleven steps brought him into the corridor: four steps more than it took Mrs. Munro, and two steps more than his average.

Naturally, he concluded when catching his breath at the front door, a degree of sluggishness on his part wasn't unexpected; he had ventured halfway around the world and back, forgoing his usual morning meal of royal jelly spread upon fried bread—the royal jelly, rich in vitamins of the B-complex and containing substantial amounts of sugars, proteins, and certain organic acids, was essential to maintaining his well-being and stamina; without its nourishment, he felt positive, his body had suffered somewhat, as had his retention.

But once outside, his mind was invigorated by the land awash in late-afternoon light. The flora posed no quandary, nor did the shadows hint at the voids where fragments of his memory should reside. Everything there was as it had been for decades—and so, too, was he: strolling effortlessly down the garden pathway, past the wild daffodils and the herb beds, past the deep purple buddleias and the giant thistles curling upward, inhaling all the while; a light breeze rustled the surrounding pines, and he savored the crunching sounds produced on the gravel from his shoes and canes. If he glanced back over his shoulder just now, he knew the farmhouse would be obscured behind four large pines—the front doorway and casements bedecked with climbing roses, the molded hoods above the windows, the exposed brick mullions of the outer walls; most of it barely visible among that dense crisscrossing of branches and pine needles. Ahead, where the path ended, stretched an undivided pasture enriched with a profusion of azaleas, laurel, and rhododendrons, beyond which loomed a cluster of freestanding oaks. And beneath the oaks—arranged on a straight-row plan, two hives to a group—existed his apiary.

Presently, he found himself pacing the beeyard as young Roger—eager to impress him with how well the bees had been tended in his absence, roving now from hive to hive without a veil and with sleeves rolled high—explained that after the swarm had been settled in early April, only a few days prior to Holmes's leaving for Japan, they had since fully drawn out the foundation wax within the frames, built honeycombs, and filled each hexagonal cell. In fact, to his delight, the boy had already reduced the number of frames to nine per hive, thereby allowing plenty of space for the bees to thrive.

"Excellent," Holmes said. "You have summered these creatures admirably, Roger. I am very pleased by your diligence here." Then, rewarding the boy, he removed the vial from his pocket, presenting it between a crooked finger and a thumb. "This was meant for you," he said, watching as Roger accepted the container and gazed at its contents with mild wonder. "*Apis cerana japonica*—or perhaps we will simply call them Japanese honeybees. How's that?"

"Thank you, sir."

The boy gave him a smile, and, gazing into Roger's perfect blue eyes, lightly patting the boy's mess of blond hair, Holmes smiled in turn. Afterward, they faced the hives together, saying nothing for a while. Silence like this, in the beeyard, never failed to please him wholly; from the way Roger stood easily beside him, he believed the boy shared an equal satisfaction. And while he rarely enjoyed the company of children, it was difficult avoiding the paternal stirrings he harbored for Mrs. Munro's son (how, he had often pondered, could that meandering woman have borne such a promising offspring?). But even at his advanced age, he found it impossible to express his true affections, especially toward a fourteen-year-old whose father had been among the British army casualties in the Balkans and whose presence, he suspected, Roger sorely missed. In any case, it was always wise to maintain emotional self-restraint when engaging housekeepers and their kin—it was, no doubt, enough just to stand with the boy as their mutual stillness hopefully spoke volumes, as their eyes surveyed the hives and studied the swaying oak branches and contemplated the subtle shifting of the afternoon into the evening.

Soon, Mrs. Munro called from the garden pathway, beckoning for Roger's assistance in the kitchen. Then, reluctantly, he and the boy headed across the pasture, doing so at their leisure, stopping to observe a blue butterfly fluttering around the fragrant azaleas. Moments before dusk's descent, they entered the garden, the boy's hand gently gripping his elbow—that same hand guiding him onward through the farmhouse door, staying upon him until he had safely mounted the stairs and gone into his attic study (navigating the stairs being hardly a difficult undertaking, though he felt grateful whenever Roger steadied him like a human crutch).

"Should I fetch you when supper's ready?"

"Please, if you would."

"Yes, sir."

So at his desk he sat, waiting for the boy to aid him again, to help him down the stairs. For a while, he busied himself, examining notes he had written prior to his trip, cryptic messages scrawled on torn bits of paper—*levulose predominates, more soluble than dextrose*—the meanings of which eluded him. He glanced around, realizing Mrs. Munro had taken liberties in his absence. The books he had scattered about the floor were now stacked, the floor swept, but—as he had expressly instructed—not a thing had been dusted. Becoming increasingly restless for tobacco, he shifted notebooks and opened drawers, hoping to find a Jamaican or at least a cigarette. After the hunt proved futile, he resigned himself with favored correspondence, reaching for one of the many letters sent by Mr. Tamiki Umezaki weeks before he had embarked on his trip abroad: *Dear Sir, I'm extremely gratified that my invitation was received with serious interest, and that you have decided to be my guest here in Kobe. Needless to say, I look forward to showing you the many temple gardens in this region of Japan, as well as—*

This, too, proved elusive: No sooner had he begun reading than his eyelids closed and his chin gradually sagged toward his chest. Then sleeping, he wouldn't feel the letter slide through his fingers, or hear the faint choking emanating from his throat. And upon waking, he wouldn't recall the field of marigolds where he had stood, nor would he remember the dream which had placed him there again. Instead, startled to find Roger suddenly leaning over him, he would clear his throat and stare at the boy's vexed face and rasp with uncertainty, "Was I asleep?"

The boy nodded.

"I see—I see—"

"Your supper will be served soon."

"Yes, my supper will be served soon," he muttered, readying his canes.

As before, Roger gingerly assisted Holmes, helping him from the chair, sticking close to him when they exited the study; the boy traveled with him along the corridor, then down the stairs, then into the dining room, where, at last slipping past Roger's light grasp, he went forward on his own, moving toward the large Victorian golden oak table and the single place setting that Mrs. Munro had laid for him.

"After I'm finished here," Holmes said, addressing the boy without turning, "I would very much like to discuss the business of the apiary with you. I wish for you to relate all which has transpired there in my absence. I trust you can offer a detailed and accurate report."

"I believe so," the boy responded, watching from the doorway as Holmes propped his canes against the table before seating himself.

"Very well, then," Holmes finally said, staring across the room to where Roger stood. "Let us reconvene at the library in an hour's time, shall we? Providing, of course, that your mother's shepherd's pie doesn't finish me off."

"Yes, sir."

Holmes reached for the folded napkin, shaking it open and tucking a corner underneath his collar. Sitting upright in the chair, he took a moment to align the flatware, arranging it neatly. Then he sighed through his nostrils, resting his hands evenly on either side of the empty plate: "Where is that woman?"

"I'm coming," Mrs. Munro suddenly called. She promptly appeared behind Roger, holding a dinner tray that steamed with her cooking. "Move aside, son," she told the boy. "You're not helping nobody like that."

"Sorry," Roger said, shifting his slender body so that she could gain entrance. And once his mother had rushed by, hurrying to the table, he slowly took a step backward—and another, and another— until he had removed himself from the dining room. However, there would be no more loitering about on his part; otherwise, he knew, his mother might send him home or, at the very least, order him into the kitchen for cleanup duty. Avoiding that eventuality, he made his escape quietly enough, doing so while she served Holmes, stealing away before she could leave the dining room and summon him by name.

But the boy didn't head outside, fleeing toward the beeyard like his mother might expect—nor did he go inside the library and prepare for Holmes's questions concerning the apiary. Instead, he crept back upstairs, entering that one room in which only Holmes was allowed to sequester himself: the attic study. In truth, during the weeks that Holmes was traveling abroad, Roger had spent long hours exploring the study—initially taking various old books, dusty monographs, and scientific journals off the shelves, perusing them as he sat at the desk. When his curiosity had been satisfied, he had carefully placed them again on the shelves, making sure they looked untouched. On occasion, he had even pretended that he was Holmes, reclining in the desk chair with his fingertips pressed together, gazing at the window, and inhaling imaginary smoke.

Naturally, his mother was oblivious to his trespassing, for if she had found out, he would have been banished from the house altogether. Yet the more he explored the study (tentatively at first, his hands kept in his pockets), the more daring he became—peeking inside drawers, shaking letters from already-opened envelopes, respectfully holding the pen and scissors and magnifying glass that Holmes had used on a regular basis. Later on, he had begun sifting through the stacks of handwritten pages upon the desktop, mindful not to leave any identifying marks on the pages while, at the same time, trying to decipher Holmes's notes and incomplete paragraphs; except most of what was read was lost on the boy—either due to the nature of Holmes's often nonsensical scribbling or as a result of the subject matter being somewhat oblique and clinical. Still, he had studied every page, wishing to learn something unique or revealing about the famous man who now reigned over the apiary.

Roger would, in fact, discover little that shed new light on Holmes. The man's world, it seemed, was one of hard evidence and uncontestable facts, detailed observations on external matters, with rarely a sentence of contemplation pertaining to himself. Yet among the many piles of random notes and writings, buried beneath it all as if hidden, the boy had eventually come across an item of true interest—a short unfinished manuscript entitled "The Glass Armonicist," the sheaf of pages kept together by a rubber band. As opposed to Holmes's other writings on the desk, this manuscript, the boy had immediately noticed, had been composed with great care: The words were easy to distinguish, nothing had been scratched out, and nothing was crammed into the margins or obscured by droplets of ink. What he then read had held his attention—for it was accessible and somewhat personal in nature, recounting an earlier time in Holmes's life. But much to Roger's chagrin, the manuscript ended abruptly after only two chapters, leaving its conclusion a mystery. Even so, the boy would dig it out again and again, rereading the text with a hope that he might gather some insight that had previously been missed.

And now, just as during those weeks when Holmes had been gone, Roger sat nervously at the study desk, methodically extracting the manuscript from underneath the organized disorder. Soon the rubber band was set aside, the pages placed near the glow of the table lamp. He studied the manuscript in reverse, briefly scanning the last few pages, while also feeling certain that Holmes had not yet had a chance to continue the text. Then he started at the beginning, bending forward as he read, turning one page over onto another page. If he concentrated without distractions, Roger believed, he could probably get through the first chapter that night. Only when his mother called his name would his head momentarily lift; she was outside, shouting for him from the garden below, searching for him. After her voice faded, he lowered his head once more, reminding himself that he didn't have much time left—in less than an hour, he was expected at the library; before long the manuscript would need to be concealed exactly as it had originally been found. Until then, an index finger slid below Holmes's words, blue eyes blinked repeatedly but remained focused, and lips moved without sound as sentences began conjuring familiar scenes within the boy's mind.

3

THE GLASS ARMONICIST

A Preface

On any given night should a stranger climb the steep stairs which conclude here in this attic, he will wander a few seconds in darkness before reaching the shut door of my study. Yet even in such pitch, a dim hue of light will steal past the closed doorway, just as it does now, and he might stand there in thought, asking himself, What sort of preoccupation keeps a man awake well after midnight? Who is it, exactly, that exists within as the majority of his countrymen slumber? And if the knob is then tried so that his curiosity could be satisfied, he will find the door locked and his entrance forbidden. And if, at last, he resigns an ear against the doorway, a faint scratching sound will likely reach him, signifying the quick movement of pen upon paper, the preceding words already drying as the following symbols arrive watery from the blackest of ink.

But, of course, it is no secret that I remain elusive at this time in my life. Nor has the chronicling of my past exploits, while apparently of infinite fascination to the reading public, ever been a gratifying endeavour for me. During the years in which John was inclined to write about our many experiences together, I regarded his skilful, if somewhat limited, depictions as exceedingly overwrought. At times, I decried his pandering to popular tastes and asked that he be more mindful of facts and figures, especially since my name had become synonymous with his often superficial ruminations. In turn, my old friend and biographer urged me to write an account of my own. "If you imagine I have done an injustice to our cases," I recall him saying on at least one occasion, "I suggest you try it yourself, Sherlock!"

"Perhaps I will," I told him, "and perhaps then you will read an accurate story, one lacking the usual authorial embellishments."

"Best of luck to you there," he scoffed. "You are going to need it."

Yet only retirement afforded me the luxury and inclination finally to engage myself with John's suggestion. The results of which, though hardly impressive, were nonetheless enlightening on a personal level, if simply to show me that even a truthful account must be presented in a manner which should entertain the reader. Realising such an inevitability, I abandoned John's form of storytelling after publishing just two stories, and, in a brief note sent to the good doctor later on,

offered a sincere apology for the derision I had heaped upon his earlier writings. His response was swift and cleverly to the point: *No
apology required, my friend. The royalties absolved you ages ago, and
continue to do so, despite my protests. J. H. W.*

As John is now once again in my thoughts, I would like to take
this opportunity to address a current irritation of mine. It has come
to my attention that my former helpmate has recently been cast in an
unfair light by both dramatists and so-called mystery novelists. These
individuals of dubious repute, whose names are not worthy of mention here, have sought to portray him as little more than an oafish,
blundering fool. Nothing could be further from reality. The very notion that I would burden myself with a slow-witted companion might
be humourous in a theatrical context, but I regard such forms of in-
sinuation as a serious insult to John and to me. It is possible that
some error of representation could have stemmed from his writings,
for he was always generous in overstating my abilities, while, at the
same time, treating his own remarkable characteristics with tremen-
dous modesty. Even so, the man I worked beside displayed a native
shrewdness and an innate cunningness which was invaluable to our
investigations. I do not deny his sporadic inability to grasp an obvious conclusion or to choose the best course of action, but rarely was
he unintelligent in his opinions and conclusions. Above that, it was
my pleasure to spend my younger days in the company of one who
could sense adventure in the most mundane of cases, and who, with
his customary humour, patience, and loyalty, indulged the eccentrici-

ties of a frequently disagreeable friend. Therefore, if the pundits are honestly inclined to pick the most foolish of the pair, then I believe, without question, they should bestow the dishonour upon me alone.

Lastly, it should be noted that the nostalgia which the reading public maintains for my former Baker Street address does not exist in me. I no longer crave the bustle of London streets, nor do I miss navigating through the tangled mires created by the criminally disposed. Moreover, my life here in Sussex has gone beyond pure contentment, and the majority of my waking hours are spent either in the peaceful solitude of my study or amongst the methodical creatures who inhabit my apiary. I will admit, however, that my advanced age has diminished my retentive abilities somewhat, but I am still fairly agile in both body and mind. Almost every week, I manage an early-evening walk down to the beach. In the afternoons, I am usually seen wandering about my garden pathways, where I tend to my herb and flower beds. But as of late, I have been consumed with the significant task of revising the latest edition of my *Practical Handbook of Bee Culture,* while alternately putting the finishing touches on my four volumes of *The Whole Art of Detection.* The latter is a rather tedious, labyrinthine undertaking, although it should stand as an indispensable collection when published.

Nevertheless, I have felt compelled to set my masterwork aside, and, at this moment, I find myself beginning the chore of transferring the past to paper, lest I forget the specifics of a case which, by whatever inexplicable rationale, sprang to mind on this night. It might come about that some of what is to be said or described henceforth is not as it was actually spoken or seen, so I shall apologise beforehand for any licence that is used to fill out the gaps and grey areas of my memory. Yet even if a degree of fiction should prevail in the following events, I guarantee that the overall account—as well as those individuals who were involved in the case—is as accurately rendered as I can make possible.

I.

The Case of Mrs. Ann Keller
of Fortis Grove

I recall that it was in the spring of the year of '02, just one month after Robert Falcon Scott's historic balloon flight in Antarctica, that I received a visit from Mr. Thomas R. Keller, a stooped, narrow-shouldered, well-dressed young man. The good doctor had yet to take up his own rooms on Queen Anne Street, but, as it happened, he was away on holiday, lazing at the seaside with the woman who would soon become the third Mrs. Watson. For the first time in many months, our Baker Street flat was all mine. As was my usual custom, I sat with my back to the window and invited my visitor into the opposite armchair, where—from his vantage point—I became obscured by the brightness of the outside light, and he—from mine—was illuminated with perfect clarity. Initially, Mr. Keller appeared uncomfort-

able in my presence, and he seemed at a loss for words. I made no effort to ease his discomfort, but used his awkward silence instead as
an opportunity to observe him more closely. I believe that it is always
to my advantage to give clients a sense of their own vulnerability, and
so, having reached my conclusions regarding his visit, I was quick to
instil such a feeling in him.

"There is a great deal of concern, I see, about your wife."

"That is correct, sir," he replied, visibly taken aback.

"Still, she is an attentive wife, for the better part. I gather, then, it
is not her fidelity which is at issue."

"Mr. Holmes, how do you know this?"

His squinting and perplexed expression tried to discern me. And
as my client awaited a response, I took it upon myself to ignite one of
John's fine Bradley cigarettes, a fair number of which I had pilfered
from the stash he kept hidden in his top desk drawer. Then having let
the young man dangle long enough, I deliberately exhaled my fumes
into the sun's rays while revealing what was so plainly evident to
my eye.

"When a gentleman enters my room in an apprehensive state, and
when he toys absently with his wedding ring as he sits before me, it
is not hard to imagine the nature of his problem. Your clothes are
new and adequately fashioned, but not professionally tailored. You
have surely noticed a slight unevenness at your cuffs, or, perhaps, the
dark brown thread used at the bottom of your left pants leg, the black
thread upon the right. But have you observed the middle button

there on your shirt which, while very similar in colour and design, is negligibly smaller than the others? This suggests that your wife has done the job for you, and that she has been diligent enough to do her best even when lacking the proper materials. As I have said, she is attentive. Why do I think it is your wife's handiwork? Well, you are a young man of modest means, clearly married, and your card has already shown me that you are a junior accountant at Throckmorton & Finley's. It would be a rare thing to meet a starting accountant with a maid and a housekeeper, would it not?"

"Nothing escapes you, sir."

"I possess no unseen powers, I can assure you, but I have learned to pay attention to what is obvious. Even so, Mr. Keller, you did not call upon me this afternoon to ponder my talents. What event transpired Tuesday last and sent you here from your home at Fortis Grove?"

"This is incredible—" he ejaculated, and again a startled look came over his hollow face.

"My dear fellow, calm yourself. Your personally delivered letter arrived on my door yesterday—a Wednesday—with your return address, yet it was dated by your own hand on Tuesday. No doubt the letter was written in the night; otherwise, you would have delivered it the same day. As you urgently requested this appointment for today—a Thursday—it would seem that something troublesome and pressing had likely occurred on Tuesday afternoon or evening."

"Yes, I wrote the letter on Tuesday night after reaching my end with Madame Schirmer. Not only is she given to meddling in my marriage but she also threatened to have me arrested—"

"To have you arrested, really?"

"Yes, those were her last words to me. She is rather an imposing woman, that Madame Schirmer. A talented musician and teacher by all accounts, but with a manner that is intimidating. I would have summoned a constable myself if it weren't for my dear Ann's sake."

"Ann is your wife, I take it."

"Quite so."

The young man took from his waistcoat a cabinet photograph and, thrusting his hand forwards, offered it for my inspection.

"This is she, Mr. Holmes."

I leaned up in my armchair. With a quick, all-comprehensive glance, I saw the features and figure of a woman of twenty-three—a single cocked eyebrow, a reluctant half smile. Yet the face was stern, giving her the appearance of one who was older than her years.

"Thank you," I said, looking up from the photograph. "She has a most unique quality about her. Now pray explain, from the beginning, what it is exactly that I should know about your wife's relationship with this Madame Schirmer."

Mr. Keller frowned miserably.

"I will tell you what I know," he said, returning the photograph to his waistcoat, "and I hope that you will be able to find reason in it.

You see, since Tuesday my brain has been muddled with this problem. I haven't slept very well the past two days, so please be patient with me if my words are unclear."

"I shall attempt to be as patient as possible."

It was wise of him to forewarn me; for if I had not expected my client's narrative to be, mostly, a rambling and inconsequential statement, then I fear my irritation would have cut him short. As it was, I readied myself by reclining into my armchair while bringing my fingertips together, and tilted my head towards the ceiling so as to listen with the greatest concentration of attention.

"You may begin."

He inhaled deeply before proceeding.

"My wife—Ann—and I were married just over two years ago. She was the only daughter of the late Colonel Bane—her father having died while she was still an infant, killed in Afghanistan during Ayub Khan's uprising—and she was raised by her mother in East Ham, where we met as children. You cannot envision a lovelier girl, Mr. Holmes. Even then I was taken with her, and, in time, we fell in love—the kind of love which is based on friendship and partnership and a desire to share both lives as if they were one. We were married, of course, and soon moved into the house at Fortis Grove. For a while, it seemed that nothing could disrupt the harmony of our little home. I do not exaggerate by saying ours was an ideal, joyful union. Obviously, there came a few rough periods, such as the protracted illness of my own dying father and the unexpected passing of Ann's mother, but we had each other, and that made all the difference. Our happiness increased when we learned of Ann's pregnancy. Then six months later, she had a sudden miscarriage. Five months after that, she was pregnant again, but soon miscarried once more. This second time, there was an excessive amount of bleeding, a haemorrhage, which nearly took her from me. While in hospital, our doctor informed her that she was probably incapable of having a baby and that any further attempts at childbirth would likely kill her. Thereafter, she began to change. These miscarriages upset and occupied her obsessively. At home, she turned somewhat morose, Mr. Holmes, despondent and indifferent, and, she told me, losing our babies was her greatest trauma.

"My antidote for her malaise was the therapeutic activity of a new preoccupation. For mental and emotional reasons alike, I thought she should take up a hobby to fill the void in her life—which I feared was growing deeper. Among my recently deceased father's possessions was an antique glass armonica. It had been a gift from his great-uncle, who, my father claimed, had purchased the instrument from Etienne-Gaspard Robertson, the famous Belgian inventor. In any case, I took the armonica home for Ann, and, with a fair amount of reluctance on her part, she finally agreed to at least give the instrument a try. Our upstairs attic is quite roomy and comfortable—we had once talked of making it the bedroom for our child—and so it was a natural environment for a tiny music den. I even polished and refurbished the armonica's casing, replaced the old spindle so the glasses would nest more securely inside each other, and fixed the foot treadle, which had been damaged years earlier. But what little interest Ann had summoned for the instrument waned almost completely from the start. She didn't like being alone in the attic, and she found it difficult creating music on the armonica. She was also bothered by the curious tones produced by the glasses as her fingers slid across their brims. The resonance of them, she explained, made her all the more sad.

"Except I wouldn't have it. You see, I believed that the advantages of the armonica were in its tones, and that these tones far surpassed the beauty of any other instrument's sound. If performed properly, its music can increase and diminish at ease by just the pressure of fingers, and its wondrous tones can be sustained for any length. No, I wouldn't have it, and I knew that if Ann could only hear the instrument played by another—a person with training and skill—then she might feel differently towards the glasses. As it happened, an associate of mine remembered attending a public recital of Mozart's Adagio and Rondo for Armonica, Flute, Oboe, Viola, and Cello, but he could only say for certain that the performance was held in a small flat above a bookstore on Montague Street, somewhere near the British Museum. Of course, I didn't need a detective to help track down the place, and so, without much footwork, I found myself inside Portman's Booksellers & Map Specialists. The proprietor then directed to me a flight of stairs which led to the very flat where my friend had heard the armonica played. I have since regretted climb-

ing those stairs, Mr. Holmes. At the time, however, I was rather ex-
cited about who might greet me after I knocked on the door."

Mr. Thomas R. Keller looked like the sort of man who it would be
tempting to bully for fun. His boyish manner was sheepish and his
wavering, soft voice carried a slight lisp as he spoke.

"And here, I take it, is where your Madame Schirmer is introduced," I said before lighting up another cigarette.

"Quite. It was she who answered the door—a very solid, manly
woman, although not really corpulent—and while she is German, my
first impression of her was still rather favourable. Without asking my
business, she invited me into her flat. She had me sit in her drawing
room, and I was given tea. I believe she just assumed I was seeking
music instruction from her, for the room itself was lined with instruments of all kinds, including two beautiful, fully restored armonicas.
I knew then that I'd found the right place—I was charmed by
Madame Schirmer's graciousness, her obvious love of the instrument—so I made my reasons for coming there known: I explained
about my wife, the tragedy of the miscarriages, how I had taken the
armonica into our house to help ease Ann's suffering, and how the
enchantment of the glasses had proved elusive to her, et cetera.
Madame Schirmer listened patiently, and when I was finished, she
suggested I bring Ann in for lessons. I couldn't have been more
pleased, Mr. Holmes. All I had wanted, truly, was for Ann to hear the
instrument played well by someone else, so this suggestion of hers ex-

ceeded my hopes. Initially, we agreed on ten lessons—twice a week, Tuesday and Thursday afternoons, full payment in advance—with Madame Schirmer offering a reduced fee because, she told me, my wife's situation was a special one. This was on a Friday. The following Tuesday, Ann would begin her lessons.

"Montague Street isn't terribly far from where I live. Instead of taking a carriage, I decided to walk home and give Ann the good news. But we ended up in a minor row, and I would have cancelled the lessons that day if I hadn't believed they might be beneficial for her. I arrived, to find the house quiet and the curtains drawn. When I called out for Ann, there was no reply. After searching the kitchen and our bedroom, I went into the study, and that's where I discovered her—dressed entirely in black, as if in mourning, with her back turned away from the door, staring idly at a bookcase while remaining perfectly still. The room was so dim, she appeared like a shadow, and when I spoke her name, she did not move to face me. I became very concerned, Mr. Holmes, that her mental state was worsening at an accelerated pace.

" 'You're home already,' said she in a tired voice. 'I wasn't expecting you this soon, Thomas.'

"I explained that I had left work early that afternoon for personal reasons. Then I told her where I'd gone, and I gave her the news about the armonica lessons.

" 'But you shouldn't have done that on my account. Naturally, you have not asked me if I wish to take these lessons.'

" 'I assumed you wouldn't mind. It can only do you good; I'm sure of it. It certainly can't be any worse than staying indoors like this.'

" 'I assume I have no choice.'

"She glanced at me, and in the darkness, I could just barely see her face.

" 'Am I not allowed any say in the matter?' she asked.

" 'Of course, you are, Ann. How can I make you do something you don't wish to do? But will you at least attend one lesson and hear Madame Schirmer play for you? If afterwards you'd rather not continue, I won't insist.'

"This request silenced her for a moment. She slowly pivoted around towards me and then lowered her head to stare at the floor. When she at last looked up, I saw the faint expression of someone who felt defeated by all, and who would acquiesce to anything, regardless of her true feelings.

" 'All right, Thomas,' said she, 'if you want me to take a lesson, I won't fight you on it, but I hope you won't expect much from me. It is you, after all, who loves the sound of the instrument, not I.'

" 'I love you, Ann, and I want you to be happy again. We both deserve at least that.'

" 'Yes, yes, I know. I am awfully troubling of late. I must tell you, however, that I no longer believe that something like happiness exists for me. I fear every individual has an inner life, with its own complications, which sometimes cannot be articulated, regardless of how one might try. So all I ask is that you be tolerant of me, and allow me the time I need to better understand myself. Meanwhile, I shall take that single lesson, Thomas, and I pray my doing so will satisfy me as much as I know it will satisfy you.'

"Fortunately—or unfortunately now—I was proven right, Mr. Holmes. After one lesson from Madame Schirmer, my wife began seeing the armonica in a more favourable light. How delighted I was with her newfound appreciation for the instrument. In fact, it seemed that by her third or fourth lesson she had made a miraculous transformation of spirit. Gone was her morbidity, as well as the listlessness which had often kept her bedridden. I admit it: During those days, I regarded Madame Schirmer as something of a godsend, and my esteem for her was unequalled. So several months later, when my wife asked if the lessons could be increased from one hour to two hours, I agreed without hesitation—especially since she had greatly improved on the glasses. Moreover, I was pleased at the many hours— afternoons and nights, sometimes an entire day—she devoted to mastering the armonica's varying tones. Besides learning Beethoven's 'Melodrama,' she developed an incredible ability to improvise her own pieces. These compositions of hers, however, were the most unusual, melancholic music I have ever heard. They were imbued with a sadness which, as she practised alone in the attic, permeated the entire house."

"This is all very interesting, in a roundabout way," I interjected, stopping his narrative, "but what—if I may kindly press you—are your exact reasons for calling upon me today?"

I could see that my client was dismayed by the sharpness of my interruption. I stared at him in an emphatic fashion, and then I composed myself, with my lids drooping and fingertips once more together, to hear the relevant facts of his problem.

"If you will allow me," he stammered, "I was just getting to that, sir. As I said, since beginning with Madame Schirmer, my wife's state of mind bettered—or at least it appeared so at first. Yet I began to sense a certain detachment in her manner, a kind of absentmindedness and an inability to engage in any prolonged conversation. In short, I soon realised that while Ann seemed to be doing well on the surface, there was something still amiss within her. I believed it was simply her preoccupation with the armonica which had distracted her, and, I hoped, she would eventually come around. But this was not to happen.

"Initially, it was just a few things I noticed—plates waiting to be washed, meals half-cooked or badly burnt, our bed left unmade. Then Ann began spending the majority of her waking hours in the attic. Often I stirred to the sound of glasses being played from above, and when I returned from work, I was welcomed home by the same noise. By that point, I had come to detest those tones which I had once enjoyed. Then, aside from our meals together, there were days that passed when I rarely caught sight of her—she would join me in our bed once I had fallen asleep, leaving at dawn, before I arose—but there was always that music, those plaintive, unending tones. It was enough to drive me mad, Mr. Holmes. The preoccupation had, in effect, become an unhealthy obsession, and I blame Madame Schirmer for that."

"Why is she responsible?" I asked. "Surely she isn't privy to the domestic problems of your household. She is, after all, only the music teacher."

"No, no, she is more than that, sir. She is, I fear, a woman with dangerous beliefs."

" 'Dangerous beliefs'?"

"Yes. They are dangerous to those who are desperately seeking hope of some sort, and who are susceptible to ludicrous falsehoods."

"And your wife falls into such a category of person?"

"I'm sorry to say she does, Mr. Holmes. To a fault, Ann has always been a very sensitive, trusting woman. It's as if she was born to feel and experience the world more acutely than the rest of us. It is both her greatest strength and weakness; if recognised by someone with devious intentions, this delicate quality can be easily exploited—and that's what Madame Schirmer has done. Of course, I didn't realise it for a long while—I was oblivious, in fact, until recently.

"You see, it was a typical evening. As is our custom, Ann and I dined quietly together, and, having swallowed a scant few bites, she promptly excused herself to go practise in the attic—this, too, had become customary. But something else was to occur soon thereafter: For earlier that day at my office—as a gift for resolving some complications with his private account—a client of mine had sent me a precious bottle of Comet wine. My intention was to surprise Ann with the wine during our supper, except, as I mentioned, she went quickly from the table before I could retrieve the bottle. So, instead, I decided to take the wine to her. With the bottle and two wineglasses in hand, I proceeded up the attic stairs. By then, she had already started playing the armonica, and its sound—extremely low tones, monotonous and sustained—transmitted its way into my body.

"When I approached the attic door, the wineglasses I was holding began vibrating, and my ears began to ache. All the same, I could hear well enough. It wasn't a musical piece she was performing, nor was she idly experimenting with the armonica. No, this was a deliberate exercise, sir—an incantation of some unholy fashion. I say *incantation* because of what I then heard next: my wife's voice addressing someone, speaking almost as lowly as the tones she was creating."

"Am I to understand that it wasn't singing you heard?"

"I wish to God it had been, Mr. Holmes. However, I assure you she was talking. Most of her utterances escaped me, but what I did hear was enough to produce a feeling of horror in my mind.

" 'I am here, James,' said she. 'Grace, come to me. I am here. Where are you hiding? I wish to see you again—' "

I raised a hand, silencing him.

"Mr. Keller, my patience is truly a limited resource, and it can withstand just so much. In attempting to put colour and life into your statement, you have continually erred by prolonging the arrival of the very issue which you wish to be resolved. If at all possible, do confine yourself to the notable features, as those will likely be the only things of any use to me."

My client said nothing for a few seconds, knitting his brows and averting his eyes from mine.

"If our child had been born a boy," he finally said, "James was to be his name—or Grace if it had been a girl."

Overcome by strong sentiment, he suddenly paused.

"Tut tut!" I said. "There is no need for displays of emotion at this juncture. Pray continue from where you left off."

He nodded, setting his lips tightly. Then he passed a handkerchief over his brow and turned his gaze to the floor.

"After setting the bottle and wineglasses down, I threw open the door. Startled, she stopped playing at once and looked upon me with wide, dark eyes. The attic was lit by candles, which were placed in a circle around the armonica, casting her in a flickering glow. In that light, with such deathly pale skin, she looked as if she might be a ghost. There was an otherworldly quality about her, Mr. Holmes. But it wasn't merely an effect of the candles which gave me this impression. It was her eyes—the way in which she stared at me, suggesting the absence of something essential, something human. Even as she spoke to me, her voice was hushed and lacked emotion.

" 'What is it, dear?' she asked. 'You frightened me.'

"I went towards her.

" 'Why you are doing this?' I cried. 'Why are you talking as if they are here?'

"She rose slowly from the armonica, and when I went to her, I saw a faint smile upon her white face.

" 'It's all right. Thomas, it's all right now.'

" 'I cannot understand,' I said. 'You were saying the names of our unborn. You spoke as if they were alive and in this very room. What is all this about, Ann? How long has this been going on?'

"She gently took hold of my arm and began moving us both away from the armonica.

" 'I must be alone when I play. Please respect that about me.'

"She was leading me to the door, but I wanted answers.

" 'Look here,' I said. 'I won't leave until you explain yourself. How long has this been going on? I insist. Why are you doing this? Is Madame Schirmer aware of what you are up to?'

"She could no longer meet my eyes. She was like a woman who had been caught in a terrible lie. It was an unexpected and cold answer that finally passed her lips.

" 'Yes,' she said, 'Madame Schirmer is fully aware of what I am doing. She's helping me, Thomas—you saw to it that she would. Good night, dear.' And with that, she shut the door on me and locked it from the inside.

"I was livid, Mr. Holmes. You can imagine that I returned downstairs in an agitated state. My wife's explanation—vague as it was— led me to one conclusion: Madame Schirmer was teaching Ann something other than music lessons, or, at the very least, she was encouraging her to perform that unnatural ritual in the attic. It was a vexing situation, especially if what I believed was correct, and I knew that only from Madame Schirmer herself could the truth be learned. My intention was to go directly to her flat that evening and discuss the matter. However, in an effort to steady my nerves, I drank far too much of the Comet wine, almost the entire bottle. Therefore, I couldn't properly call on her until the following morning. But once I did arrive at her flat, Mr. Holmes, I was as sober and determined as a man could be. Madame Schirmer had hardly opened the door when I confronted her with my concerns.

" 'What rubbish have you been teaching my wife?' I demanded. 'I want you to tell me why she talks to our unborn children—and please don't pretend you know nothing, because Ann has already told me enough.'

"There was an awkward silence, and she was some little time before speaking. Then she asked me inside and sat with me in the drawing room.

" 'Your wife, Herr Keller, is this bothered, unhappy woman,' said she. 'These lessons she has from me, they don't really interest her. She keeps her thoughts always on the babies—no matter what, always the babies—and the babies are the problem, no? But, of course, you want her to play, and she wants the babies—so I do something for both of you, right? And now she plays most beautifully. I think she is happier, don't you?'

" 'I don't understand. What is it that you've done for the both of us?'

" 'It is nothing too difficult, Herr Keller. It is the nature of the glasses, you know—the echoes of the divine harmony—I teach her about this thing.'

"You cannot fathom the nonsense that she went on to explain to me."

"Oh, but I can," I said. "Mr. Keller, I have some basic knowledge regarding the unusual history surrounding this particular instrument. There was a time when certain disturbances were attributed to glass music. This produced panic in the general population of Europe, and led to the armonica's decline in popularity. That is why encountering one—let alone hearing one performed—is a unique opportunity indeed."

"What sort of disturbances?"

"Everything from nerve damage to nagging depression, as well as domestic disputes, premature births, any number of mortal afflictions—even convulsions in household pets. No doubt your Madame Schirmer is familiar with the police decree that once existed in various German states, a proclamation which banned the instrument altogether for the sake of public order and health. Naturally, as your wife's melancholy antedates her usage of the instrument, we can likely rule it out as the source of her troubles.

"However, there is another side to the armonica's story, one which Madame Schirmer was hinting at by mentioning 'the echoes of the divine harmony.' There are some—those adhering to the idealistic musings of men like Franz Mesmer, Benjamin Franklin, and Mozart—

who feel glass music promotes a kind of human harmony. Others hold the fervent belief that listening to the sounds produced on glasses can cure maladies of the blood, while others—and I suspect this Madame Schirmer is among them—maintain that the sharp, penetrating tones travel swiftly from this world into the hereafter. They are of the opinion that an extremely gifted player of glass can readily summon the dead, and that, as a result, the living might again communicate with their departed loved ones. This is what she explained to you, is it not?"

"It is exactly so," my client said with a rather surprised air.

"And at that point you released her from your employment."

"Yes—but how—"

"My boy, it was an inevitability, wasn't it? You believed she was responsible for your wife's occultist behaviour, so the intention, surely, was already there before you went to see her that morning. In any event, if she were still kept in your service, she would hardly have threatened you with arrest. Now please forgive these occasional interruptions. They are needed to expedite what might otherwise prove redundant to my mind. Proceed."

"What else, I ask you, could I have done? I had no other choice. Imagining myself to be fair, I didn't insist she refund the fee for the remaining lessons, nor did she make an offer to do so. Nonetheless, I was shocked at her composure. As I told her that she was no longer needed, she smiled and nodded in agreement.

" 'My dear sir, if you think it is the best for Ann,' said she, 'then I, too, think it is the best for Ann. You are the husband, after all. I wish you both live a long, happy life together.'

"I should have known better than to accept her at her word. When I went from her flat that morning, I believe she knew well enough that Ann was under her influence, and that my wife wasn't about to walk away from her. I realize now that she is a conniving woman of the worst sort. It's all quite evident in hindsight: the way she had initially offered me a discount rate and then—once poor Ann had been taken in by her rubbish—suggested extending the hourly lessons in order to get more from my pocket. I worry, too, that she has designs on the inheritance left by Ann's mother, which— while not greatly substantial—is still a rather tidy sum. I am absolutely positive of this, Mr. Holmes."

"It had not occurred to you at the time?" I asked.

"No," he answered. "My only concern was how Ann might respond to the news. I spent an uneasy day pondering the situation at work and debating the appropriate words with which to tell her. After returning home that evening, I asked Ann into my study, and, as she sat before me, I calmly spoke my mind. I pointed out that she had been neglecting her chores and responsibilities of late, and that her obsession with the armonica—it was the first time I had ever classified it as such—was putting a strain on our marriage. I told her that each of us had certain obligations to the other: Mine was to provide a secure, sound environment for her; hers was to maintain the duties and upkeep of the household for me. Moreover, I said, I was deeply

bothered by what I had discovered going on in the attic, but that I
didn't blame her for mourning the loss of our unborn. Then I discussed my visit with Madame Schirmer. I explained that there would
be no more armonica lessons, and that Madame Schirmer had agreed
that it was probably for the best. I took her hand, and I stared directly
into her inexpressive face.

" 'You are forbidden to see that woman again, Ann,' I said, 'and
tomorrow I am removing the armonica from the house. It is not my
intention to be cruel or unreasonable in this matter, but I need my
wife back. I want you back, Ann. I want us to be like we once were.
We must restore order to our life.'

"She began weeping, but they were tears of remorse and not
anger. I knelt beside her.

" 'Forgive me,' I said, and put my arms around her.

" 'No,' she whispered in my ear, 'it is I who should ask your for-
giveness. I am so confused, Thomas. I feel as if I can do nothing right
anymore, and I don't understand why.'

" 'You mustn't give in to that, Ann. If you will just trust me, you
will see that everything is all right.'

"She promised me then, Mr. Holmes, that she would strive to be a
better wife. And she seemed to honour that promise. In fact, I had
never seen her make such a prompt turnabout before. Of course,
there were moments when I sensed those deeper currents raging quietly within her. On occasion, her mood grew sombre—as if something
oppressive had entered her thoughts—and, for a while at least, she

did devote an inordinate amount of attention to cleaning the attic. But by then the armonica was gone, so I wasn't overly concerned. And why should I have been? The chores were all completed by my return from work. After supper, we enjoyed each other's company, just as we had during better times, sitting together and talking for hours in the front room. It was as if happiness had returned to our home."

"I am delighted for you," I said blandly, lighting my third cigarette. "Yet I remain perplexed as to why you have chosen to consult me. It is an intriguing story on some level, to be sure. But you appear agitated about something else, and I do not understand why. You seem well capable of handling matters for yourself."

"Please, Mr. Holmes, I need your help."

"I can't help you without knowing the true nature of your problem. As it is, there is no puzzle here."

"But my wife keeps disappearing!"

" 'Keeps disappearing'? Am I to gather, then, that she keeps reappearing, as well?"

"Yes."

"How often has this happened?"

"Five times."

"And when did her disappearing act commence?"

"Just over a fortnight ago."

"I see. On a Tuesday, more than likely. Then again on the subsequent Thursday. Speak up if I am mistaken, but the following week it would be the same—and Tuesday last, of course."

"Precisely."

"Excellent. Now we are getting somewhere, Mr. Keller. Clearly, your story concludes at Madame Schirmer's front door, but do tell it to me anyway. There may be one or two particulars that I have yet to glean for myself. If you will be so kind as to begin with the first disappearance, although it really is inaccurate to describe her waywardness as such."

Mr. Keller looked sadly at me. Then he glanced at the window, shaking his head solemnly.

"I have thought too much on this," he remarked. "You see, as my midday tends to be rather busy, the errand boy usually brings in my meal. But my work was less consuming that day, so I decided to go home and join Ann for lunch. When I found her missing, I wasn't terribly concerned. In fact, of late I have encouraged Ann to get out of the house on a regular basis, and, taking my advice, she has begun enjoying afternoon walks. I assumed this was where she had gotten off to, so I wrote her a note and headed to my office."

"And where does she claim these walks lead her?"

"To the butcher, or the marketplace. She has also grown quite fond of the public park at the Physics and Botanical Society, and says she spends hours there reading amongst the flowers."

"Indeed, it would be an ideal place for that sort of leisurely pursuit. Continue with your statement."

"I returned home that evening, only to discover she was still gone. The note I had put on the front door remained, and there wasn't any trace of her having been back. At that point, I became worried. My first thought was to go in search of her, but no sooner had I stepped outside than Ann wandered through the gate. How tired she looked, Mr. Holmes, and the very sight of me seemed to produce some hesitation in her. I asked why she was so late coming in, and she explained that she had fallen asleep at the Physics and Botanical Society. It was an unlikely but hardly implausible answer, and I refrained from pressing her further. Frankly, I was just relieved to have her home again.

"Two days later, however, the same thing occurred. I arrived home and Ann was gone. She arrived shortly thereafter, explaining that she had once more napped underneath a tree in the park. The following week, it happened again, exactly as before—on Tuesdays and Thursdays only. Had the days been different, my doubts would not have arisen so readily, nor would I have sought to verify my suspicions this past Tuesday. Knowing that her previous armonica lessons began at four and concluded at six, I departed work early and took up an inconspicuous position across the street from Portman's. At almost a quarter past four, a vague feeling of relief impressed itself upon me, but just as I was about to vacate my position, I spotted her. She was walking nonchalantly along Montague Street—on the other side of the road—holding high the parasol I had given her for her birthday. My heart sank at that moment, and I continued standing there, not going after her or calling her name, only watching as she shut the parasol and then stepped into Portman's."

"And does your wife make a habit of arriving late for appointments?"

"On the contrary, Mr. Holmes. She believes punctuality is a virtue—until recently, that is."

"I see. Do go on, by all means."

"You might well imagine the upset that finally stirred within me. Seconds later, I was racing up the stairs to Madame Schirmer's flat. Already I could hear Ann playing the armonica—those awful, disagreeable tones of hers—and the very sound of it simply furthered my ire, and I struck with all my fury at the door.

" 'Ann!' I cried. 'Ann!'

"But it wasn't my wife who met me. It was Madame Schirmer. She opened the door and gazed upon me with the most venomous expression I have ever witnessed.

" 'I wish to see my wife, immediately!' I exclaimed. 'I know she is in there!' Just then, the music abruptly ceased from inside her flat.

" 'Go home to see this wife of yours, Herr Keller!' said she in a low voice, stepping forwards and shutting the door behind herself. 'Ann is my student no more!' She kept one hand on the doorknob, and her massive body blocked the doorway, preventing me from rushing past her.

" 'You deceived me,' I told her, speaking loudly enough for Ann to hear me. 'Both of you have, and I won't stand for it! You are a vile, wicked person!'

"Madame Schirmer had grown fierce with anger, and, indeed, I was so angry myself that my own words slurred from me as if I were intoxicated. Looking back, I realise now that my behaviour was somewhat irrational, yet this awful woman had betrayed me and I was fearful for my wife.

" 'I just do my teaching,' she said, 'but you make this trouble for me. You are a drunk man, so you think about this tomorrow and feel mad over yourself! I will talk to you no more, Herr Keller, so you never knock like this on my door again!'

"At this, my temper erupted, Mr. Holmes, and I am afraid that I raised my voice beyond reason.

" 'I know she has been coming here, and I am certain that you are continuing to sway her unduly with your devilish notions! I have no idea what you hope to gain by doing so, but if it is her inheritance you seek, I can assure you that I shall do all that is humanly possible to prevent you from touching it! Let me warn you, Madame Schirmer, that until my wife is free of your influence, you shall be hindered by me at every turn, and I won't allow myself to be fooled any further by whatever you might say to appease me!'

"The woman's hand slid from the knob, her fingers curling into a fist, and she seemed on the verge of striking me. As I have said, she is a large, sturdy German, and I have no doubt that she could easily overtake most men. Nevertheless, she restrained her hostility and said, 'The warning is mine, Herr Keller. You go and never come again.

If you bring the trouble around another time, I can have you arrested!" Then she turned upon her heels and entered her flat, slamming the door on me.

"Badly shaken, I left at once and headed home, with the full intention of castigating Ann upon her return. I was sure she had heard
me arguing with Madame Schirmer, and I was rather upset that she
had remained hiding in that woman's drawing room instead of showing herself. For my part, I had no reason to deny I was spying on her;
she was, by that afternoon, fully aware of that fact. However, to my
complete and thorough amazement, she was already home when I arrived there. And this is what I cannot figure out: It would have been
impossible for her to leave Madame Schirmer's before I did, especially since the flat itself is on the second floor. Yet even if she had
managed it somehow, she would hardly have been able to have my
supper cooking by the time I arrived. I was, and still am, baffled by
how she pulled it off. During our meal, I waited for her to make some
mention of my argument with Madame Schirmer, but she said absolutely nothing about it. And when I asked what she had done that
afternoon, she replied, 'I started a new novel, and earlier I took a brief
stroll through the Physics and Botanical Society's grounds.'

" 'Again? Haven't you tired of it by now?'

" 'How could I? It's such a lovely spot.'

" 'You haven't encountered Madame Schirmer on these strolls of
yours, have you, Ann?'

" 'No, Thomas, of course not.'

"I asked her if she might be mistaken, and, seemingly annoyed by my assertion, she insisted otherwise."

"Then she is lying to you," I said. "Some women have a remarkable talent for making men believe what they already know to be false."

"Mr. Holmes, you do not understand. Ann is incapable of uttering a meaningful lie. It isn't in her nature. And if she had, I would have seen right through her and confronted her at that moment. But, no, she wasn't lying to me—I saw it in her face, and I am convinced she has no knowledge of my row with Madame Schirmer. How that is possible is beyond me. Yet I am positive that she was there—just as I am positive that she has told me the truth—and I am at a loss to make sense of any of it. This is why I urgently wrote to you that night and asked for your advice and assistance."

Such was the puzzle which my client had presented me. Trifling as it was, however, there were several points about it which I found engaging. Drawing then upon my well-established method of logical analysis, I began eliminating rival conclusions, until only one remained, for it seemed very few possibilities could determine the reality of the matter.

"At this book and map shop," I asked, "did you, to the best of your belief, notice any other employees aside from the proprietor?"

"I recall just the old proprietor, no one else. I am of the feeling that he runs the place by himself, although he doesn't appear to be getting on well."

"How so?"

"I meant to say that he appears in poor health. He has an incessant cough, which sounds rather severe, and his eyesight is clearly failing him. When I first went there and asked the whereabouts of Madame Schirmer's flat, he used a magnifying glass to view my face. And this last time, he didn't even seem to realise I had entered his shop."

"Too many years hunched over texts by lamplight, I suspect. All the same—while I am extremely knowledgeable of Montague Street and its environs—I will admit that this particular shop is unfamiliar to me. Is it an amply stocked place, do you know?"

"Indeed I do, Mr. Holmes. It is a small place, mind you—I believe it was a family's household once—but each room contains row upon row of books. The maps, it appears, are kept elsewhere. A sign at the front of the shop requests that customers take their map enquiries to Mr. Portman personally. In fact, I don't remember seeing a single map in the shop."

"By chance, did you ask Mr. Portman—for I assume that is the proprietor's name—if he had seen your wife enter his shop?"

"There was no need to. As I said, the man's eyesight is quite horrid. In any case, I observed her entering the place myself, and my eyesight is more than adequate."

"I do not question your vision, Mr. Keller. Still, the matter itself is unremarkable, yet there are a couple of things which should be settled in person. I will go with you to Montague Street at once."

"At once?"

"It is Thursday afternoon, is it not?" Tugging at my watch chain, I soon determined the time to be approximately half past three. "And I see that if we depart now, we might make it to Portman's before your wife does." Rising to fetch my overcoat, I added, "We must be circumspect from this point on, for we are dealing with the emotional complexities of at least one troubled woman. Let us hope that your wife is as reliable and consistent in her actions as my watch here. Although it may weigh in to our advantage if she chooses once again to be late upon arrival."

Then with some haste, we ventured out from Baker Street, and promptly found ourselves mixing amidst the crowded din of London's busy thoroughfares. And while making our way towards Portman's, I became keenly aware that the problem which Mr. Keller had offered me was, upon pondering its details, of little or no importance. Indeed, the case would surely fail to stir even the literary musings of the good doctor. It was, I realise now, the sort of minor affair which I would have jumped at in my formative years as a consulting detective, but which, by the twilight of my career, I mostly saw fit to send elsewhere; more often than not, I referred these sorts of matters to a choice few of the younger upstarts—usually Seth Weaver, or Trevor of Southwark, or Liz Pinner—all of whom displayed a degree of promise in the consulting detective trade.

I must confess, however, that my own regard for Mr. Keller's dilemma was not found at the conclusion of his long-winded account, but instead rested solely on two unrelated and yet private fascinations: the musical wonderment generated from the ill-famed glass armonica—an instrument which I had often wished to experience for myself—and that alluring, curious face I had glimpsed in the photograph. Suffice it to mention, I can explain the appeal of one better than I can the other, and I have since decided that my short-lived predisposition for the fairer sex was aroused by John's oft-stated belief concerning the health benefits derived from female companionship. Aside from assuming such about those irrational feelings of mine, I remain truly at a loss to make sense of the attraction which was summoned by the common, unremarkable photograph of a married woman.

4

WHEN ASKED by Roger how the two Japanese honeybees came into his possession, Holmes stroked the length of his beard and then—after some thought—mentioned the apiary he had discovered at the center of Tokyo: "Pure luck finding it—would have missed seeing the place if I had gone by car with my luggage, but being cooped up at sea, I needed the exercise."

"Did you walk far?"

"I believe so—yes, in fact, I am certain I did, although I cannot accurately recall the exact distance."

They were in the library, seated across from each other—Holmes reclining with a glass of brandy, Roger leaning forward with the vial of honeybees sandwiched between his clasped hands.

"You see, it was an excellent opportunity for a stroll—the weather was ideal, very pleasant—and I was eager for a look around the city." Holmes's manner was relaxed and effusive, his gaze on the boy as he recounted that morning in Tokyo. He would, of course, omit the embarrassing details—such as the fact he had gotten lost in the Shinjuku business district while searching for the railroad station, and that as he wandered the narrow streets, his normally infallible sense of direction abandoned him altogether. There was no point in telling the boy that he had almost missed the train for the port city of Kobe, or that, until finding relief at the apiary, he had observed the worst aspects of postwar Japanese society: men and women living in makeshift huts and packing crates and corrugated iron lean-tos in the busiest parts of the city; housewives with babies on their backs lined up to purchase rice and sweet potatoes; individuals crammed into packed cars, sitting on coach roofs, clinging to engine cowcatchers; the countless hungry Asian bodies moving past him on the street, those ravenous eyes glancing every so often at the disoriented Englishman walking among them (carried forward by two canes, his muddled expression impossible to read beneath the long hair and beard).

Ultimately, Roger learned only of the encounter with the urban bees. The boy remained thoroughly fascinated by what he heard nonetheless, his blue-eyed stare never once straying from Holmes; his visage passive and accepting, his eyes open wide, Roger's pupils stayed fixed on those venerable, reflective eyes, as though the boy were seeing distant lights shimmering along an opaque horizon, a glimpse of something flickering and alive existing just beyond his reach. And, in turn, the gray eyes that focused sharply on him—piercing and kind at the same instant—endeavored to bridge the lifetime that separated the two of them, attempting to do so as brandy was sipped, and the vial's glass grew warmer against soft palms, and that seasoned, well-lived voice somehow made Roger feel much older and more worldly than his years.

As he journeyed deeper and deeper into Shinjuku, Holmes explained, his attention was drawn to worker bees foraging here and there, buzzing around the limited patches of flowers beneath street trees and in the flowerpots left outside of residences. Then, attempting to pursue the workers' route, sometimes losing track of one but soon spotting another, he was led to an oasis within the city's heart: twenty colonies by his count, each capable of producing a sizable amount of honey every year. What shrewd creatures, he found himself thinking. For surely the foraging sites of the Shinjuku colonies varied from season to season. Perhaps they flew greater distances in September, when flowers were rare, while traveling much less distance while the summer and spring flowers bloomed, for once the cherry blossoms came out in April, they would be hemmed in by a food-rich environment. Better still, he told Roger, the shorter foraging range increased the colonies' foraging efficiency; thus, considering the decreased competition for nectar and pollen from poor urban pollinators like syrphid, flies, butterflies, and beetles—more profitable food sources were evidently located and exploited at a closer range in Tokyo than in the outlying areas.

Yet Roger's initial query regarding the Japanese honeybees was never addressed (the boy being far too polite to press it). Even so, Holmes hadn't forgotten the question. The answer, however, wasn't forthcoming, lingering instead like a name suddenly caught at the tip of the tongue. Yes, he had brought the honeybees back from Japan. Yes, they were intended as a gift for the boy. But the manner in which they had come into Holmes's possession was unclear: maybe at the Tokyo apiary (though highly unlikely, since he was preoccupied with finding the railroad station), or maybe during his travels with Mr. Umezaki (for they had covered a lot of ground once he had arrived in Kobe). This apparent lapse, he feared, was a result of changes in his frontal lobe due to aging—how else could one explain why some memories stayed intact, while others were substantially impaired? Strange, too, that he could recall with complete clarity random moments from his childhood, like the morning he entered the fencing salon of Maître Alphonse Bencin (the wiry Frenchman stroking his bushy military mustache, gazing warily at the tall, lean, shy boy standing before him); whereas now, on occasion, he might check his pocket watch and find it impossible to account for previous hours of his day.

Still, as opposed to whatever knowledge was forfeited, he believed a greater degree of recollection always prevailed. And on subsequent evenings following his return home, he sat at the attic desk and—alternating between work on his unfinished masterwork (*The Whole Art of Detection*) and revising his thirty-seven-year-old *Practical Handbook of Bee Culture* for a new printing from Beach & Thompson—invariably turned his mind toward where he had been. Then it wasn't impossible that he might find himself there, waiting on the railroad platform in Kobe after the long train ride, looking for Mr. Umezaki, glancing at those moving about him—a smattering of American officers and soldiers wandered among Japanese locals, businessmen, families; the cacophony of dissimilar voices and swift footsteps resonated across the platform, heading off into the night.

"Sherlock-san?"

As if materializing from nowhere, a slender man wearing an alpine hat, a white open-necked shirt, shorts, and tennis shoes appeared beside him. In his company was another man, somewhat younger, dressed in exactly the same attire. Both identical men stared at him through wire-rimmed glasses, and the older of the two—possibly in his mid-fifties, Holmes assumed, although it was difficult saying for sure with Asian men—stepped in front of him, bowing; the other promptly did likewise.

"I suspect you must be Mr. Umezaki."

"I am, sir," said the older one, remaining bowed. "Welcome to Japan, and welcome to Kobe. It is our honor to meet you at last. We are also honored to have you as a guest in our home."

And while Mr. Umezaki's letters had revealed a keen grasp of English, Holmes was pleasantly surprised by the man's British-tinged accent, suggesting an extensive education beyond the Land of the Rising Sun. Yet all he really knew of the man was that they shared a passion for prickly ash, or, as it was called in Japanese, *hire sansho*. It was this equal interest that had initiated their lengthy correspondence (Mr. Umezaki having first written after reading a monograph Holmes had published years ago, entitled *The Value of Royal Jelly, with Further Comment Upon the Health Benefits of Prickly Ash*). But because the shrub thrived mostly near the sea of its native Japan, he hadn't actually experienced it firsthand, or tasted the cuisine made with its leaves. Furthermore, during the travels of his youth, the opportunities to visit Japan were never seized. When Mr. Umezaki's invitation came, he realized time might not afford him another chance to explore those glorious gardens he had only read about—or, for once in his life, to behold and sample the unusual sprawling plant that had long fascinated him so, an herb whose qualities he suspected might prolong one's life in the same manner as his beloved royal jelly.

"Let us say a mutual honor, shall we?"

"Yes," said Mr. Umezaki, becoming upright. "Please, sir, let me introduce my brother. This is Hensuiro."

Hensuiro continued bowing, his eyes half-closed: "*Sensei*—hello, you are very great detective, very great—"

"Hensuiro is it?"

"Thank you, *sensei,* thank you—you are very great—"

How puzzling the pair suddenly seemed: One brother spoke English without effort, while the other brother could barely speak the language. Shortly thereafter, as they went from the railroad station, Holmes noticed a peculiar sway in the younger brother's hips— as though the weight of the luggage Hensuiro now toted had somehow given him a feminine swagger—and concluded it was of a natural disposition, rather than an affectation (the luggage, after all, wasn't that heavy). When finally reaching a tram stop, Hensuiro put the bags down and offered up a pack of cigarettes: "*Sensei*—"

"Please," Holmes said, taking a cigarette, bringing it to his lips. Illuminated beneath the streetlight, Hensuiro lit a match, cupping the flame. Leaning toward the match, Holmes saw the delicate hands flecked with red paint, the smooth skin, the trimmed fingernails, which were dirty around the edges (the hands of an artist, he decided, and the fingernails of a painter). Then savoring the cigarette, he peered down the dark street, spotting in the distance the shapes

of people strolling an intimate quarter aglow with neon signs. Somewhere jazz music was playing, faint but lively, and between drags on
the cigarette, he breathed in the fleeting scent of charred meat.

"I imagine you're hungry," said Mr. Umezaki, who, since their
going from the station, had kept silently beside him.

"Indeed," Holmes said. "I am rather tired, as well."

"If that's the case, why don't we get you settled in at the house.
We'll have supper served there tonight, if you'd like."

"An ideal suggestion."

Hensuiro began talking, speaking in Japanese to Mr. Umezaki;
those dainty hands gestured wildly—for a moment touching his
alpine hat, then repeatedly indicating a shape like a small tusk near
his mouth—as a cigarette bounced precariously on his lips. Afterward, Hensuiro smiled broadly, nodding at Holmes, bowing slightly.

"He wonders if you brought your famous hat," said Mr. Umezaki,
looking slightly embarrassed. "The deerstalker, I believe it's called.
And your big pipe—did you bring it along?"

Hensuiro, still nodding, pointed simultaneously at his alpine hat
and his own cigarette.

"No, no," Holmes replied, "I am afraid I never wore a deerstalker,
or smoked the big pipe—mere embellishments by an illustrator, intended to give me distinction, I suppose, and sell magazines. I didn't
get much say in the matter."

"Oh," said Mr. Umezaki, his face registering disillusionment—
the expression quickly mirrored by Hensuiro when the truth was re-
layed (the younger man promptly bowing, seemingly ashamed).

"Really, there is no need for that," said Holmes, who was accus-
tomed to such questions and, truth be known, derived a modicum of
perverse satisfaction in dispelling the myths. "Tell him it is quite all
right, quite all right."

"We had no idea," Mr. Umezaki explained, before calming
Hensuiro.

"Few do," Holmes said lowly, exhaling smoke.

Soon the tram appeared, rattling toward them from where the neon signs glowed, and, as Hensuiro took up the luggage, Holmes found himself gazing down the street once again. "Do you hear music?" he asked Mr. Umezaki.

"Yes. In fact, I hear it often, throughout the night sometimes. There're not many tourist sights in Kobe, so we make up for it in nightlife."

"Is that so," Holmes said, squinting, trying without success for a better glimpse at the bright clubs and bars beyond (the music now becoming lost with the tram's clamorous approach). Eventually, he found himself riding farther from the neon signs, going through a district of closed shops, empty sidewalks, and darkened corners. Seconds later, the tram entered a realm of ruins, of burned-out sites ravaged during the war—a desolate landscape lacking streetlights, the crumbling silhouettes made clear only by the full moon above the city.

Then, as if Kobe's forsaken avenues deepened his own fatigue, Holmes's eyelids shut and his body slumped on the tram seat. The long day had finally consumed him, and, minutes later, what little energy he had left would be used for stirring in his seat and hiking up a hillside street (Hensuiro leading the way, Mr. Umezaki gripping him by the elbow). As his canes tapped along the ground, a warm buffeting wind from the sea pressed over him, carrying with it the essence of salt water. Breathing in the night air, he envisioned Sussex and the farmhouse he'd nicknamed "La Paisible" (*My peaceful place,* he'd once called it in a letter to his brother Mycroft), and the coastline of chalk cliffs visible through the attic study's window. Wishing for sleep, he saw his tidy bedroom at home, his bed with the sheets pulled back.

"Nearly there," said Mr. Umezaki. "You see before you my inheritance."

Ahead, where the street ended, stood an unusual two-story house. Anomalous in a country of traditional *minka* dwellings, Mr. Umezaki's

residence was clearly of the Victorian style—painted red, encircled by
a picket fence, the front yard approximating an English garden.
Whereas blackness loomed behind and around the property, an ornate
cut-glass fixture cast light across the wide porch, presenting the house
like a beacon underneath the night sky. But Holmes was far too exhausted to comment on any of it, even when following Hensuiro into
a hallway lined with impressive displays of Art Nouveau and Art Deco
glass objects.

"We collect Lalique, Tiffany, and Galle, among others," said Mr.
Umezaki, guiding him forward.

"Evidently," Holmes remarked, feigning interest. Thereafter, he
felt ethereal, as if drifting through a tedious dream. In hindsight, he
could recall nothing else of that first evening in Kobe—not the meal
he ate, or the conversation they shared, or being shown to his room.
Nor could he remember meeting the sullen woman known as Maya,
though she had served him supper, had poured his drink, had no
doubt unpacked his luggage.

Yet there she was the next morning, drawing the curtains, waking him. Her presence wasn't startling, and while having been half-
conscious when they'd met previously, he regarded her immediately
as a familiar face, albeit a dour one. Is she Mr. Umezaki's wife?
Holmes wondered. Maybe a housekeeper? Wearing a kimono, her
graying hair done in a more Western fashion, she appeared older than
Hensuiro, but not much older than the refined Umezaki. Still, she
was an unattractive woman, rather homely, with a round head, flat
nose, and eyes slanted into two thin slits, giving her a myopic, mole-
like quality. Without question, he concluded, she must be the housekeeper.

"Good morning," he uttered, watching her from his pillow. She
didn't acknowledge him. Instead, she opened a window, letting the
sea air waft inside. Then she exited the room, promptly entering
again with a tray, upon which steamed a cup of breakfast tea beside
a note written by Mr. Umezaki. Using one of the few Japanese words

he actually knew, he blurted out *"Ohayo"* as she set the tray on the bedside table. Once again, she ignored him, this time going into the adjacent bathroom and running him a bath. He sat up, chagrined, and drank the tea, doing so while reading the note:

> Must do some business.
> Hensuiro awaits downstairs.
> Back before dusk falls.
> Tamiki

"Ohayo," he said to himself, speaking with disappointment and with the concern that his being there had possibly disrupted the household (perhaps the invitation wasn't meant to be accepted, or perhaps Mr. Umezaki was disappointed by the less than vibrant gentleman he had found waiting at the station). He felt relief when Maya had gone from the room, but it was overshadowed by the thought of Hensuiro and an entire day without proper communication, and by the notion of gesticulating whatever was important—food, drink, lavatory, nap. He couldn't explore Kobe alone, lest insulting his host when it was realized he had sneaked out on his own. As he bathed, the rumbling of unease gained momentum. Though worldly by most standards, he had spent almost half his life sequestered on the Sussex Downs, and now he felt ill-equipped to function within such an alien country, especially without a guide who spoke proper English.

But after dressing and meeting Hensuiro downstairs, his worries vanished. "Good more-knee-eng, *sensei,*" Hensuiro stammered, smiling.

"Ohayo."

"Oh, yes, *ohayo*—good, very good."

Then, as Hensuiro repeatedly nodded with approval at his chopsticks abilities, Holmes ate a simple breakfast consisting of green tea and a raw egg stirred into rice. Before midday, they were walking together outside, enjoying a beautiful morning canopied by a clear blue sky. Hensuiro, like young Roger, gripped him at the elbow, casually directing him along, and, having slept so well, invigorated, too, from his bath, he felt as if he were experiencing Japan anew. In daylight, Kobe was entirely different from the desolate place he had viewed through the tram window: The ruined buildings were nowhere in sight; the streets teamed with foot traffic. Vendors occupied the central square, where children ran about. Chatter and boiling water erupted inside a multitude of noodle shops. On the northern hills of the city, he spied an entire neighborhood of Victorian and Gothic homes, which, he suspected, must have originally belonged to foreign traders and diplomats.

"What, if I might ask, does your brother do, Hensuiro?"

"*Sensei*—"

"Your brother—what does he do—his job?"

"This—no—I not understand, just a little understand, not many."

"Thank you, Hensuiro."

"Yes, thank you—thank you very much."

"You are excellent company on this pleasant day, regardless of your deficiencies."

"I think so."

However, as the walk progressed, as they turned corners and crossed busy streets, he began recognizing signs of hunger all around. The shirtless children in the parks didn't run like the other children; rather, they stood inert, as if languishing, their pronounced rib cages framed by bone-defined arms. Men begged in front of the noodle shops, and even those who looked fed—the shopkeepers, the patrons, the couples—wore similar expressions of yearning, although less obvious. Then it seemed to him that the flux of their daily lives masked a noiseless despair: Behind the smiles, the nods, the bows, the general politeness, there lurked something else that had grown malnourished.

5

DURING HIS TRAVELS, every now and then, Holmes would again sense an immense want permeating human existence, the true nature of which he couldn't fully comprehend. And while this ineffable longing had skirted his country life, it still saw fit to visit him on occasion, becoming more and more evident among the strangers who continually trespassed upon his property. In earlier years, the trespassers were usually a mixed assortment of drunken undergraduates wishing to laud him, London investigators seeking help with an unsolved crime, the occasional young men from the Gables—a well-known coaching establishment some half a mile away from Holmes's estate—or holidaying families, there in the hope of catching a glimpse of the famous detective.

"I am sorry," he told them without exception, "but my privacy must be respected. I will ask you to please leave the grounds now."

The Great War brought him some peace, as fewer and fewer people knocked on his door; this occurred, too, while the second Great War raged across Europe. But between both wars, the encroachers returned in force, and the old conglomeration was gradually replaced by another assortment: autograph seekers, journalists, reading groups from London and elsewhere; those gregarious individuals contrasted sharply with the crippled veterans, the contorted bodies confined forever to wheelchairs, the various breathing mutations, or the literal basket cases appearing like cruel gifts on his front steps.

"I am sorry—I truly am—"

What was sought by one group—a conversation, a photograph, a signature—was easy to deny; what was desired by the other, however, was illogical but harder to rebuke—just the laying on of his hands, perhaps a few words whispered like some healing incantation (as if the mysteries of their ailments might at last be solved by him and him alone). Even so, he remained firm with his refusals, often admonishing the caretakers who had inconsiderately pushed the wheelchairs past the NO TRESPASSING signs.

"Please go this instant. Otherwise, I will inform Anderson of the Sussex Constabulary!"

Only recently had he begun to bend his own rules, sitting for a while with a young mother and her infant. She had first been seen by Roger, crouched beside the herb garden, her baby wrapped in a cream-colored shawl and its head cradled at her exposed left breast. As the boy led him to her, Holmes pounded his canes along the pathway, grumbling so she might hear, saying aloud that entry into his gardens was strictly prohibited. Upon seeing her, his anger dissipated, but he hesitated before going any closer. She gazed up at him with wide, sedated pupils. Her dirty face betrayed loss; her unbuttoned yellow blouse, muddied and torn, hinted at the miles she had walked to find him. Then she held the shawl out toward him, offering her infant with soiled hands.

"Get to the house," he ordered Roger in a low voice. "Call Anderson. Tell him it is an emergency. Say that I am waiting in the garden."

"Yes, sir."

He had observed what the boy had not: the tiny corpse held by its mother's trembling hands, its purple cheeks, its blue-black lips, the numerous flies crawling on and encircling the handwoven shawl. Once Roger was on his way, he put the canes aside and, with some effort, sat down by the woman. Again she thrust the shawl toward him, so he gently accepted the bundle, holding the baby against his chest.

By the time Anderson arrived, Holmes had given the infant back to her. For a while, he stood beside the constable there on the pathway, both men watching as the bundle was held at the woman's breast, her fingers repeatedly pressing a nipple against the baby's rigid lips. Coming from the east, ambulance sirens rang out, drawing nearer, eventually ceasing near the gate of the property.

"Do you think it's a kidnapping?" whispered Anderson, stroking his slightly curled mustache, remaining openmouthed after he spoke, his gaze frozen on the woman's chest.

"No," answered Holmes, "I believe it is something far less criminal than that."

"Really," the constable replied, and Holmes detected displeasure in his tone: For a great mystery wasn't presenting itself after all, nor would the constable be involved in working a case with his childhood hero. "So what are your thoughts, then?"

"Look at her hands," Holmes told him. "Look at the dirt and mud underneath her fingernails, on her blouse, on her skin and clothing." She has been in the earth, he figured. She has been digging. "Look at her muddy shoes—fairly new and showing few signs of wear. Still, she has walked a distance, but no further than Seaford. Look at her face and you'll recognize the grief of a mother who has lost her newborn. Contact your associates in Seaford. Ask about a child's grave that was dug up during the night, the body taken—and ask if the child's mother has gone missing. Ask if the infant's name might be Jeffrey."

Anderson looked swiftly at Holmes, reacting as if he'd been slapped. "How do you know this?"

Holmes shrugged ruefully. "I don't—at least not for certain."

Mrs. Munro's voice carried from the farmhouse yard, instructing the ambulance men where to go.

Appearing forlorn in his uniform, Anderson cocked an eyebrow while tugging his mustache. He said, "Why'd she come here? Why'd she come to you?"

A cloud passed over the sun, casting a long shadow across the gardens.

"Hope, I suspect," said Holmes. "It seems I am known for discovering answers when events appear desperate. Beyond that, I wouldn't care to speculate."

"And what about it being called Jeffrey?"

Holmes explained: He had asked the infant's name while holding the shawl. "Jeffrey," he thought he'd heard her say. He asked how old. She stared miserably at the ground, saying nothing. He asked where the child had been born. She said nothing. Had she traveled far?

"Seaford," she had muttered, brushing a fly off her forehead.

"Are you hungry?"

Nothing.

"Would you like something to eat, dear?"

Nothing.

"I believe you must be quite famished. I believe you need water."

"I believe it's a stupid world," she finally said, reaching for the shawl.

And if he had then addressed her forthrightly, he would have been inclined to agree.

6

I N K O B E A N D , subsequently, on their travels westward, Mr.
Umezaki sometimes inquired about England, asking—among
other things—if Holmes had seen the Bard's birthplace in Stratford-
upon-Avon, or strolled within the mysterious Stonehenge circle,
or visited Cornwall's scenic coastline, which had inspired so many
artists over the centuries.

"Indeed," he usually answered before elaborating.

And had the great Anglican cities survived the devastation of the
war? Had the spirit of the English people remained intact throughout the Luftwaffe's aerial bombings?

"For the most part, yes. We have an indomitable character, you
know."

"Victory tends to underscore that, wouldn't you say?"

"I suppose so."

Then returning home, it was Roger posing questions about Japan
(although asking in a less specific manner than Mr. Umezaki had).
Following an afternoon of removing overgrown grass from around
the hives, of pulling weeds so that the bees could come and go without obstruction, the boy escorted him to the nearby cliffs, where,
minding every step, they proceeded down a long, steep path that

eventually ended at the beach below. There, in either direction, stretched miles of scree and shingles, interrupted only by shallow inlets and tide pools (filled afresh with each flow, existing as ideal watering places). In the distance, on a clear day, the little cove that held the village of Cuckmere Haven was seen.

Presently, their clothing lay neatly on the rocks, and both he and the boy eased into a favored tide pool, reclining while the water rose to their chests. Once settled—their shoulders just above the currents, the afternoon sunlight shimmering off the sea beyond—Roger glanced toward him and, shadowing his eyes with a hand, said, "Sir, does the Japanese ocean look anything like the Channel?"

"Somewhat. At least what I saw of it—salt water is salt water, is it not?"

"Were there lots of ships?"

Shielding his own eyes, Holmes realized that the boy was now staring at him inquisitively. "I believe so," he said, unsure if the numerous tankers, tugboats, and barges drifting through his memory had been seen in a Japanese or an Australian port. "It is an island nation, after all," he reasoned. "They, like us, are never far from the sea."

The boy let his feet float up, absently wiggling his toes in the surface foam.

"Is it true? Are they a little people?"

"It's quite true, I'm afraid."

"Like dwarves?"

"Taller than that. On average about your height, my boy."

Roger's feet sank, the wiggling toes disappearing.

"Are they yellow?"

"What do you mean exactly? Skin or constitution?"

"Their skin—is it yellow? Do they have big teeth, like rabbits?"

"Darker than yellow." He pressed a fingertip into Roger's tanned shoulder. "Closer to this color, you see?"

"What about their teeth?"

He laughed and said, "I cannot say with certainty. On the other hand, I surely would recall a predominance of lagomorph incisors, so I suspect it is safe to say they have teeth much like yours and mine."

"Oh," Roger muttered, but he said no more for the moment.

The gift of the honeybees, Holmes figured, had sparked the boy's curiosity: those two creatures in the vial, similar to yet different from the English honeybees, suggesting a parallel world, where everything was comparable but not quite the same.

Only later, when they began climbing the steep path, did the questioning resume. Now the boy wanted to know if the Japanese cities still bore traces of Allied bombing. "In places," Holmes answered, aware of Roger's preoccupation with airplanes and attack and fiery death—as if some resolution regarding the father's untimely fate might be found in the sordid details of war.

"Did you see where the bomb got dropped?"

They had stopped to rest, sitting for a while on a bench that marked the path's middle point. Stretching his long legs toward the cliff edge, Holmes gazed out at the Channel, thinking, the Bomb. Not the incendiary variety, nor the antipersonnel model, but the atomic kind.

"They call it *pika-don*," he told Roger. "It means 'flash-bang'— and yes, I saw where one was dropped."

"Did everyone look ill?"

Holmes continued to stare at the sea, observing the gray water now reddened by the sun's descent. He said, "No, most didn't look visibly ill. However, quite a few seemed so—it is a difficult thing to describe, Roger."

"Oh," the boy replied, looking at him with a slightly puzzled expression, but he said nothing more.

Holmes found himself considering that most unfortunate event in the life of a hive: the sudden loss of the queen, when no resources were available from which to raise a new one. Yet how could he explain the deeper illness of unexpressed desolation, that imprecise pall harbored en masse by ordinary Japanese? It was hardly perceptible upon such reticent people, but it was always there—roaming the Tokyo and Kobe streets, visible somehow on the solemn young faces of repatriated men, within the vacant stares of malnourished mothers and children, and hinted at by a popular saying from the previous year. *"Kamikaze mo fuki sokone."*

On his second evening with his Kobe hosts, while sharing sake inside a cramped drinking establishment, Mr. Umezaki translated the saying: " 'The Divine Wind didn't blow'—that's basically what it means." He had said this after a drunken patron—dressed shabbily in former military attire, staggering wildly from table to table—was escorted outside, yelling as he went, *"Kamikaze mo fuki sokone! Kamikaze mo fuki sokone! Kamikaze mo fuki sokone!"*

As it happened, just prior to the drunk's outburst, they had been discussing postsurrender Japan. Or rather, Mr. Umezaki, straying abruptly from a conversation regarding their travel itinerary, asked Holmes if he, too, found the Allied occupation rhetoric of freedom and democracy at odds with the continual suppression of Japanese poets, writers, and artists. "Don't you find it somewhat baffling that many are starving, yet we aren't allowed to criticize the occupation forces openly? For that matter, we can't grieve as a whole for our losses and mourn together as a nation, or even create public eulogies for our dead, in case such an evocation is perceived as a promotion of militaristic spirit."

"Frankly," Holmes admitted, bringing his cup to his lips, "I know little about it. I am sorry."

"No, please, I'm sorry for mentioning it." Mr. Umezaki's already-flushed face burned brighter, then slackened with fatigue and a presentiment of intoxication. "Anyway, where were we?"

"Hiroshima, I believe."

"That's right, you were interested in visiting Hiroshima—"

"Kamikaze mo fuki sokone!" the drunk began yelling, startling everyone except Mr. Umezaki. *"Kamikaze mo fuki sokone!"*

Unfazed, Mr. Umezaki poured himself another drink, and one for Hensuiro, who had repeatedly downed his sake in one swallow. Following the drunk's shouting and prompt removal, Holmes found himself studying Mr. Umezaki, and Mr. Umezaki—his demeanor becoming increasingly somber with each drink—stared thoughtfully at the tabletop, the downcast glower on his face protruding like the pout of a scolded child (an expression appropriated by Hensuiro, whose normally cheerful appearance took on a grim, withdrawn look). At last, Mr. Umezaki glanced toward him. "So, where were we again? Ah, yes, our journey west—and you wanted to know if Hiroshima might be on our way. Well, I can tell you it is."

"I very much wish to see the place, if you are agreeable."

"Certainly, I'd like to see it, too. To be honest, I haven't been there since before the war—other than passing through by train."

But Holmes detected apprehension in Mr. Umezaki's voice, or possibly, he second-guessed, it was simply weariness saturating his host's tone. After all, the Mr. Umezaki who had greeted him that afternoon appeared run-down from his business dealings elsewhere, as opposed to the attentive and affable fellow who had met him at the railroad station the day before. Now, having taken a satisfying nap after exploring the city alongside Hensuiro, it was his turn to be wide-awake during the evening, whereas Mr. Umezaki conveyed a heavy and deep-rooted exhaustion (a lassitude made less burdensome with a steady intake of alcohol and nicotine).

Holmes had recognized the signs earlier that day, when opening the door to Mr. Umezaki's study, finding him standing there beside his desk, lost in thought, a thumb and index finger pressing against his eyelids, an unbound manuscript held loosely at his side. Because Mr. Umezaki still wore his hat and jacket, it was evident he had just come home.

"Pardon me," Holmes said, feeling suddenly intrusive. However, he had stirred within a silent house, where the doors were shut and no one else was seen or heard. Still, without intending to, he had violated his own code: Throughout his life, he had believed a man's study was hallowed ground, a sanctuary for reflection and a retreat from the outside world, meant for important work, or, at least, the private communion with the written texts of others. Therefore, the attic study of his Sussex home was the room he cherished the most, and while he never made it explicitly known, both Mrs. Munro and Roger understood they wouldn't be welcomed inside if the door was closed. "I didn't mean to interrupt you. It appears my advancing years usher me into rooms for no obvious reason."

Mr. Umezaki glanced up, showing little surprise, and said, "On the contrary, I'm glad you're here. Come in, please."

"Really, I'll not bother you any further."

"Actually, I thought you were asleep. Otherwise, I'd have invited you to join me. So do come in, have a look around. Tell me what you think of my library."

"Only if you insist," Holmes said, advancing toward the teak bookshelves, which covered an entire wall, noticing Mr. Umezaki's activities while going forward: the manuscript being placed at the center of the uncluttered desk, the hat then removed and set carefully over it.

"I apologize about my business obligations, but I trust my comrade took good care of you."

"Oh, yes, we had a pleasant day together—language obstacles aside."

Just then, Maya called from down the hallway, her voice sounding somewhat irritated.

"Excuse me," Mr. Umezaki said. "I won't be a minute."

"Take your time," Holmes said, now standing before the extensive rows of books.

Again, Maya called out, and Mr. Umezaki walked hurriedly in her direction, forgetting to close the door as he went. For a few moments after he had gone, Holmes gazed at the books, his eyes roving from shelf to shelf. Most of the books were fine hardbound editions, the majority of which had Japanese characters on the spines. Even so, one shelf held nothing but Western works, organized thoughtfully into separate categories—American literature, English literature, plays, a large portion devoted to poetry (Whitman, Pound, Yeats, various Oxford textbooks regarding the Romantic poets). The shelf below it was devoted almost exclusively to Karl Marx, although several volumes by Sigmund Freud were squeezed in at the end.

As Holmes turned and looked around, he saw that Mr. Umezaki's study, though small, was arranged efficiently: a reading chair, a floor lamp, a few photographs, and what appeared to be a framed university diploma hung high behind the desk. Then he caught the incomprehensible banter of Mr. Umezaki and Maya, their discussion fluctuating from heated debate to sudden quiet, and he was about to go and peep into the hallway, when Mr. Umezaki returned, saying, "We've had some confusion regarding the supper menu, so I fear we'll be eating later than usual. I hope you don't mind."

"Not at all."

"In the meantime, I believe I would like a drink. There's a bar not too far, rather comfortable, probably as good a place as any to discuss our travel schedule—if that's all right."

"Sounds delightful."

So out they'd gone for a while, walking leisurely to the cramped drinking establishment as the sky darkened, staying at the bar much longer than was intended, then headed back only after the drinking crowd grew too large and too loud. Then it was a simple supper consisting of fish, some vegetables, steamed rice, and miso soup—each dish served unceremoniously in the dining room by Maya, who refused any offer to join them. But the joints of Holmes's fingers ached from working the chopsticks, and no sooner had he lowered them than Mr. Umezaki suggested they retire to his study. "If you will, there's something I wish to show you." And with that, the two went from the table, going together into the hallway, leaving Hensuiro alone with what remained of their meal.

His recollection of that night in Mr. Umezaki's study remained quite vivid, even though, at the time, the alcohol and the food had tired him. Yet, as opposed to earlier, Mr. Umezaki was the enlivened one, smiling as he offered Holmes his reading chair, then producing a lit match before a Jamaican could be retrieved. Once comfortable in the chair—the canes across his lap, the cigar burning at his lips—Holmes watched as Mr. Umezaki opened a desk drawer and removed a slender hardbound book from within.

"What do you make of this?" Mr. Umezaki asked, coming forward, the book held out for him to take.

"A Russian edition," Holmes said, accepting the volume, immediately noting the imperial crests adorning the otherwise bare cover and spine. With further inspection—his fingers touching the reddish binding and gold inlay around the crests, his eyes momentarily scanning the pages—he concluded it was an extremely unique translation of a very popular novel. *"The Hound of the Baskervilles*—a one-off printing, I suspect."

"Yes," said Mr. Umezaki, sounding pleased. "Fashioned exclusively for the Czar's private collection. I understand he was a great follower of your stories."

"Was he?" said Holmes, handing the book back.

"Very much so, yes," Mr. Umezaki replied, crossing back over to his desk. Depositing the rare volume inside the drawer, he added, "As you can imagine, this is the most valuable item in my library—though well worth the price I paid for it."

"Indeed."

"You must own a good many books regarding your adventures—different printings, numerous translations, various editions."

"Actually, I possess none—not even the flimsy paperbacks. Truthfully, I've only read a handful of the stories—and that was many years ago. I couldn't instill in John the basic difference between an induction and a deduction, so I stopped trying, and I also stopped reading his fabricated versions of the truth, because the in-

accuracies drove me mad. You know, I never did call him Watson—
he was John, simply John. But he really was a skilled writer, mind
you—very imaginative, better with fiction than fact, I daresay."

Mr. Umezaki's gaze was on him, and there was a touch of bewilderment in his eyes. "How can that be?" he asked, lowering himself
to his desk seat.

Holmes shrugged, exhaling smoke, saying, "Simply the truth, I
am afraid."

But it was what occurred thereafter that remained clear in his
mind. For Mr. Umezaki—still flushed from drinking, drawing a
long breath, as though he, too, were smoking—paused thoughtfully
before asserting himself. Then grinning, he confessed he wasn't too
surprised to learn the stories weren't entirely accurate. "Your ability—or perhaps I should say the character's ability—to draw definitive conclusions from often tenuous observations always struck me as
fanciful, don't you think? I mean, you don't seem anything like the
person I've read so much about. How do I say it? You seem less ex-
travagant, less colorful."

Holmes sighed reproachfully, briefly waving a hand, as if clearing
the smoke. "Well, you are referring to the arrogance of my youth. I
am an old man now, and I have been retired since you were but a
child. It is rather shameful in hindsight, all the vain presumption of
my younger self. It really is. You know, we bungled a number of important cases—regrettably. Of course, who wants to read about the
failures? I certainly don't. But I can tell you this with a fair degree
of certainty: The successes may have been exaggerated; however,
those fanciful conclusions you mention were not."

"Really?" Mr. Umezaki paused again, taking another long
breath. Then he said, "I wonder what you know of me. Or is your talent retired, as well?"

It was possible, Holmes considered upon reflection, that Mr.
Umezaki did not use those exact words. Nevertheless, he remembered tilting his head back, bringing his stare to the ceiling. With

the cigar fuming in one hand, he began slowly at first: "What do I know of you? Well, your command of English suggests a formal education abroad—from the old Oxford editions on the bookshelves, I would say you studied in England, and the diploma on the wall there should prove me correct. I submit that your father was a diplomat with strong preferences for all things Western. Why else would he favor such a nontraditional dwelling as this—your inheritance, if memory serves—or, for that matter, send his son to study in England, a country where he no doubt had dealings?" He closed his eyes. "As for you specifically, my dear Tamiki, I can easily gather that you are a man of letters and well read. Actually, it is amazing how much can be learned about people from the books they own. In your case, there is an interest in poetry—especially Whitman and Yeats— which tells me you have an affinity for verse. However, not only are you a reader of poetry but you often write it, too—so frequently, in fact, that you probably didn't realize that the note you left me this morning was actually in haiku form—the five-seven-five variety, I believe. And while I have no way of knowing unless I look, I imagine the manuscript sitting on your desk contains your unpublished work. I say *unpublished* because you were careful to conceal it beneath your hat earlier. Which brings me to your business trip. If you came home with your own manuscript—somewhat dispirited, I should add—then I suspect you took it with you this morning. But what sort of business requires a writer to take along an unpublished text? And why would he come home in such a mood, the text still in hand? Likely a meeting involving a publisher—which didn't go favorably, I gather. So while one could assume it was the quality of your writing preventing publication, I believe otherwise. I submit that it is the content of your writing that is in question, not the quality. Why else would you express indignation over the continual suppression of Japanese poets, writers, and artists by Allied censors? But a poet who devotes a large portion of his library to Marx is hardly a champion of the emperor's militaristic spirit—in all likelihood, sir, you are something of an armchair Communist—which, of course, means you are deemed worthy of censorship by both the occupying forces and those who still hold the emperor in high regard. The very fact that you referred to Hensuiro as your comrade this evening—a strange word for one's own brother, I think—hints at your ideological leanings, as well as your idealism. Of course, Hensuiro isn't your brother, is he? If he were, your father would undoubtedly have sent him in your footsteps to England, giving him and me the luxury of better communication. Curious, then, that the two of you share this home, and dress so alike, and that you continually substitute *we* for *I*—in much the same manner as married couples do. Naturally, this is none of my concern, although I'm convinced you were raised as an only child." A mantelpiece clock began chiming, and Holmes opened his eyes, fixing his stare on the ceiling. "Lastly—and I pray you won't take offense—I have wondered how you manage to survive so comfortably during these troubled days. You show no signs of poverty, you maintain a housekeeper, and you are quite proud of your expensive collection of Art Deco glassware—all of this being a notch or two above the bourgeoisie, wouldn't you agree? On the other hand, a Communist dealing goods in the black market is slightly less hypocritical—especially if he is offering his bounty at a fair price and at the expense of the capitalist hordes occupying his country." Sighing deeply, Holmes fell silent. Finally, he said, "There are other particulars, I am sure, but they escape me at the moment. You see, I am not as retentive as I once was." At this point, he lowered his head, brought the cigar to his mouth, and gave Mr. Umezaki a weary glance.

"It's remarkable." Mr. Umezaki shook his head with a gesture of disbelief. "Absolutely incredible."

"No need, really."

Mr. Umezaki attempted to appear unfazed. He fished a cigarette from a pocket, holding it between his fingers without bothering to light it. "Aside from one or two errors, you've completely undressed me. Still, I've had minor involvement in the black market, but only as an infrequent buyer. In truth, my father was a very wealthy man and made sure his family was taken care of, but that doesn't mean I can't appreciate Marxist theory. Also, it isn't exactly accurate to say I maintain a housekeeper."

"Mine is hardly an exact science, you know."

"It's impressive nonetheless. I will say your observations about me and Hensuiro aren't terribly surprising. Without being too blunt—you are a bachelor who lived with another bachelor for many years."

"Purely platonic, I assure you."

"If you say so." Mr. Umezaki continued looking at him, momentarily awestricken. "It really is remarkable."

Holmes's expression became puzzled: "Am I mistaken—the woman who cooks your meals and tends your house—Maya—she is your housekeeper, correct?" For clearly Mr. Umezaki was a bachelor by choice, yet it struck him odd just then that Maya behaved more like a put-upon spouse than hired help.

"It's semantical, if that's what you mean—but I don't like to think of my mother as such."

"Naturally."

Holmes rubbed his hands together, puffing blue fumes, hoping to mask what was, in reality, a bothersome oversight on his part: the forgetting of Mr. Umezaki's relation to Maya, something he had surely learned when introductions were made. Or perhaps, he entertained, the oversight was his host's—perhaps he was never told to begin with. Regardless, it wasn't worth fretting over (an understandable mistake, as the woman appeared too young to be Mr. Umezaki's mother anyway).

"Now if you will excuse me," Holmes said, holding the cigar a few inches from his mouth. "I have become rather tired—and we are starting early tomorrow."

"Yes, I'll be turning in shortly myself. May I say first that I'm truly grateful for your visit here."

"Nonsense," Holmes said, standing with his canes, the cigar at one side of his mouth, "it is I who is grateful. Sleep well."

"You, too."

"Thank you, I will. Good night."

"Good night."

With that, Holmes made his way into the dim corridor, stepping where the hall lights were extinguished and everything ahead of him was steeped in shadow. Yet some illumination prevailed amid the darkness, spilling past an ajar door up ahead. Toward the light he ambled, bringing himself to stand before that brightened doorway. And peeking inside the room, he observed Hensuiro at work: shirtless within a sparsely furnished parlor, stooping in front of a painted canvas that—from Holmes's vantage point—depicted something like a bloodred landscape littered with a multitude of geometric shapes (straight black lines, blue circles, yellow squares). Peering closer, he saw finished paintings of various sizes stacked along the barren walls—primed in red, and, of those he could see plainly, bleak (crumbling buildings, pale white bodies surfacing lengthwise through the crimson, twisted arms, bent legs, grasping hands, and faceless heads presented as a visceral pile). Dotting the wooden flooring, sprinkled haphazardly around the easel, were countless drops and splashes of paint, appearing like the spattering of blood loss.

Later, when settled in bed, he would ponder the poet's suppressed relationship with the artist—the two men posing as brothers, yet living as a couple beneath the same roof, no doubt within the same sheets, judged by the critical glare of the disapproving but loyal Maya. To be sure, it was a clandestine life, one of subtlety and complete discretion. But he suspected there were other secrets as well, possibly one or two delicate matters soon to be imparted—for Mr. Umezaki's letters, he now suspected, had further motives beyond

what was written. So an invitation had been offered, and it had been
accepted. Come the next morning, he and Mr. Umezaki would begin
their travels, leaving Hensuiro and Maya alone in the big house.
How deftly you've lured me here, he thought before sleeping. Then,
at last, he drifted off with eyes half-open, eventually dreaming as a
familiar low, buzzing suddenly pricked up his ears.

PART
II

7

HOLMES WOKE, gasping. What had happened?

Seated at his desk, he glanced toward the attic window. Outside, the wind was blustering, monotonous and steadfast, humming against the panes, billowing through the gutters, swaying pine limbs in the yard, no doubt ruffling the blooms of his flower beds. Other than the gusts beyond the closed window and the emergence of night, everything in his study remained as it had been prior to his drifting off. The shifting hues of dusk framed between the parted curtains were replaced now by pitch-blackness, yet the table lamp cast the same glow across his desktop; and there, spread haphazardly before him, were the handwritten notes for *The Whole Art of Detection*'s third volume—page after page of various musings, the words often scrawled into the margins—scattershot from line to line, and, in a way, lacking any conceivable order. Whereas the first two volumes had proved a rather effortless undertaking (both written concurrently over a fifteen-year period), this latest endeavor was hampered by an inability to concentrate fully: He would sit down and promptly fall asleep, pen in hand; he would sit down and find himself staring out the window instead, sometimes for what seemed hours; he would sit down and begin writing an erratic series of sen-

tences, most unrelated and free-flowing, as if something palpable
might evolve from the mess of ideas.

What had happened?

He touched his neck, rubbing his throat lightly. Only the wind,
he thought. That swift humming at the window, filtering into his
sleep, startling him awake.

Just the wind.

His stomach grumbled. And then he realized supper had been
missed again—Mrs. Munro's Friday usual of roast beef and Yorkshire
pudding with side dishes—and that he was sure to find a tray in the
hallway (the roasted potatoes having grown cold beside the locked
attic door). Kind Roger, he thought. Such a good boy. Because during the past week—while he had remained sequestered within the
attic, forgoing supper and his normal activities in the beeyard—the
tray had always found its way up the stairs, waiting to be encountered whenever he stepped into the hallway.

Earlier that day, Holmes had felt some degree of guilt about having neglected his apiary, so following breakfast he had wandered
toward the beeyard, catching sight of Roger ventilating the hives
from afar. Anticipating hot weather and with the nectar flow at its
most vigorous, the boy was wisely offsetting the upper supers on
each hive, allowing an air current to push through the entrance and
out the top, thereby aiding the fluttering wings, which, aside from
also helping cool the hives, could better evaporate the nectar stored
in the supers. Then whatever guilt Holmes had felt vanished; for the
bees were being properly tended, and it was evident that his casual,
if not deliberate, tutelage of Roger had reached fruition (the beeyard
considerations, he was pleased to observe, were in the boy's capable,
attentive hands).

Soon enough, Roger would start harvesting the honey on his
own—gingerly removing the frames one at a time, calming the bees
with a puff of smoke, using an uncapping fork to lift the wax covers
off the cells—and in the days to come a small amount of honey

would flow through a double strainer into a honey bucket, followed thereafter by larger amounts. And from where he stood on the garden pathway, Holmes could imagine himself again in the beeyard with the boy, instructing Roger about the simplest method in which a novice could produce comb honey.

After placing a super on a given hive, he had previously told the boy, it was better to use eight extracting frames rather than ten, doing so only when the nectar flow was in progress. Then the remaining two frames should be set in the middle of the super, making sure that unwired comb foundation was used. If everything was done properly, the colony would draw the foundation, filling the two frames with honey. Once the comb-honey frames became filled and capped, they should be immediately replaced with more comb foundation—providing, of course, that the flow was proceeding as expected. In the event that the flow appeared less profuse than what was desired, it was wise, then, to replace the unwired comb foundation with a wired extracting foundation. Obviously, he pointed out, the hives must be inspected frequently in order to best decide which method of extraction was appropriate.

Holmes had walked Roger through the entire regimen, showing the boy each step of the process, feeling positive that—as the honey was ready for harvest—Roger would heed his instruction by the letter. "You understand, my boy, that I am entrusting this task to you because I believe you are fully capable of managing it without error."

"Thank you, sir."

"Do you have any questions?"

"No, I don't think so, no," replied the boy, speaking with a gentle enthusiasm, which somehow gave the false impression that he was smiling—even though his expression was serious and mindful.

"Very good," Holmes said, shifting his gaze from Roger's face to the surrounding hives. He didn't realize that the boy remained staring at him, didn't notice that he was being looked upon with the same kind of quiet reverence that he himself reserved only for the beeyard. Instead, he pondered the comings and goings of the apiary's inhabitants, the busy, diligent, active communities of the hives. "Very good," he repeated, whispering to himself on that afternoon in the recent past.

Turning around on the garden pathway, returning slowly to the house, Holmes knew Mrs. Munro would eventually do her part, filling jar after jar with the honey surplus, delivering a batch to the vicarage, to the charity mission, to the Salvation Army when running her errands in town. By providing these gifts of honey, Holmes believed he was also doing his part—making available the viscid material from his hives (something which he regarded as a wholesome by-product of his true interests: bee culture and the benefits of royal jelly), giving it to those who would fairly disburse the many unlabeled jars (on condition that his name would never become associated with what was given), and providing a beneficial sweetness to the less fortunate of Eastbourne and, hopefully, elsewhere.

"Sir, it's God's blessed work you're doing," Mrs. Munro had once told him. "Sure enough, it's His will you're following—the ways you help them who've been living without."

"Don't be ludicrous," he'd replied disdainfully. "If anything, it is you following my will. Let us remove God from the equation, shall we?"

"As you like," she'd said in a humoring tone. "But if you ask me, it's God's will, that's all."

"My dear woman, you were never asked to begin with."

What could she know about God anyway? The personification of her God, Holmes figured, was surely the popular one: a wrinkled old man sitting omnisciently upon a throne of gold, reigning over creation from within puffy clouds, speaking both graciously and commandingly at the same instant. Her God, no doubt, wore a flowing beard. For Holmes, it was amusing to think that Mrs. Munro's Creator probably looked somewhat like himself—except her God existed as a figment of imagination, and he did not (at least not entirely, he reasoned).

However, sporadic references to a divine entity aside, Mrs. Munro proclaimed no open affiliation with a church or a religion, nor had she made any obvious effort toward insinuating God into her son's thoughts. The boy, it was clear, held very secular concerns, and, truth be known, Holmes found himself gladdened by the youngster's pragmatic character. So now on that windy night, there at his desk, he would jot several lines for Roger, a few sentences he wanted the boy to read sometime later.

Placing a clean sheet of paper before him and bringing his face to hover just above the desktop, he began writing:

> Not through the dogmas of archaic doctrines will you gain your greatest understandings, but, rather, through the continued evolution of science, and through your keen observations of the natural environment beyond your windows. To comprehend yourself truly, which is also to comprehend the world truly, you needn't look any farther than at what abounds with life around you—the blossoming meadow, the untrodden woodlands. Without this as mankind's overriding objective, I don't foresee an age of actual enlightenment ever arriving.

Holmes put his pen down. Twice, he considered what was written, speaking the words aloud, changing nothing. Afterward, he folded the paper into a perfect square, pondering an acceptable location in which to store the note for the time being—a place where it wouldn't be forgotten, a place where he could retrieve it with ease. The desk drawers were out of the question, as the note would soon become lost among his writings. Likewise, the disorganized, overstuffed file cabinets would be too risky, and so would the confounding enigmas that were his pockets (often small items went in without much thought—bits of paper, broken matches, a cigar, stems of grass, an interesting stone or shell found upon the beach, those unusual things gathered during his walks—only to vanish or appear later as if by magic). Someplace reliable instead, he decided. Someplace appropriate, memorable.

"Where then? Think . . . "

He surveyed the books stacked along one wall.

"No . . ."

Pivoting the chair, he glanced at the bookshelves beside the attic doorway, narrowing his gaze to a single shelf reserved solely for his own published editions.

"Perhaps . . ."

Moments later, he stood before those early volumes and various monographs of his, an index finger pushing a horizontal line across the dust-coated spines—*Upon Tattoo Marks, Upon the Tracing of Footsteps, Upon the Distinction Among the Ashes of 140 Tobacco Forms, A Study of the Influence of a Trade Upon the Form of the Hand, Malingering, The Typewriter and Its Relation to Crime, Secret Writings & Ciphers, Upon the Polyphonic Motets of Lassus, A Study of the Chaldean Roots in the Ancient Cornish Language, The Use of Dogs in the Work of the Detective*—until arriving at the first magnum opus of his latter years: *Practical Handbook of Bee Culture, with Some Observations Upon the Segregation of the Queen.* How immense the book felt when taken off the shelf, the hefty spine cradled by his palms.

Between chapter 4 ("Bee Pasturage") and chapter 5 ("Propolis"), Roger's note was stuck like a bookmark—because, Holmes had decided, the rare edition would be a fitting gift for the boy's next birthday. Of course, being one who seldom acknowledged such anniversaries, he needed to ask Mrs. Munro when the auspicious day was celebrated (had the occasion come already, or was it imminent?). Still, he envisioned the surprised look spreading on Roger's face as the book was presented, then the boy's fingers slowly turning the pages while reading alone in his cottage bedroom—where, eventu-

ally, the folded note would get discovered (a more prudent, less offi-
cious manner in which to deliver an important message).

Confident that the note now resided within an assured location,
Holmes placed the book on the shelf. When turning and going
toward the desk, he was relieved that his attention could again focus
on work. And once settled in his chair, he stared intently at the
handwritten pages covering the desktop, each filled with a multitude
of hastily conceived words, inked characters like a child's scrawl—
but just then the strands of his memory began unwinding, leaving
him unsure of what those pages might actually pertain to. Soon the
receding threads floated away, disappearing into the night like leaves
whisked from the gutters, and for a spell, he remained staring at the
pages, while not questioning or recalling or thinking anything.

Yet his hands kept busy even as his mind was at a loss. His fingers roamed about the desktop—sliding over the many pages before him, randomly underlining sentences—ultimately rummaging
through the stacks of papers without any apparent reason. It was as
if his fingers were operating of their own accord, searching for something that had recently been forgotten. Pages and pages were set
aside, one upon another—creating an entirely new stack near the
center of the desk—until, at last, his fingers lifted that unfinished
manuscript that was held together by a single rubber band: "The
Glass Armonicist." Initially, he gazed blankly at the manuscript, appearing indifferent to its rediscovery; nor did he discern in any way
that Roger had repeatedly studied the text, the boy sneaking into the
attic on occasion to check if the story had been elaborated or finished.

But it was the manuscript's title that finally eased Holmes from
his stupor, producing a curious, modest smile within his beard; for if
the words had not been written clearly at the top, appearing above
the first section, he might have put the manuscript into the new
stack, where the text would once more become obscured beneath
subsequent and unrelated jottings. Now his fingers removed the rubber band, letting it drop to the desktop. Thereafter, he reclined in

his chair, reading the incomplete story as if it had been written by someone else. Nevertheless, the recollection of Mrs. Keller suddenly persisted with a certain amount of clarity. He could behold her photograph. He could easily summon her upset husband sitting across from him at Baker Street. Even when pausing for a few seconds, glancing upward at the ceiling, he could still place himself back in time—venturing out from Baker Street with Mr. Keller, mixing amid the crowded din of London's thoroughfares as they made their way toward Portman's. He could, on that night, occupy the past better than the present, doing so as the wind murmured ceaselessly against the attic panes.

8

II.

A Disturbance at Montague Street

At precisely four o'clock, my client and I were positioned beside a lamppost, waiting across the street from Portman's, but Mrs. Keller had not yet arrived. As it happened, we were also loitering within sight of the shuttered rooms I had leased on Montague Street when I first came up to London in 1877. Clearly, there was no reason to share such personal information with my client, or to impart that— during my youthful tenure within that terrace development—Port- man's shop was once a female boardinghouse of some dubious repute. Even so, the area itself had changed little since I lodged there, and consisted mostly of identical common-walled dwellings, the ground floors dressed in white stone, the upper three levels showing brick.

And yet standing there, my eyes travelling from those windows of the past to the present locale before me, I was touched by a degree of sentiment for what had escaped me over the years: the anonymity of my formative consulting detective practice, the liberty of coming and going without recognition or diversion. So while the street endured as it always had, I understood that my older incarnation differed somewhat from the man I had been when living there. Early on, disguises were previously donned only as a means for infiltration and observation, a way in which to blend effortlessly into various parts of the city while gaining information. Amongst the numerous roles I assumed, there was a common loafer, a rakish young plumber named Escott, a venerable Italian priest, a French *ouvrier*, even an old woman. However, towards my career's end, I had resorted to carrying upon me at all times a fake moustache and a pair of eyeglasses, doing so for the sole purpose of evading the widespread followers of John's accounts. No longer could I go about my business unidentified, nor could I sup in public without strangers accosting me midmeal, wishing to converse with me and shake my hand, asking intolerable questions regarding my calling. Therefore, it might seem an imprudent oversight—as I quickly realised while hurrying with Mr. Keller from Baker Street—that I was able to start forth on the case while forgetting to bring along my facade. For as we rushed to

Portman's, we found ourselves engaged by a workman of the amiable and simpleminded variety, to whom I would offer a few curt words.

"Sherlock Holmes?" said he, suddenly joining us as we made our way along Tottenham Court Road. "Sir, it is you, is it not? I have read all your stories, sir." My reply was given with the gesturing of a hand, which I waved briskly in the air, as if to cast him aside. But the fellow was not to be deterred; he set his senseless gape upon Mr. Keller, saying, "And I should think this is Dr. Watson."

Surprised by the workman, my client glanced at me with an uneasy expression.

"What an absurd notion," I said demurely. "If I am Sherlock Holmes, then pray explain how it is possible for this much younger gentleman to be the doctor?

"I don't know, sir. But you are Sherlock Holmes—I ain't easily flat, I can tell you that."

"Perhaps a touch glocky?"

"No, sir, I wouldn't say I am." Sounding a tad doubtful and confused, the workman paused in his tracks as we continued onwards. "Are you on a case?" he soon called after us.

Again I gestured my hand in the air, addressing him no more. This was how I usually dealt with the unwanted attention of strangers. Moreover, had the workman truly been accustomed to the narratives of John, he would have surely known that I never wasted words or disclosed my thoughts while a case was under consideration. Yet my client seemed dismayed by my abruptness, although he said nothing of it, and the two of us continued silently together on our journey to Montague Street. Then having taken up our position near Portman's, I began to ask something which had crossed my mind earlier while en route: "A final question regarding payment of—"

My remark was cut in on by Mr. Keller, who spoke with urgency as his thin white fingers gripped at his lapel.

"Mr. Holmes, it is true that I exist on a modest wage, but I will do whatever is necessary to reward you for your services."

"My dear boy, my profession is its own reward," I said, smiling. "Should I be put to any expenses—which I do not foresee in this matter—you are free to defray them at a time which best suits your modest wage. And now if you can contain yourself for a moment, I beg you to let me finish the question I was attempting to ask: How is it that your wife could pay for these clandestine lessons?"

"I cannot tell," he answered. "Nevertheless, she has her own means."

"You are referring to her inheritance."

"I am."

"Very good," I said, surveying the human traffic on the other side of the street—my view obstructed every so often by four-wheelers, hansoms, and, what was becoming a less singular apparition by those days, at least two clamorous transporters of the upper class: the automobile.

Believing my case to be almost complete, I waited expectantly for

Mrs. Keller's approach. When, after the passing of several minutes, she failed to materialise, I found myself wondering if she might not have entered Portman's ahead of schedule. Or perhaps she was, in reality, completely aware of her husband's suspicions and had decided against showing herself. As I was about to suggest the latter possibility, my client's gaze narrowed; nodding his head, he said lowly, "There she is," and with that his body was eager for pursuit.

"Steady," I said, bracing a hand upon his shoulder. "At the moment, we should maintain our distance."

And then I, too, glimpsed her as she walked idly toward Portman's, a slower form moving gradually amidst swifter currents. The bright yellow parasol floating above her was at odds with the woman beneath it; for Mrs. Keller, a diminutive wisp of a creature, was in the conventional costume of a grey day dress—the austere pigeon-breast look and the waist line dipping in front to accentuate the S curve of her corset shape. She wore white gloves, and one of those adorned hands cradled a rather small brown-covered book. Upon reaching the entrance of Portman's, she brought the parasol down and tugged it shut, tucking it then under an arm before venturing inside.

My client's shoulder resisted my grip, but I prevented his rushing ahead of me by asking, "Is your wife in the habit of applying perfume?"

"Yes, she is."

"Excellent," I said, releasing my hold and stepping past him into the street. "Let's see what all this is about, shall we?"

My senses are—as my friend John certainly noted—remarkably attuned perceivers, and I have long upheld the belief that the prompt outcome of a given case often relies on the immediate recognition of perfumes; therefore, criminal experts would be well advised to learn how to distinguish them. Regarding Mrs. Keller's scent of choice, it was that sophisticated blend of roses complemented by a hint of spice, the lingering of which was first detected in the entryway of Portman's shop.

"The fragrance is Cameo Rose, is it not?" I whispered after my client. But as he had already charged beyond me in haste, no reply was forthcoming.

Still, the farther we went, the stronger the odour became, until, pausing briefly to discern its course, I felt that Mrs. Keller was somewhere very close to us. My eyes darted around the cramped, dusty establishment—rickety bookcases tilting unevenly from one end of the shop to the other, with volumes filling the shelves and, as well, stacked haphazardly along the dim aisles; yet she was nowhere to be seen, nor was the elderly proprietor, who I had imagined would be sitting behind the counter by the entryway, his face peering down at some obscure text. In fact, devoid of both staff and patrons, Portman's gave the eerie impression of having been vacated; no sooner had that thought crossed my mind than, as if to underscore the unusual aura of the place, I caught the faint sound of music coming from upstairs.

"It's Ann, Mr. Holmes. She's at it now; she's playing!"

I suppose truly to claim such ethereal abstraction as being music was inaccurate; for the delicate sounds which reached my ears lacked form, arrangement, or simple melody. However, the magnetism of the instrument had its effect: the varying tones converged into a single sustained harmony which was at once discordant and captivating; enough so that my client and I were drawn in its direction. With Mr. Keller leading the way, we passed between bookcases and reached a flight of stairs near the back.

But while climbing upwards towards the second story, I realized that the odour of Cameo Rose had not travelled beyond the ground floor. I glanced back, surveyed the shop below, again saw no one about, stooped for a better view, and, with no success, contrived to bring my stare over the tops of bookcases. This hesitation on my part prevented me from stopping the fervour of Mr. Keller's fist upon Madame Schirmer's door, a short-lived pounding which resonated along the corridor and silenced the instrument. Nonetheless, the case was, to a certain degree, finished by the time I joined him there. Without a doubt, I knew Mrs. Keller had gone elsewhere, and whoever was practising on the armonica would prove to be someone other than she. Ah, that I should reveal so much when attempting my own narrative. I cannot hide the truth as John could, nor do I possess his talent of withholding the relevant points in order to fashion a superficially significant conclusion, alas.

"Calm yourself, man," said I, admonishing my companion. "By no means should you display yourself so."

Mr. Keller frowned gravely and held his gaze at the door. "You must forgive me," said he.

"There is nothing to forgive. But as your furore may impede our progress, I shall speak on your behalf from here on."

The silence which ensued in the wake of my client's angry knocking was then vanquished by the quick, equally pounding steps of Madame Schirmer. The door was thrown open and she appeared then with inflamed features and ruffled demeanour, as brawny a woman as I have ever encountered. Before she could utter a heated word, I stepped forwards and handed her my calling card, saying, "Good afternoon, Madame Schirmer. Could you be so gracious as to grant us a little of your time?"

Considering me momentarily with a questioning glance, she proceeded to shoot her formidable stare to my companion.

"I promise we shan't keep you but a few minutes," I continued, tapping my finger against the card she was holding. "Perhaps you are familiar with me."

Disregarding my presence altogether, Madame Schirmer spoke harshly: "Herr Keller, don't come here like this again! I won't have this interruption! Why must you come and create these problems for me? And for you, sir," she added, fixing her stare upon me, "the same goes, too. That's right! You are his friend, no? So you go away with him and never come back to me like this! I have no more patience for these people like you!"

"My dear woman, please," said I, extracting the card from her hand and lifting it in front of her face.

To my surprise, the sight of my name provoked an adamant shaking of her head. "No, no, you are not this person," said she.

"I assure you, Madame Schirmer, that I am none other than he."

"No, no, you are not him. No, I have seen this person often, you know."

"And pray tell me when the acquaintance was made?"

"In the magazine, of course! This detective is much taller, right? With the black hair, and the nose, and the pipe. You see, it was never you."

"Ah, the magazine! It is a somewhat intriguing misrepresentation. On that we can agree. I fear I do my caricature an injustice. If only the majority of people I meet could perceive me as wrongly as you do, Madame Schirmer, then my liberty might be less hampered."

"You are ridiculous!" With that, she crushed the card and threw it at my feet. "So you go from me now, or the constables are coming for you!"

"I cannot leave here," said Mr. Keller firmly, "until I see Ann with my very own eyes."

Our inconvenienced antagonist suddenly stomped on the floor, doing so repeatedly, until the noise of it reverberated beneath us.

"Herr Portman," she cried out afterwards, her emphatic voice echoing past us into the corridor, "there is trouble with me now! Go for the constables! There are two burglars at the door! Herr Portman—"

"Madame Schirmer, it is of no use," said I. "It seems Mr. Portman has gone out for a while." Then I turned to my client, who looked deeply chagrined. "You should also be aware, Mr. Keller, that Madame Schirmer is completely within her rights and that we have no legal status to go within her flat. However, she must understand that your action is governed solely by concern for your wife. I venture to hope that if we were allowed to have just two minutes inside with Madame Schirmer, we could certainly put this issue to rest."

"The wife is not here with me," said the displeased woman. "Herr Keller, I have told you this enough. Why do you come here and give me your problems? I can ring up the police on you, you know!"

"There is no reason for that," I said. "I am fully conscious of the fact that Mr. Keller has accused you unjustly, Madame Schirmer. But any interference by the police would only complicate what is, in truth, a rather sad affair." I leaned forwards and whispered several words into her ear. "You see," I then said when moving back from her, "your assistance would be most valuable."

"How could I know this?" she gasped, her expression transforming from annoyance to regret.

"Indeed," I answered sympathetically. "My trade, I am sorry to say, is sometimes a woeful business."

As my client's face focused on me with confusion, Madame

Schirmer stood in thought for a moment, her massive arms akimbo. Then she nodded and stepped aside, gesturing for us to enter: "Herr Keller, I think it is not your fault. Come inside, if you wish to see for yourself, poor man."

We were shown into a bright, sparsely decorated drawing room, with a low ceiling and half-opened windows. An upright piano was in one corner, a harpsichord and a good many percussion instruments in another, and, put side by side, two impressively refurbished armonicas sat nearest the windows. These instruments, with a number of small wickerwork chairs placed at or around them, were the only objects in what was an otherwise-barren room. Save for a square of Wilton in the centre, the discoloured brownish slats of the floor remained exposed; the white-painted walls were also unadorned, allowing for the sound waves to reflect in such a way as to produce a distinct echoing timbre.

It was not, however, the contrivances of the drawing room which immediately caught my attention, nor was it the scent of spring flowers wafting through the open windows; rather, it was the fidgeting, slight form sitting before an armonica: a boy of no older than ten, with red hair and freckled cheeks, turning nervously in his seat to view us as we came into the room. Seeing the child, my client stopped in his steps; his eyes then darted about while Madame Schirmer watched from the entryway, her arms folded at her waist. I, on the other hand, proceeded towards the boy, addressing him with the warmest of intonations: "Hello there."

"Hello," said the child shyly.

Glancing back at my client, I smiled and said, "I take it that this young man is not your wife."

"You know he isn't" was my client's bristling reply. "But I cannot understand it. Where is Ann?"

"Patience, Mr. Keller, patience."

I drew up one of the chairs to the armonica and sat beside the boy, while my eyes travelled round and over the instrument, taking in every detail of its design.

"Pray what is your name, child?"

"Graham."

"Now then, Graham," said I, noting that the old glasses were thinner in the treble and thus were easier to make sing, "is Madame Schirmer teaching you well?"

"I believe so, sir."

"Hum," said I thoughtfully, lightly running a fingertip across the brims of the glasses.

The opportunity to inspect an armonica—especially a model in such pristine condition—had never before presented itself. What I had known previously was that the instrument was played upon when sitting directly in front of the set of glasses, spinning them by means of a foot treadle, and wetting them on occasion with a moistened sponge. I was also aware that both hands were required, allowing different parts to be performed simultaneously. However, while actually looking closely at the armonica, I observed that the glasses were blown into the shape of hemispheres, with each having an open socket in the centre. The largest and highest pitched of the glasses was G. To distinguish the glasses, each—save the semitones, which were white—was painted inside with one of the seven prismatic colours: C, red; D, orange; E, yellow; F, green; G, blue; A, indigo; B, purple; and C, red again. The thirty or so glasses varied in size from about nine inches in diameter to no more than three inches; fixed upon a spindle, they sat within a three-foot-long case, which—tapered in its length to adapt to the conical shape of the glasses and fastened to a frame with four legs—lifted on hinges from the middle of its height. The spindle was cast of hard iron, and, made to turn on brass gudgeons on either end, it crossed the case horizontally. On the widest side of the case was a square shank, upon which a mahogany wheel was fixed. It was the wheel which served as a fly to make the motion steady, doing so when the spindle and the glasses were rotated by the action of the foot. With a strip of lead concealed near its circumference, the wheel appeared to be some eighteen inches in diameter, and, approximately four inches from the axis, an ivory pin was fixed to its face; around the neck of the pin was placed a loop of string, which travelled up from the moveable treadle to provide its motion.

"It is a remarkable contraption," said I. "Am I to understand that the tones are best drawn out when the glasses turn from the ends of the fingers, not when they turn to them?"

"Yes, it is so," Madame Schirmer replied from behind us.

Already the sun was angling for the horizon, its light reflecting off the glasses. Graham's wide-eyed stare had slowly become a squint, and the sound of my client's restless sighs took advantage of the room's acoustics. Carried from outside, the bouquet of daffodils tingled in my nostrils, an onionlike smell, hinting of mould; I am not alone in my dislike of the flower's subtle qualities, as deer, too, are repelled by it. Then giving the glasses a final touch, I said, "If circumstances were different, I should ask you to play for me, Madame Schirmer."

"Of course, this we can always arrange, sir. I am available for the private performance; that is what I do sometimes, you know."

"Naturally," said I, rising from the seat. Gently patting the boy's shoulder, I continued: "I believe we have monopolised enough of your lesson, Graham, so we shall now leave you and your teacher in peace."

"Mr. Holmes!" my client ejaculated in protest.

"Really, Mr. Keller, there is nothing else for us to learn here, aside from what Madame Schirmer offers at a price."

And with that, I pivoted upon my heels and set across the drawing room, where I was followed by the woman's dumbfounded stare. Mr. Keller rushed to join me in the hallway, and as we exited the flat, I called back to her while shutting the door: "Thank you, Madame Schirmer. We won't bother you again, although I suspect you might be engaged by me at a later date for a lesson or two. Good-bye."

But once we had started down the corridor, the door was flung open and her voice chased after me: "Is this true, then? Are you him in the magazine?"

"No, my dear lady, I am not him."

"Ha!" said she, and the door slammed shut.

It wasn't until my client and I had reached the bottom of the stairs that I paused to calm him; for his face had become flushed and darkened from encountering the boy instead of his wife. His brows were drawn into two crooked, thick lines, while his eyes shone out beneath them with an almost irrational pall. His nostrils, too, flexed with the deepest of vexations, and his mind was so absolutely confounded by the whereabouts of his wife that the whole of his expression conveyed a significant question mark.

"Mr. Keller, I assure you that all is not as grave as you imagine it to be. In fact, while granting some deliberate omissions on her part, your wife has been mostly honest in her account to you."

The grimness of his expression lessened somewhat. "You have evidently seen more upstairs than was visible to me," said he.

"Perhaps, but I wager that you saw exactly what I did. However, I may have discerned a little more. Even so, you must allow me one week to bring the matter to a satisfactory conclusion."

"I am in your hands."

"Very good. I ask now that you promptly return to Fortis Grove, and when your wife arrives, you should mention nothing of what has occurred here today. It is very essential, Mr. Keller, that you should adhere to my advice in every respect."

"Yes, sir. I shall endeavour to do so."

"Excellent."

"I wish to know something first, Mr. Holmes. What was it you spoke in Madame Schirmer's ear which gained us entrance into her flat?"

"Oh, that," I remarked, with a flick of the hand. "It is a simple but effective untruth, one I have used previously in similar instances; I told her that you were a dying man, and I said your wife had abandoned you in your time of need. The very fact that it was whispered should have revealed it as a lie—yet it rarely fails as a skeleton key of sorts."

Mr. Keller stared at me with a look of slight distaste.

"Tut, man," said I, and turned from him.

Then going to the front of the shop, we at last happened upon the elderly proprietor, a little wrinkled fellow, who had resumed his place behind the counter. Sitting there in a soil-stained gardening smock, hunched over the text of a book, the man clutched a magnifying glass in a trembling hand and was using it to read. Near him were brown gloves, which he had apparently just shuffled off, laying them on the counter. Twice, the man rattled out a cough of the harshest kind, startling us both. But I lifted a finger to my lips so that my companion would remain silent. Still, as Mr. Keller had mentioned earlier, the man seemed oblivious to anyone being in the shop, even as I came within two feet of him, peering down at the large book which held his attention: a volume on the art of topiary. The pages I could see were illustrated with carefully rendered drawings of shrubs and trees trimmed into the shapes of an elephant, a cannon, a monkey, and what appeared to be a canopic jar.

We soon made our way outside as quietly as possible, and in the waning sunshine of late afternoon, I requested one last thing of my client before departing. "Mr. Keller, you have something which may prove useful to me for the time being."

"You have but to name it."

"Your wife's photograph."

My client nodded reluctantly.

"Certainly, if you need it."

He reached inside his coat and retrieved the photograph, offering it to me while appearing wary to do so.

Without hesitation I slipped the photograph into my pocket, saying, "I thank you, Mr. Keller. Then there is no more to be done today. I wish you a very pleasant evening."

And that was how I left him. With his wife's image upon me, I wasted not a moment in taking my retreat. Along the road moved buses and traps, hansoms and four-wheelers, bearing the figures of those riding home or elsewhere, while I weaved around fellow pedestrians on the paved walk, strolling in a deliberate pace towards Baker Street. A few country carts rolled past, displaying what remained of the vegetables which had been carried into the metropolis at dawn. Shortly, I knew well enough, the thoroughfares surrounding Montague Street would become as hushed and inanimate as any village after nightfall; and I, by then, would be leaning back in my chair, watching as the blue smoke from my cigarette floated to the ceiling.

9

B Y SUNRISE, the note for Roger had escaped Holmes's consciousness altogether; it would stay inside the book until, several weeks later, he retrieved the volume for research purposes and found the folded sheet flattened between the chapters (a curious message in his own hand, yet one he couldn't fathom having written). There were other folded sheets as well, all hidden throughout his many attic books and ultimately lost—urgent missives never sent, odd reminders, lists of names and addresses, the occasional poem. He wouldn't recall concealing a personal letter from Queen Victoria, or a playbill kept since his brief engagement with the Sasanoff Shakespearean Company (playing Horatio in an 1879 London stage production of *Hamlet*). Nor would he remember putting away for safekeeping a crude but detailed drawing of a queen bee among the pages of M. Quinby's *Mysteries of Beekeeping Explained*—the picture having been done by Roger when the boy was twelve, and slipped beneath the attic door two summers ago.

Regardless, Holmes wasn't unaware of his memory's increasing fallibility. He believed he was capable of incorrectly revising past events, especially if the reality of those events were beyond his grasp. But, he wondered, what was revised and what was true? And what was known for certain anymore? More importantly, what exactly had been forgotten? He couldn't say.

Even so, he adhered to the consistent tangibles—his land, his home, his gardens, his apiary, his work. He enjoyed his cigars, his books, a glass of brandy sometimes. He favored the evening breezes, and the hours after midnight. Without a doubt, he knew that Mrs. Munro's chatty presence often annoyed him, yet her soft-spoken son had always been a dear, welcomed companion; but here, too, his mental revisions had changed what was, in fact, the truth: For he hadn't taken kindly to the boy upon first sight—that shy, awkward youngster peeking sullenly at him from behind his mother. In the past, he had made it an unwavering rule never to hire a housekeeper with children, except that Mrs. Munro, recently widowed and in need of steady employment, had come highly recommended. More-over, finding reliable help had become quite difficult—particularly when being isolated in the country—so, he had told her plainly that she could stay as long as the boy's activities were restricted to the guest cottage, as long as his work wasn't disrupted by whatever ruckus her child might produce.

"No worries there, sir, I promise. My Roger won't cause you trouble. I'll see to that."

"It is understood, correct? I may be retired—however, I am still a very busy man. Needless distractions of any sort are simply not tolerated."

"Yes, sir, I understand that well enough. Don't concern yourself a bit over the boy."

"I won't, my dear, although I suspect you should."

"Yes, sir."

Then almost a year passed before Holmes saw Roger again. One afternoon while strolling about the west corner of his property, near the guest cottage where Mrs. Munro dwelled, he glimpsed the boy at a distance, watching as Roger entered the cottage with a butter-

fly net in hand. Thereafter, he spotted the solitary boy more frequently—traversing the meadows, doing schoolwork in the gardens,
studying the scree upon the beach. But it wasn't until encountering
Roger in the beeyard—finding the boy facing the hives, one hand
holding the wrist of the other, inspecting a single sting at the center
of his left palm—that Holmes at last dealt with him directly. Seizing the boy's stung hand, he used a fingernail to brush the stinger
off, explaining, "It was wise you resisted grasping the stinger; otherwise, you would have surely emptied the entire poison sac into
your wound—so use your fingernail, brush it away like this, and
don't compress the sac, understand? You were saved just in time—
see, here, it has hardly begun swelling. I have had much worse, I assure you."

"It doesn't hurt too bad," said Roger, looking at Holmes with his
eyes screwed up, as if the sun shone brightly on his face.

"It will soon—but only a little, I expect. Should it get worse, try
soaking your hand in salt water or onion juice—that usually cures
the smart."

"Oh."

And while Holmes expected tears from the boy (or, at the very
least, some embarrassment at having been caught in the beeyard), he
was impressed by how quickly Roger's attention then went from his
wound to the hives—transfixed, it seemed, with apiary life, the light
clustering of bees roaming before or after flight near the hive entrances. Had the boy cried once, had he shown even the slightest lack
of courage, Holmes would never have urged him forward, leading
him to a hive and lifting the top so Roger could see the world within
(the honey chamber with its white wax cells, the larger cells that
housed the drone brood, the darker cells below where the worker
brood lived); he would never have given the child a second thought,
or considered the boy to be of a like mind. (It is often the case, he
had thought, that exceptional children usually come from mundane

parents.) Nor would he have invited Roger to return the next afternoon, allowing the boy to witness firsthand the March chores: checking the hive's weekly weight, combining colonies when a queen ceased functioning in one, making sure enough food was available to the brood nests.

Subsequently, as the boy went from curious spectator to valued helper, Roger was given the clothing Holmes no longer wore—light-colored gloves and a veiled beekeeper's hat—which were then dispensed with once he grew comfortable handling the bees. Soon it became an effortless, innate association. After school, on most afternoons, the boy joined Holmes in the beeyard. During the summer, Roger awoke early and was busy at the hives when Holmes arrived there. While they tended the hives—or sometimes sat quietly in the pasture—Mrs. Munro brought them sandwiches, tea, perhaps something sweet she had created that morning.

On the hottest of days—following whatever work was done, when the refreshing waters of the tide pools beckoned—they hiked the winding cliff trail, where Roger walked beside Holmes, picking rocks off the steep path, peering repeatedly at the ocean below, stooping every so often to study something found along the way (broken bits of seashells, or a diligent beetle, or a fossil embedded within the cliff wall). A warm salty smell increased with their descent, as did Holmes's delight at the boy's inquisitiveness. It was one thing to take notice of an object, but an intelligent child, like Roger, had to inspect and touch carefully those things that drew his attention. Holmes was positive there was nothing too remarkable on the path, yet he was inclined to pause with Roger, contemplating all that enticed the boy.

When first traveling the trail together, Roger gazed up at the expansive rugged folds towering above and asked, "Is this cliff only chalk?"

"It is made of chalk, and it is made of sandstone."

Within the strata beneath the chalk was gault clay, greensand, and Wealden sands in successive order, explained Holmes as they continued downward; the clay beds and the thin layer of sandstones were covered with chalk, clay, and flint added throughout the aeons by countless storms.

"Oh," said Roger, absently veering toward the path's rim.

Dropping a cane, Holmes pulled him back. "Careful, my boy. You must mind your step. Here, take my arm."

The trail itself was barely wide enough for a full-grown adult, let alone an elderly man and a boy walking side by side. The path was about three feet across, and in places erosion had narrowed its width considerably; the pair, however, managed together without much trouble—Roger keeping mostly near the sheer edge, Holmes moving inches from the cliff wall as the boy gripped his arm. After a while, the path broadened in a spot, providing an overlook and a bench. Although it had been Holmes's intention to continue to the bottom (for the bathing pool could only be reached during daylight; otherwise, the evening tide swallowed the entire shore), the bench suddenly felt a more convenient location in which to rest and converse. Sitting there with Roger, Holmes dug a Jamaican from his pocket but soon realized he had no matches; instead, he chewed on the cigar, savoring the sea air, eventually following the boy's stare to where seagulls circled and swooped and cried out.

"I've heard the nightjars, have you? I heard them last night," Roger said, his memory stirred by the seagulls' squalling.

"Did you? How fortunate."

"People call them goatsuckers, except I don't believe they feed on goats."

"Insects, for the most part. They catch their prey on their wings, you know."

"Oh."

"We have owls, as well."

Roger's expression brightened. "I've never seen one. I'd like one for a pet, but my mother doesn't think birds are good pets. I think they'd be nice to have around the house, though."

"Well then, perhaps we can catch you an owl some night. We have plenty on the property, so one won't be missed, surely."

"Yes, I'd like that."

"Of course, we had best keep your owl in a place where your mother won't find it. My study is a possibility."

"Wouldn't she look there?"

"No, she wouldn't dare. But if she did, I would tell her it belonged to me."

A mischievous grin formed on the boy's face: "She'd believe you, too. I know she would."

Letting on that he wasn't being serious about the owl, Holmes gave Roger a wink. All the same, he appreciated the boy's confidence—the sharing of a secret, the covert alliances inherent to a friendship—and this pleased Holmes so much that he found himself offering what he'd ultimately forgotten to say: "In any case, Roger, I will speak with your mother. I suspect she will allow you a parakeet." Then to further their camaraderie, he promised that they would start earlier the next afternoon and reach the tide pools well before dusk approached.

"Should I fetch you?" asked Roger.

"Indeed. You will find me at the hives."

"When, sir?"

"Three is early enough, don't you imagine? That should allow ample time for the hike and a bathe and the stroll back up. I fear we started off too late today to complete the journey."

Already the waning sunlight and the burgeoning ocean breeze enveloped them. Holmes inhaled deeply, squinting his eyes against the setting sun. With his sight blurred, the ocean beyond appeared like a blackened expanse fringed with a massive fiery eruption. We should begin heading up the cliff, he thought. But Roger seemed to be in no hurry. Neither was Holmes, who glanced sideways at the boy and beheld that intent young face tilted toward the sky, those clear blue eyes fixed on a seagull circling high overhead. A little while longer, Holmes told himself, smiling as he observed Roger's lips parting in strange fascination, the boy somehow undaunted by the sun's brilliant glare or the wind's persistent rush.

10

MANY MONTHS afterward, Holmes would find himself alone within Roger's cramped bedroom (the first and last time he ever set foot among the boy's few possessions). On an overcast, gray morning—with no other soul present at the guest cottage—he unlocked Mrs. Munro's gloomy living quarters, going inside to where the impermeable drapes remained drawn, and the lights were kept off, and the woodsy barklike smell of mothballs obscured whatever else he inhaled. Every three or four steps, he paused, peering ahead into the darkness, and readjusted his grip on the canes, as if anticipating some vague, unimaginable form to emerge out of the shadows. Then he continued forward—the taps of his canes falling less heavily and wearily than his footsteps—until making his way past Roger's open doorway, entering the only cottage room that wasn't sealed wholly from daylight.

It was, in fact, a very tidy room, far from what Holmes had expected to discover—the careless, random droppings of a boy's vibrant life, that clutter. A housekeeper's son, he concluded, was surely more inclined than most children to maintain an ordered space—unless, of course, his bedroom was also tended by the housekeeper. Still, as the boy was rather fastidious by nature, Holmes felt positive it was

Roger who had organized his things so dutifully. Furthermore, the pervasive mothball smell hadn't yet filtered into the bedroom, suggesting the absence of Mrs. Munro's bearing; instead, a musty but not unpleasant, somewhat earthy aroma was evident. Like dirt during a good rain, he thought. Like fresh soil on the hands.

For a while, he sat at the edge of the boy's neatly made bed, taking in the general surroundings—the walls painted baby blue, the windows covered by transparent lace curtains, the various oak furnishings (nightstand, single bookcase, chest of drawers). Peering through the window directly above a student's writing desk, he noticed the crisscrossing of slender branches just outside, which appeared somewhat ethereal behind the gauze of lace, scraping almost noiselessly against the panes. And then his attention turned toward the personal, those things Roger had left there: six textbooks stacked on the writing desk, a sagging schoolbag hung from the closet doorknob, the butterfly net propped upright in a corner. Eventually, he stood, wandering slowly about, moving from wall to wall like one respectfully surveying a museum exhibit, then stopping briefly to take closer looks, resisting the urge to touch certain belongings.

But what he observed didn't surprise him, or offer any new insights into the boy. There were books about bird-watching and bees and warfare, several tattered science-fiction paperbacks, a good many *National Geographic* magazines (spanning two shelves, arranged chronologically), and there were rocks and seashells found at the beach, assorted by size and likeness, lined up in equal-numbered rows on the chest of drawers. Aside from the six textbooks, the writing desk displayed five sharpened pencils, drawing pens, blank paper, and the vial containing the Japanese honeybees. Everything had been ordered, given a proper place, aligned; so, too, were the objects occupying the nightstand—scissors, a bottle of rubber cement, a large scrapbook with an unadorned black cover.

Nevertheless, the most revealing items, it seemed, had ended up either taped or hung on the walls: Roger's colorful drawings—

nondescript soldiers firing brown rifles at one another, green tanks exploding, violent red scribbles bursting like explosions from chests or the foreheads of cross-eyed faces, yellow antiaircraft fire streaming upward toward a blue-black bomber fleet, massacred stick figures strewn about a bloodied battlefield as an orange sun rose or set on the pink horizon); three framed photographs, sepia-toned portraits (a smiling Mrs. Munro holding her infant son while the young father stood proudly beside her, the boy posing with his uniformed father on a train platform, toddler Roger running into his father's outstretched arms (each photograph—one near the bed, one near the writing desk, one near the bookcase—showed a stocky, strong-looking man, a square, ruddy face, sandy hair combed straight back, the benevolent eyes of someone who was now gone and someone who was terribly missed).

Yet, of all the things there, it was the scrapbook that, in the end, held Holmes's attention the longest. Returning to the boy's bed, he sat and stared at the nightstand, considering the scrapbook's black cover, the scissors, the rubber cement. No, he told himself, he wouldn't pry into the pages. He wouldn't snoop any more than he already had. Best not, he warned himself, reaching for the scrapbook—and with that, he left his better thoughts unheeded.

Thereafter, he leisurely perused the pages, his gaze lingering for a while on a series of intricate collages (photographs and words clipped from assorted magazines, then glued together shrewdly). The first third of the scrapbook betrayed the boy's interest in nature, in wildlife and foliage. Upright grizzly bears roamed forests near spotted leopards that lounged within African trees; cartoon hermit crabs hid with snarling pumas amid a cluster of Van Gogh sunflowers; an owl and a fox and a mackerel lurked beneath an aggregate of fallen leaves. What soon followed, however, was increasingly less scenic, although similar in design: The wildlife became British and American soldiers, the forests became the bombed-out ruins of cities, and the leaves became either corpses or single words—DEFEATED, FORCES, RETREAT—scattered across the pages.

Nature complete in and of itself, man forever at odds with man—the yin-yang of the boy's worldview, Holmes believed. For he assumed the initial collages—those at the front of the scrapbook—had been done years earlier, while Roger's father was still alive (the curled, yellowed edges of the cut images suggested this, as did the lack of odor from the rubber cement). The rest, he decided after sniffing at the pages, examining the seams of three or four collages, had been fashioned little by little over the recent months, and appeared more complicated, artful, and methodical in their layout.

Even so, the final piece of Roger's handiwork was unfinished; in actuality, with only one image centered on the page, it appeared to have been just begun. Or, Holmes wondered, had the boy intended it to be seen as such—a desolate monochromatic photograph floating in a void of blackness; a stark, puzzling, yet emblematic conclusion to all that had preceded it (the vivid overlapping imagery, the fauna and wilderness, those grim, determined men of war). The photograph itself was no mystery; Holmes knew the place well enough, had glimpsed it with Mr. Umezaki in Hiroshima—that former prefectural government building reduced to skeletal remains by the atomic blast ("the Atom Bomb Dome," Mr. Umezaki had called it).

But alone on the page, the building resonated utter annihilation, much more so than when seen in person. The photograph had been taken weeks, possibly days, after the bomb was dropped, revealing an immense city of rubble—no humans, no tramcars or trains, nothing recognizable save the ghostly shell of the prefectural building existing above the flattened, burned landscape. Then what preceded the final piece—unused scrapbook paper, page after page of black—simply underscored the disquieting impact of that sole image. And suddenly, when closing the scrapbook, Holmes was overcome by the weariness he had carried into the cottage. *Something has gone amiss* with the world, he found himself thinking. *Something has changed in the marrow, and I'm at a loss to make sense of it.*

"So what is the truth?" Mr. Umezaki had once asked him. "How do you arrive at it? How do you unravel the meaning of something that doesn't wish to be known?"

"I don't know," Holmes uttered aloud, there in Roger's bedroom. "I don't know," he said again, lowering himself to the boy's pillow and shutting his eyes, the scrapbook held against his chest: "I haven't a clue. . . ."

Holmes drifted away after that, though not into the sort of sleep that came from total exhaustion, or even a restless slumber in which dreams and reality were interlaced, but rather a torpid state submerging him into a vast stillness. Presently, that expansive, downreaching sleep delivered him elsewhere, tugging him from the bedroom where his body rested.

11

HAVING CARRIED the shared suitcase Holmes and Mr. Umezaki would be taking aboard the morning train (the two men having packed lightly for their sight-seeing journey), Hensuiro saw them off at the railroad station, where, tightly clasping Mr. Umezaki's hands, he whispered fervently in his companion's ear. Then before they entered the coach, he stepped in front of Holmes, bowing deeply, and said, "I see you—again—very again, yes."

"Yes," Holmes said, amused. "Very, very again."

And when the train departed the station, Hensuiro remained on the platform, his arms raised and waving amid a crowd of Australian soldiers, his swiftly receding but stationary figure eventually diminishing altogether. Soon the train gathered its westward momentum, and both Holmes and Mr. Umezaki sat rigidly in their adjacent second-class seats, watching with sidewise stares as Kobe's buildings gradually gave way to the lush terrain that moved and shifted and flashed beyond the window.

"It's a lovely morning," Mr. Umezaki remarked, a comment he would repeat several times throughout their first day of travel (the lovely morning becoming a lovely afternoon and, finally, a lovely evening).

"Quite," was Holmes's consistent reply.

Yet during the start of the trip, the men spoke hardly a word to each other. They sat quietly, self-contained and remote in their respective seats. For a while, Mr. Umezaki occupied himself by writing inside a small red journal (further haiku, Holmes figured), while Holmes, fuming Jamaican in hand, contemplated the blurs of scenery outside. It was only after departing the station at Akashi—when the jarring start of the train's movement shook the cigar from Holmes's fingers, sending it rolling across the floor—that real conversation ensued (initiated by Mr. Umezaki's general curiosity, and ultimately encompassing a number of subjects preceding their arrival at Hiroshima).

"Allow me," said Mr. Umezaki, rising to fetch the cigar for Holmes.

"Thank you," said Holmes, who then, having already lifted himself some, eased back down, placing the canes lengthwise over his lap (but at an angle so as to avoid bumping Mr. Umezaki's knees).

Once settled again in their seats, with the countryside sweeping past, Mr. Umezaki touched the stained wood of one cane. "They're finely crafted, are they not?"

"Oh, yes," said Holmes. "I have had them at least twenty years, quite possibly longer. They are my durable companions, you know."

"Have you always walked with both?"

"Not until recently—recently for me, that is—actually, about the last five years, if memory serves."

Then Holmes, feeling the desire to elaborate, explained: In fact, he really required only the support of the right cane while walking; the left cane, however, had an invaluable dual purpose—to give him support should he lose hold of the right cane and find himself stooping to retrieve it, or to stand in as a quick replacement should the right cane ever become irretrievable. Of course, he went on, lacking the sustained nourishment of royal jelly, the canes would serve him no useful function whatsoever, as he was convinced he'd surely be confined to a wheelchair.

"Is that so?"

"Unquestionably."

With that, their mutual exchange began in earnest, for both were eager to discuss the benefits of royal jelly, especially its effects in halting or controlling the aging process. Mr. Umezaki had, as it turned out, interviewed a Chinese herbalist before the war regarding the beneficial qualities of that viscous milky white secretion: "The man was clearly of the opinion that royal jelly could cure menopause and male climacteric, as well as liver disease, rheumatoid arthritis, and anemia."

"Phlebitis, gastric ulcer, various degenerative conditions," Holmes interjected, "and general mental or physical weakness. It also nourishes the skin, erases facial blemishes, wrinkles, while also preventing the signs of normal aging or even premature senility." How amazing it was, Holmes mentioned, that such a powerful substance, the chemistry of which was still not completely known, could be produced by the pharyngeal glands of the worker bee—creating queens from ordinary bee larvae, healing a multitude of mankind's ills.

"Though try as I may," said Mr. Umezaki, "I've found little or no evidence to support the claims of its therapeutic usefulness."

"Ah, but there is," replied Holmes, smiling. "We have studied royal jelly a long, long while, haven't we? We know it is full of protein and lipids, fatty acids and carbohydrates. That said, neither of us has come close to discovering all it contains, so I rely on the only evidence I truly possess, which is my own good health. But I take it you are not a regular user."

"No. Aside from writing one or two magazine articles, my interest is purely casual. I'm afraid, however, that I lean toward the skeptic's side on the matter."

"What a shame," said Holmes. "I was quite hoping you might spare a jar for my journey back to England—I have gone awhile without, you know. Nothing that can't be remedied upon my arrival home, although I do wish I had remembered to pack a jar or two— at least enough for a daily dose. Fortunately, I have brought more than enough Jamaicans, so I am not completely lacking in what I require."

"We might still find you a jar along our way."

"Such bother, don't you think?"

"It's hardly a bother."

"That is quite all right, really. Let us just consider it the price I must pay for forgetting. It seems even royal jelly cannot prevent the inevitable loss of retention."

And here, too, was another springboard in their conversation, be- cause now Mr. Umezaki, scooting closer to Holmes, speaking lowly, as if his question was of the utmost importance, could ask him about his renowned faculties; more specifically, he wanted to know how Holmes had mastered the ability to perceive so easily what others of- ten missed. "I'm aware of your belief in pure observation as a tool for achieving definitive answers—except I'm puzzled by the way in which you actually observe a given situation. From what I've read, as well as experienced firsthand, it appears that you don't merely ob- serve, but you also use recall effortlessly, almost photographically— and somehow this is how you arrive at the truth."

" 'What is truth? asked Pilate,' " Holmes said, sighing. "Frankly, my friend, I've lost my appetite for any notion of truth. For me, there simply is what is—call that truth, if you must. Better put—and I am understanding this with a fair amount of hindsight, mind you— I am drawn toward that which is clearly seen, gathering as much as I can from the external, and then synthesizing whatever is gathered into something of immediate value. The universal, mystical, or long- term implications—those places where truth, perhaps, resides—are of no interest."

Yet what of recall? Mr. Umezaki wondered. How was it used?

"In terms of forming a theory, or reaching a conclusion?"

"Yes, exactly."

As a younger man, Holmes would then tell him, visual recall was fundamental to his capacity for solving certain problems. For when he examined an object or investigated a crime scene, everything was instantaneously converted into precise words or numbers corresponding with the things he observed. Once the conversions formed a pattern in his mind (a series of particularly vivid sentences or equations that he could both utter and visualize), they locked themselves into his memory, and while they might stay dormant during those times when he was caught up with other considerations, they would immediately emerge whenever he turned his attention to the situations that had generated them.

"Over time, I have realized my mind no longer operates in such a fluid manner," Holmes continued. "The change has been by degrees, but I sense it fully now. My means for recall—those various groupings of words and numbers—aren't as easily accessible as they were. Traveling through India, for example, I stepped from the train somewhere in the middle of the country—a brief stop, a place I had never seen before—and was promptly accosted by a dancing, half-naked beggar, a most joyous fellow. Previously, I would have observed everything around me in perfect detail—the architecture of the station building, the faces of people walking by, the vendors who were selling their goods—but that rarely happens anymore. I don't remember the station building and I cannot tell you if there were vendors or people nearby. All I recall is a toothless brown-skinned beggar dancing before me, an arm outstretched for a few pence. What matters to me now is that I possess that delightful vision of him; where the event took place is of no account. Had this occurred sixty years ago, I would have been quite distraught for being unable to summon the location and its minutiae. But now I retain only what is necessary. The minor details aren't essential—what appears in my mind these days are rudimentary impressions, not all the frivolous surroundings. And for that I'm grateful."

For a moment, Mr. Umezaki said nothing, his face taking on the distracted, thoughtful look of someone processing information. Then he nodded and his expression softened. When he spoke again, his voice sounded almost tentative. "It's fascinating—how you describe it."

But Holmes was no longer listening. Down the aisle, the passenger car door had opened and a slender young woman with sunglasses on had entered the carriage. She wore a gray kimono and held an umbrella at her side. She headed waveringly in their direction, pausing every few steps as if to steady herself; then, still standing in the aisle, she gazed at a nearby window, drawn for a while by the fast-moving landscape—her profile suddenly displaying a broad, disfiguring keloid scar, which slithered like tentacles from underneath her collar (up her neck, over her jawline, across the right side of her face, vanishing into her immaculate black hair). When at last she came forward, passing them without notice, Holmes found himself thinking, You were once an enticing girl. Not so long ago, you were the most beautiful vision someone had ever seen.

12

THEY ARRIVED at Hiroshima Station in the early afternoon, and found themselves departing the train and entering a crowded, boisterous area of black-market stalls—the banter of haggling, the passing of illicit goods, the occasional tantrum thrown by a weary child—but after the monotonous rumble and steady vibrations inherent to railway travel, such human clamor was a welcome relief. They were, as Mr. Umezaki pointed out, entering a city newly reborn on the principles of democracy—where, just that month, a mayor had been chosen by popular vote during the first postwar election.

But when glimpsing Hiroshima's outskirts from within the passenger car, Holmes had seen very little that indicated a bustling city was nearby; instead, he had noticed clusters of temporary wooden shacks, like impoverished villages existing at close proximity to one another, separated only by wide fields strewn with tall horseweeds. When the train slowed on its approach to the dilapidated station, he realized that the horseweeds—sprouting thickly over a dark, uneven terrain of charred earth and concrete slabs and debris—were, in fact, thriving upon the burned-out land in which office buildings, entire neighborhoods, and business districts had stood.

The normally detested horseweed, Holmes then learned from Mr. Umezaki, was an unexpected blessing following the war. In Hiroshima, the plants' sudden emergence—offering a sense of hope and rebirth with its budding—had dispelled the widely accepted theory that the city would remain an infertile place for at least seventy years. There and elsewhere, its abundant growth had prevented mass death through starvation: "The leaves and flowers became a main ingredient in dumplings," Mr. Umezaki said. "Not too appetizing—believe me, I know—but those who couldn't continue on an empty stomach ate them to relieve the hunger."

Holmes had continued to look out the window, searching for a more definitive sign of the city, but, as the train moved into the rail yard, he could see just the wooden shacks—increasing in number, with some of the vacant lots around them transformed into modest vegetable gardens—and the Enko River, which ran parallel to the tracks. "As my stomach is a bit empty at the moment, I wouldn't mind sampling the dumplings myself—sounds like a most singular concoction."

Mr. Umezaki had nodded in agreement. "They are singular, it's true—except hardly in the best sense."

"Seems intriguing nonetheless."

But while Holmes had hoped for a late lunch of horseweed dumplings, it was another local specialty that eventually appeased him—a Japanese-style pancake covered in a sweet sauce, stuffed inside with whatever the customer chose from the menu list, and sold by any number of street vendors or makeshift noodle shops around Hiroshima Station.

"It's called *okonomi-yaki*," Mr. Umezaki explained later, while he and Holmes sat at a noodle shop counter, watching the cook create their lunch with great skill upon a large iron plate (their appetites further aroused by the sizzling fragrances wafting toward them). He went on to mention that he had first tried the dish when he was a boy, doing so while he vacationed in Hiroshima with his father. Since that childhood trip, he had visited the city a handful of times, usually staying only long enough to exchange trains, but sometimes an *okonomi-yaki* vendor would be at the station. "It's always impossible for me to resist it—the very smell conjures up that weekend with my father. You see, he had brought us to visit Shukkei-en Garden. Except rarely do I think of him and me being here together—or together at all, for that matter—unless *okonomi-yaki* is in the air."

Then during their meal, Holmes paused between bites, poking the interior pocket of the pancake with a chopstick and eyeing that mixture of meat, noodle, and cabbage, then said, "It is an uncomplicated creation, though rather exquisite, don't you agree?"

Mr. Umezaki looked up from the pancake piece held by his chopsticks. He appeared preoccupied with chewing and did not reply until he had swallowed. "Yes," he said at last. "Yes—"

Afterward, having been given hasty, vague directions by the busy cook, they headed for Shukkei-en Garden, a seventeenth-century refuge that Mr. Umezaki knew Holmes would enjoy seeing. Toting their suitcase at his side, leading the way along sidewalks teeming with foot traffic, ambling by crooked telephone poles and bent pine trees, he painted a vivid portrait, the details being extracted from his boyhood memories of the place. For the garden, he told Holmes, was a landscape in miniature, with a pond based on China's famous Xi Hu lake, and consisted of streams, islets, and bridges that appeared much larger than they actually were. An unimaginable oasis, Holmes realized when trying to envision the garden—impossible to conceive of, it seemed, in a flattened city struggling with reconstruction (the noises of which surrounded them—the beating of hammers, the groan of heavy equipment, the workmen moving down the street with lumber on their shoulders, the patter of horses and cars).

In any case, Mr. Umezaki readily admitted, the Hiroshima of his youth no longer remained, and he feared the garden had probably been badly damaged by the bomb. All the same, he believed something of its original charm might still remain intact—possibly the small stone bridge crossing a clear pond, maybe the stone lantern built in the image of Yang Kwei Fei.

"I suppose we will know soon enough," said Holmes, eager to leave the sun-drenched streets for a serene, relaxing environment, somewhere he could pause awhile amid the shade of trees and wipe the sweat from his forehead.

But when nearing a bridge that went across the Motoyasu River, at the city's barren center, Mr. Umezaki sensed a wrong turn had been made along the way, or that he had somehow misheard the cook's swiftly spoken instructions. Yet neither stopped, compelled instead to go forward toward what loomed ahead: "The Atom Bomb Dome," said Mr. Umezaki, pointing at the reinforced-concrete dome that had been stripped bare by the blast. His index finger climbed up past the building, indicating the hard blue sky. And there, he revealed, was where the great flash-bang had occurred, that inexplicable *pika-don,* engulfing the city in a massive firestorm; its wake then bringing days of black rain—fast-falling radioactivity mixed with the ashes of homes, trees, and bodies that had been obliterated by the blast and were sent swirling into the atmosphere.

As they approached the building, the breeze off the river started to blow more freely and the warm afternoon suddenly felt cooler. The sounds of the city, muted by the breeze, were less bothersome as they paused for a smoke—Mr. Umezaki setting the suitcase at their feet before lighting Holmes's cigar, both then sitting on a fallen concrete column (a convenient ruin, around which grew various weeds and wild grass). Other than what appeared to be a smattering of newly planted trees, the area provided little else in the way of shade; it was mostly an open stretch of land, which—absent of anyone else other than an elderly woman accompanied by two younger women—resembled a deserted, hurricane-swept shore. A few yards away, at the fence that encircled the Atom Bomb Dome building, they could see the women, each one kneeling and dutifully placing a paper crane necklace among the thousands of necklaces that were already there.

Then inhaling and releasing smoke between pursed lips, they sat mesmerized by the sight of the reinforced-concrete structure—a ravaged symbol standing close to ground zero, a forbidding memorial to the dead. After the blast, it was one of the few buildings not reduced to melted rubble—the skeletal steel frame of the dome arching above the ruins and prominent against the sky—while almost everything else below it had fragmented and burned and disappeared. Inside, there were no floors, as shock waves had collapsed the interior material into the basement, leaving only the vertical walls in place.

Yet, for Holmes, the building conveyed a kind of hopefulness, although he wasn't exactly sure why. Perhaps, he mused, the hope manifested from the sparrows perched along the building's rusted girders and the patches of blue sky present within the hollowed dome—or perhaps, in the aftermath of unfathomable destruction, the building's defying perseverance was in and of itself a harbinger of hope. But several minutes earlier—as he had first glimpsed the building—the very propinquity of the dome, suggesting so much violent death, filled him with profound regrets for where modern science had ultimately brought mankind: this uncertain age of atomic alchemy. He'd recalled the words of a London physician he'd once interrogated, an intelligent, thoughtful individual who, without any conceivable motive, had killed his wife and three children with strychnine, and who, subsequently, had set his own house on fire. When repeatedly asked about the reasons for his crime, the physician, refusing to speak, finally wrote three sentences on a sheet of paper: *There is a great weight beginning to push down on all sides of the earth at once. Because of it, we must stop ourselves. We must stop; otherwise, the earth will reach a complete standstill and cease to go round from all we have pressed upon it.* Only now, many years since, could he attach some modicum of meaning to that cryptic explanation, however tenuous it might be.

"We haven't much time," said Mr. Umezaki, dropping the butt

of his cigarette, then crushing it underfoot. He consulted his watch. "No, I'm afraid not much time at all. If we want to see the garden and catch the ferry for Miyajima, we should probably be going—that is, if we want to make the spa near Hofu by evening."

"Of course," said Holmes, situating his canes. As he rose off the column, Mr. Umezaki excused himself, wandering over to the women so he could get proper directions for Shukkei-en Garden (his friendly greeting and inquisitive voice carrying in the breeze). Still savoring his cigar, Holmes watched Mr. Umezaki and the three women, all standing beneath the somber building, smiling together in the afternoon sunlight. The elderly woman, whose creased face he could see quite plainly, was smiling in an unusually blissful manner, betraying the childlike innocence that sometimes reemerged with old age. Then, as if on cue, the three bowed, and Mr. Umezaki, after doing the same, about-faced sharply and walked quickly away from them, his smile promptly dissolving behind a stoic, somewhat grim expression.

1 3

As at the Atom Bomb Dome, a high fence surrounded Shukkei-en Garden, put there in order to prevent entrance. Mr. Umezaki, however, was undeterred, and, as had apparently been done by others, he found a fissure in the fence (mangled open with wire cutters, Holmes suspected, and pulled back with gloved hands, creating a wide-enough gap for a body to squeeze through). Presently, they found themselves strolling on the interconnected, circuitous footpaths, which were powdered with a grayish soot and wound around dark, lifeless ponds or the sticklike remains of charred plum and cherry trees. Maintaining a leisurely pace, they often stopped to look off the paths, taking in the burned, fragile remnants of the historical garden—the blackened vestiges of tea-ceremony rooms, a meager grouping of azaleas where once hundreds, possibly thousands, had flourished.

But Mr. Umezaki kept silent about all they observed and—much to Holmes's dismay—ignored whatever questions were asked regarding the garden's previous splendor; moreover, he showed an infuriating hesitation to stay beside Holmes—sometimes walking ahead, or abruptly lagging behind on the paths while Holmes, unaware, went forward. In fact, after getting directions from the women, Mr. Umezaki's mood had turned rather sullen, suggesting some unwanted information had been passed on. Most likely, Holmes imagined, that the garden of his memory had become an inhospitable, restricted domain—a place where public access was now forbidden.

Except, as was soon evident, they were not the only trespassers there. Coming toward them on a path was a sophisticated-looking man—in his late forties or early fifties, shirtsleeves rolled to his elbows—holding the hand of a cheerful small boy, who skipped alongside him in blue shorts and a white shirt. As the two approached, the man nodded politely at Mr. Umezaki and spoke something in Japanese, and when Mr. Umezaki replied, he nodded politely again. It seemed the man wished to say more, but the boy tugged at his hand, urging him on, so the man simply continued nodding and walked by.

When Holmes asked what the man had said, Mr. Umezaki shook his head and shrugged. The brief encounter, Holmes realized, had had an unsettling effect upon Mr. Umezaki. Repeatedly glancing over his shoulder, Mr. Umezaki appeared distracted and, walking close to Holmes for a while, gripping the suitcase handle with whitened knuckles, looked as if he had met an apparition. Then, before once more hurrying ahead, he said, "How odd. . . . I believe I have just passed myself with my father, though my younger brother—my actual brother, not Hensuiro—is nowhere to be seen. As you were convinced I was an only child, and having lived the majority of my life without a sibling, I didn't see any point in mentioning him to you. You see, he died of tuberculosis—in fact, he died only a month or so after we strolled this very pathway together." He glanced back while quickening his steps. "How very strange, Sherlock-san. It was many years ago, and yet now it doesn't seem so distant at all."

"It is true," Holmes said. "The disregarded past has sometimes startled me with vivid and unexpected impressions—moments I had scarcely remembered until they revisited me."

The footpath brought them to a larger pond and curved toward a stone bridge that arched over the water. With several tiny islands dotting the pond—each bearing traces of tearooms and huts and other bridges—the garden suddenly felt vast and far from any city. Farther ahead, Mr. Umezaki had stopped, waiting for Holmes to join him; then both men stared for a time at a monk sitting cross-legged on one of the islands, his robed body upright and perfectly still, like a statue, his shaved head lowered in prayer.

Holmes stooped near Mr. Umezaki's feet, taking a turquoise-colored pebble from the path and dropping it into a pocket.

"I don't believe there is such a thing as fate in Japan," Mr. Umezaki eventually said, his gaze fixed on the monk. "Following my brother's death, I saw less and less of my father. He traveled a lot in those days, mostly to London and Berlin. With my brother gone—his name was Kenji—and my mother's grief pervading our household, I wanted terribly to accompany him on his trips. But I was a schoolboy, you see, and my mother needed me near her more than ever. My father was encouraging, though: He promised if I learned English and did well in school, then someday I might travel abroad with him. So, as you can imagine an eager child doing, I spent my free hours learning to read and write and speak English. I suppose, in a way, that kind of diligence fostered the resolve I needed for becoming a writer."

When they began walking again, the monk lifted his head, tilting it to the sky. He chanted lowly under his breath, a guttural, droning sound that drifted across the pond like ripples.

"A year or so later," Mr. Umezaki continued, "my father sent me a book from London, a fine edition of *A Study in Scarlet*. It was the first novel I read from start to finish in English, and it was my introduction to Dr. Watson's writings concerning your adventures.

Regrettably, I wouldn't read the English editions of his other books
for quite a while—not until I'd gone from Japan to attend school in
England. You see, because of my mother's state of mind, she refused
to allow any books dealing with you—or England—to be read in our
home. In fact, she got rid of that edition my father sent me—finding where I'd hidden it, disposing of it without asking my permis-
sion. Luckily, I'd already finished the last chapter the night before."

"A rather harsh reaction on her part," said Holmes.

"It was," said Mr. Umezaki. "I was angry at her for weeks. I refused to speak to her, or to eat her meals. It was a difficult period for
everyone."

They came to a range of hillocks on the pond's northern shore,
where—past the garden property—a neighboring river and distant
hills provided a pleasant backdrop. A deliberately placed boulder
was nearby, functioning as a kind of natural bench, its upper half
having been leveled and smoothed. So Holmes and Mr. Umezaki sat,
enjoying a good overview of the garden grounds from their vantage
point.

Sitting there, Holmes felt as worn down as that age-old boulder,
resting by hillocks, somehow remaining present when everything
else that had been previously recognized was receding or gone.
Across the pond, beyond the opposite bank, were the curious shapes
of fallow trees—the crooked, unproductive limbs of which no longer
shielded the garden from the city's houses and busy streets. For a
while, they stayed there, saying very little and contemplating the
view, until Holmes—pondering what Mr. Umezaki had told him—
said, "I pray I am not being too inquisitive, but I take it your father
is no longer living."

"My mother was less than half his age when they married," Mr.
Umezaki said, "so I'm quite sure he's dead, though I have no idea
where or how he passed on. To be honest, I was hoping you could
tell me."

"How exactly do you propose I do that?"

Bending forward, Mr. Umezaki pressed his fingertips together; then he glanced at Holmes with intent eyes. "During our correspondence, was my name not familiar to you?"

"No, I cannot say that it was. Should it have been?"

"My father's name, then—Umezaki Matsuda, or Matsuda Umezaki."

"I am afraid I don't understand."

"It appears you had some dealings with my father while he was in England. I've been uncertain on how to broach the subject with you, because I feared you might question my reasons for inviting you here. I suppose I assumed you'd make the connections on your own and somehow be more forthcoming."

"And when would these dealings have occurred? For I assure you I possess no memory of them."

Nodding gravely, his fingers now unlatching the traveling bag at his feet, Mr. Umezaki proceeded to open the suitcase on the ground, digging deliberately through his own clothing, and retrieving a letter, which he unfolded and handed to Holmes. "This arrived with the book my father sent. It was for my mother."

Holmes brought the letter near his face, scrutinizing what he could.

"It was written forty, maybe forty-five years ago, correct? See how the paper has yellowed considerably along the edges, and how the black ink has turned bluish." Holmes gave the letter to Mr. Umezaki. "The contents, unfortunately, are lost on me. So if you will please do me the honor—"

"I'll do my best." With his expression remote and transfigured, Mr. Umezaki began translating: "After consulting with the great detective Sherlock Holmes here in London, I realize that it is in the best interest of all of us if I remain in England indefinitely. You will see from this book that he is, indeed, a very wise and intelligent man, and his say in this important matter should not be taken lightly. I have already made arrangements for the property and my finances to be placed in your care, until such a time as Tamiki can take over these responsibilities in adulthood." Then Mr. Umezaki began folding the letter, adding as he did so, "The letter was dated March twenty-third. The year was 1903—which means I was eleven and he was fifty-nine. We never heard from him again—nor was any further information discovered as to why he felt compelled to stay in England. In other words, this is all we know."

"That is regrettable," said Holmes, watching as the letter was placed back inside the suitcase. It was not possible, at that moment, to tell Mr. Umezaki that he believed his father was a liar. But he could address his own mystification, explaining that he wasn't sure if a meeting with Matsuda Umezaki had ever happened. "It is conceivable that I may have met him—then again, I may not have. You have no idea how many people came to us during those years, literally thousands. Yet very few stand out in my mind, although I think a Japanese man in London certainly would, don't you? Still, one way or the other, it really does escape me. I am sorry, for I know that isn't very helpful."

Mr. Umezaki waved his hand, a dismissive gesture, which, as if by choice, caused him suddenly to cast off his serious demeanor. "It's hardly worth the trouble," he said, his voice becoming casual in tone.

"I care little about my father—he disappeared so long ago, you understand, and he's buried in my childhood, along with my brother. It's for my mother that I had to ask you—because she has always wondered. To this day, in fact, she continues to agonize. I realize I should have discussed this with you earlier, but it was difficult bringing it up in her presence, so I chose our travels to do so."

"Your discretion and your devotion to your mother," Holmes said genially, "are commendable."

"I appreciate that," said Mr. Umezaki. "And please, this small matter mustn't cloud the true reasons for why you're here. My invitation was sincere—I want that made clear—and we have much to see and talk about."

"Naturally," said Holmes.

Except nothing of substance was said for a good while after that exchange, aside from brief generalities spoken mostly by Mr. Umezaki ("I fear we should be going. We don't want to miss our ferry."). Nor did either man feel inclined to prompt a conversation—not as they left the garden, not even when they found themselves on a ferry bound for Miyajima Island (keeping silent even when glimpsing the huge red torii that stood above the sea). Then their awkward silence would only increase, staying with them as they rode the bus to Hofu, and as they settled in for the evening at Momiji-so Spa (a resort where, according to legend, a white fox had once nursed its wounded leg in the healing hot springs, and where, while sinking into a tub of the famed water, one might spy the fox's face floating amid the steam. It dissipated only just before supper, when Mr. Umezaki looked straight at Holmes and smiled broadly, saying, "It's a lovely evening."

Holmes smiled in return, though without enthusiasm. "Quite" was his concise reply.

14

B UT IF Mr. Umezaki had, with a slight raising of his hand, discarded the issue of his father's disappearance, then it was Holmes who was preoccupied by the quandary of Matsuda. For the man's name, he later became convinced, had a vaguely recognizable ring (or was this sense, he wondered, based solely on the already-familiar surname?). And so during their second overnight stay—while eating fish and drinking sake at a Yamaguchi inn—he inquired further about the father, his initial question being met with a lingering, uncomfortable stare from Mr. Umezaki. "Why are you asking me this now?"

"Because my curiosity has gotten the better of me, I am sorry to say."

"Is that so?"

"I am afraid it is."

Thereafter, all questions received thoughtful answers, with Mr. Umezaki growing increasingly effusive as his cup was repeatedly emptied and refilled. Though by the time both men reached intoxication, Mr. Umezaki occasionally stopped in midsentence, unable to complete what he had been saying. For a while, he stared hopelessly at Holmes, his fingers tightening around his cup. Soon he ceased talking altogether, and it would be Holmes, for once, helping him to stand, to walk from the table, to go unsteadily forward. Presently, they would retire into their respective rooms, and the next morning—when sight-seeing at three nearby villages and shrines—no mention was made of the previous evening's discussion.

That third day of travel would stay with Holmes as the highlight of his entire trip. Both he and Mr. Umezaki, while feeling the disagreeable aftereffects of having drunk too much, were in great spirits, and it was a glorious spring day. Sitting on buses, bumping through the countryside, their conversation drifted from subject to subject in a natural, lighthearted manner. They talked of England, and they talked of beekeeping; they talked of the war, and they talked of travels both had undertaken in their youth. Holmes was surprised to hear that Mr. Umezaki had visited Los Angeles and shaken hands with Charles Chaplin; in turn, Mr. Umezaki was fascinated by Holmes's account of his adventures in Tibet, where he had visited Lhasa and spent some days with the Dalai Lama.

Their amicable, easy exchange carried on through the morning and into the afternoon—while exploring goods at a village bazaar (Holmes purchasing an ideal letter opener: a *kusun-gobu* short sword), and witnessing an unusual spring fertility festival in another village, the two chatting surreptitiously as a procession of priests, musicians, and locals dressed like demons paraded down the street: the men hoisting erect wooden phalluses, the women embracing smaller carved penises swathed in red paper, the spectators touching the tips of passing phalluses to ensure good health for their children.

"How remarkable," commented Holmes.

"I thought you might find this of interest," said Mr. Umezaki.

Holmes grinned slyly. "My friend, I suspect this is much more to your liking than mine."

"You're probably right," agreed Mr. Umezaki, smiling while his fingertips reached out for an oncoming phallus.

But the ensuing evening was like the one before: another inn,

supper together, rounds of sake, cigarettes and cigars, and more questions regarding Matsuda. Since it was impossible for Mr. Umezaki to
know everything concerning his father—especially after the questioning went from the general to the specific—his replies were often
indefinite, or answered simply with a shrug, or by saying, "I don't
know." Still, Mr. Umezaki didn't begrudge the probing, even if
Holmes's inquiries brought back unhappy memories of childhood
and the agony of his mother's grief. "She destroyed so much—almost
anything my father had touched. Twice, she set fire to our house, and
she also tried persuading me to join her in a suicide pact. She wanted
us to walk together into the sea and drown ourselves; it was her idea
of avenging my father's wrong against us."

"I take it, then, that your mother has a distinct dislike for me.
The woman can hardly contain her contempt—I sensed it early on."

"No, she isn't very fond of you—but, honestly, she isn't very fond
of anyone, so you needn't take it too personally. She hardly acknowl-
edges Hensuiro, and she dislikes the path I've taken in life. I haven't
married; I live with my companion—she blames these things on my
father's abandonment of us. In her mind, a boy can never become a
man unless he has a father to teach him what it means."

"Was I not, supposedly, decisive in that choice of abandonment?"

"She thinks so."

"Well, I must take it personally. How could I not? I pray you
don't share her feelings."

"No, not at all. We are different creatures of reason, my mother
and I. I hold nothing against you. You are—if I may say—a hero of
mine, and a newfound friend."

"You flatter me," said Holmes, proffering his cup for a toast. "To
newfound friends—"

Then surfacing on Mr. Umezaki's face throughout the evening
was a trusting, attentive expression. Indeed, Holmes perceived the
expression as one of faith: that Mr. Umezaki—in speaking of his
father, in relating what he knew—believed the retired detective

might shed some welcome light on the disappearance, or, at the very least, provide a few insights once the questioning had concluded. Only later, when it was clear Holmes had nothing to reveal, did a separate expression become evident—a sorrowful face, somewhat morose. Canker and melancholy, thought Holmes, after Mr. Umezaki berated a waitress who had accidentally spilled fresh sake on their table.

Subsequently, on the last leg of their trip, there came long periods of introspection between the two, punctuated only by the exhalations of tobacco smoke. On board the train headed for Shimonoseki, Mr. Umezaki kept busy by writing inside his red journal, and Holmes—his thoughts now preoccupied with what he had learned of Matsuda—stared out the window, following the course of a slender river that curved alongside steep mountains. At times, the train wound near country residences, each house having a single twenty-gallon barrel set beside the river's bank (the words on the side of the barrels, Mr. Umezaki had explained earlier, meant "Fire-Prevention Water"). Along the way, Holmes observed various small villages, with mountains towering beyond them. To reach the summits of those mountains, he imagined, was to stand above the prefecture and command a breathtaking view of everything below—the valleys, the villages, the distant cities, maybe the entire Inland Sea.

While surveying that scenic terrain, Holmes mulled over all Mr. Umezaki had told him concerning his father, forming in his mind a basic portrait of the vanished man—someone whose presence he could almost summon from the past: the thin features and the tall stature, the distinctive shape of his gaunt face, the goatee of a Meiji intellectual. Yet Matsuda was also a diplomat-statesman, serving as one of Japan's leading foreign ministers, before disgrace shortened his term. Even so, he endured as an enigmatic character, known for his skill with logic and debate, and for his vast understanding of international policies. Most notable among his many accomplishments was a book documenting Japan's war with China, written while he was residing in London and detailing, among other things, the secret diplomacy that occurred prior to the war's outbreak.

Ambitious by nature, Matsuda's political aspirations began during the Meiji Restoration, when he entered government service despite his parents' wishes. Considered an outsider because he wasn't associated with any of the favored four Western clans, his abilities were impressive enough that eventually the governorship of a number of prefectures was offered to him, and while in that post, he made his first visit to London in 1870. On the heels of resigning his gubernatorial position, he was selected to join the expanding Foreign Ministry, but his promising career ended three years later as his dissatisfaction with the clan-dominated government found him plotting its overthrow. The failed conspiracy led to a lengthy imprisonment, where—rather than languishing behind bars—he continued doing important work, such as translating Jeremy Bentham's *Introduction to the Principles of Morals and Legislation* into the Japanese language.

After his prison release, Matsuda married his girl-like wife, and in time she gave him two sons. Meanwhile, he spent several years traveling abroad, frequently coming and going from Japan, making London his European home base, while journeying often to Berlin and Vienna. This was a long period of study for him, his main interest being constitutional law. And while he was widely considered to be a scholar with a profound knowledge of the West, his beliefs were always those of an autocrat: "Make no mistake," Mr. Umezaki had said on that second evening of questioning, "my father believed a single, absolute power should rule its people—I think this is why he preferred England to America. I also think his dogmatic beliefs made him too impatient to be a successful politician, let alone a good father and husband."

"And you imagine he remained in London until his death?"

"It's more than likely."

"And you never sought him out while attending school there?"

"Briefly, yes—except it proved impossible to find him. Frankly, I didn't try hard enough, but I was a young man and taken with my new life and new friends—and felt no urgent need to contact the man who had abandoned us long ago. In the end, I deliberately gave up on any effort to locate him, feeling somehow liberated in that decision. He was, after all, of another world by then. We were strangers."

Yet decades later, Mr. Umezaki confessed, he would come to regret that decision. Because now he was fifty-five—only four years younger than his father had been when they last saw each other—and he fostered a growing emptiness inside himself, a black space where the absence of his father dwelled. Moreover, he was convinced that his father must have shared the same empty place for the family he'd never see again; with Matsuda's passing, that murky, vacuous wound had somehow found its way into his surviving son, eventually festering within as a frequent source of bewilderment and distress, existing as an unresolved problem of an aging heart.

"Then it is not just for your mother's sake that you require some answers?" Holmes had asked, his words suddenly tainted by intoxication and weariness.

"No, I suppose it's not," answered Mr. Umezaki with a degree of despair.

"You are really seeking the truth for yourself, correct? It is—in other words—important to grasp the facts of the matter for your own well-being."

"Yes." Mr. Umezaki reflected for a moment, peering into his sake glass before glancing again at Holmes. "So what is the truth? How do you arrive at it? How do you unravel the meaning of something that doesn't wish to be known?" He kept his eyes on Holmes, in the expectation that such questioning would produce a definitive starting point; if Holmes responded, the disappearance of his father and the greatest pain of his childhood might begin to be dealt with.

But Holmes was quiet, seemingly lost in thought; his inward

expression as he sat thinking generated an optimistic twinge in Mr. Umezaki. Without a doubt, Holmes was sorting through the vast index of his memory. Like the contents of a file buried deep inside a forgotten cabinet, the once-known specifics surrounding Matsuda's forsaking of his family and homeland would, when at last retrieved, give way to an invaluable amount of information. Soon Holmes's eyes would close (the old detective's ruminating mind, Mr. Umezaki felt certain, was already reaching into that cabinet's darker recesses), and almost imperceptibly, a faint snoring would then be heard.

PART

III

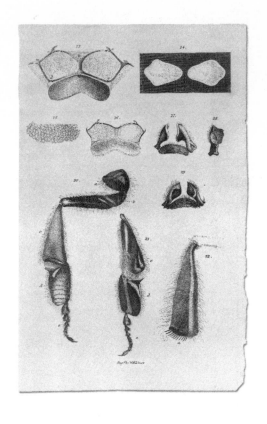

15

IT WAS HOLMES—after waking at his desk with numbed feet, and then taking a stroll outside to bolster his circulation—who discovered Roger on that late afternoon, finding him very near the beeyard and partially concealed amid the adjacent pasture's higher grass. The boy was stretched out upon his back, arms along his sides, lounging there and gazing upward at the slow-moving clouds far above. And before stepping any closer or saying Roger's name, Holmes, too, pondered those clouds, wondering what it was exactly that held the boy's attention so rigidly—for nothing extraordinary could be spotted, nothing at all save the gradual evolving of cumulus and the expansive cloud shadows that periodically muted sunlight and swept across the pasture like waves rushing over a shoreline.

"Roger, my boy," Holmes eventually said, lowering his stare while wading forward through the grass, "your mother has, unfortunately, requested your help in the kitchen."

As it happened, Holmes had had no intention of venturing into the beeyard. He'd simply planned a brief walk around the gardens, checking the herb beds, yanking the occasional weed, patting down loose soil with a cane. Except Mrs. Munro had caught him as he went past the kitchen doorway, wiping flour on her apron, asking if he might be good enough to fetch the boy for her. So Holmes agreed, although not without reluctance, because there was still unfinished work awaiting him in the attic, and because a hike beyond the gardens inevitably became a protracted but welcome distraction (once setting foot within the beeyard, he was sure to remain at the apiary until dusk, peeking into hives, rearranging the brood nest, removing unneeded combs).

Some days later, however, he'd realize that Mrs. Munro's request was a dismally fortuitous one: Had she gone for the boy herself, she'd never have looked any farther than the beeyard, at least not initially; she'd never have observed the high grass trampled into a fresh trail in the pasture, or—then traveling alongside that narrow, curving course—noticed Roger resting motionless, facing such massy white clouds. Yes, she'd have shouted his name from the garden pathway, but with no answer forthcoming, would have imagined him being elsewhere (reading at the cottage, chasing butterflies in the woods, maybe picking shells off the beach). She wouldn't have grown suddenly concerned. A troubled expression wouldn't have spread on her face—as her legs parted the grass, as she went to him and repeated his name.

"Roger," said Holmes. "Roger," he whispered while standing over the boy, pressing a cane gently against his shoulder.

Ultimately, when locked again inside his study, he'd recall only the boy's eyes—those dilated pupils transfixed on the sky, somehow conveying rapture—and he'd think little more of what had been quickly fathomed there amid the gently shuddering grass: Roger's swollen lips and hands and cheeks, the countless weltlike stings that formed irregular patterns on the boy's neck, face, forehead, ears. Nor would Holmes ponder the few words he had then uttered while crouched by Roger, such gravely spoken words that, if heard by another, would have rung impossibly cold, unimaginably callous.

"Quite dead, my boy. Quite dead, I fear. . . ."

But Holmes was well acquainted with death's unwelcome arrival—or at least he wished to believe so—and hardly did its sudden visitations surprise him anymore. During the long expanse of his life, he'd knelt near a multitude of corpses—women, men, children, and animals alike, often complete strangers, though sometimes acquaintances—observing the conclusive ways in which quietus had left its calling card (blue-black bruises along one side of a body, discolored skin, curled fingers frozen with rigor, that sickly sweet smell inhaled into the nostrils of the living: any number of variations but always the same undeniable theme). *Death, like crime, is commonplace,* he'd once written. *Logic, on the other hand, is rare. Therefore, maintaining a logical mental inclination, especially when facing mortality, can be difficult. However, it is always upon logic rather than upon death that one should dwell.*

And so, too, amid the high grass was logic brought out like a shield of sterling armor to repel the heartbreaking discovery of the boy's body (forget the slight dizziness Holmes felt taking hold, or the trembling of his fingers, or the befuddling anguish that was starting to blossom in his mind). Roger being gone was of no importance at the moment, he convinced himself. What mattered now was how Roger had reached his end. But without even examining the body—without even bending, studying that inflamed, swollen face—the scenario of Roger's demise was understood.

The boy had been stung, of course. Stung repeatedly, Holmes knew upon first glance. Before Roger had succumbed, his skin had become flushed, accompanied by a burning pain, generalized itching. He'd fled his attackers, perhaps. In any case, he'd wandered from the hives into the pasture, likely disoriented, pursued by the swarm. There was no indication of vomit on his shirt or around his lips and chin, although the boy had surely ached from abdominal cramps, nausea. His blood pressure would have dropped, creating a feeling of weakness. The throat and mouth had no doubt swelled, preventing him from swallowing or calling for help. Alterations of heart rate would have followed, as well as difficulty breathing, and probably a notion of impending doom (he was an intelligent child, so he would've sensed his fate). Then, as if slipping past a trapdoor, he had collapsed in the grass and become unconscious—dying, remarkably, with eyes wide open.

"Anaphylaxis," Holmes muttered, brushing dirt flecks off the boy's cheeks. Severe allergic reaction, he concluded. One sting too many. The extreme end of the allergic spectrum, a relatively immediate and uncomfortable death. He brought his forlorn stare to the sky, watching as the clouds progressed overhead, aware of dusk's increasing eminence at day's end.

What mishap occurred? he finally asked himself, struggling with his canes to stand upright. What did the boy do—what provoked the bees so? For the beeyard appeared as serene as it usually did; when crossing the apiary earlier, searching for Roger and speaking the boy's name, Holmes had witnessed no swarm, no agitated activity at the hives' entrances, nothing out of the ordinary. Furthermore, not a single bee hovered in proximity to Roger now. Regardless, the apiary deserved closer consideration; the hives required proper inspection. Overalls, gloves, a hat, and a veil needed to be worn, lest a similar fate as the boy's await Holmes. But first the authorities had to be informed, and Mrs. Munro told, and Roger's body carried away.

Already the sun was dipping toward the west, and behind the fields and woods, the horizon glowed faintly white in the distance. Going unsteadily from Roger, Holmes made his way across the pasture, forging his own crooked trail in order to avoid the beeyard altogether, stepping through the grass until reaching the gravel of the garden pathway; there, he paused, looking back at the tranquil beeyard and the grassy spot where the boy lay unseen, both places now awash in golden sunlight. Just then, he spoke beneath his breath, flustered at once by the insignificance of his own silent words.

"What are you saying?" he suddenly said aloud, pounding his

canes on the gravel. "What—are you—" A worker bee whizzed by, trailed by another, restraining him with their buzzing.

The blood had drained from his face, and his hands shook while clutching at the cane handles. Attempting to regain composure, he inhaled deeply and then turned quickly to the farmhouse. But he couldn't yet proceed, because everything ahead of him—the garden rows, the house, the pine trees—was only vaguely tangible. For a moment, he remained perfectly still, confounded by all around and before him: How is it possible, he questioned, that I've blundered into someplace that isn't mine? How did I lead myself here?

"No," he said, "no, no—you are mistaken—"

He shut his eyes, inhaling air into his chest. He had to concentrate, not just to recover himself but also to vanquish the sense of unfamiliarity, for the pathway was his design, the garden, too—there were wild daffodils nearby; even closer at hand were purple buddleias. If his eyes were to open, Holmes was positive, he'd certainly recognize his giant thistles; he'd see his herb beds. And at last parting his eyelids, he saw the daffodils, the buddleias, the thistles, the pine trees farther on. Then he urged his legs forward, doing so with a fair degree of grim determination.

"Of course," he mumbled, "of course—"

That night, Holmes would stand at the attic window, looking out into the darkness. As if by choice, he'd fail to examine the previous moments that had sent him up into the study, the specifics of all that was said and explained—the brief conversation with Mrs. Munro after he entered the farmhouse, her voice calling to him from the kitchen: "Did you find him?"

"Yes."

"Is he on his way?"

"I am afraid so—yes."

"About time, I'll say."

Or the hushed phone call notifying Anderson of the boy's passing, telling the constable where the body could be found, and a warning to Anderson and his men to keep clear of the apiary: "There is something amiss with my bees, so be careful. If you will tend to the boy and inform his mother, I will tend to the hives and then reveal tomorrow what was learned."

"We'll be right there. And I'm sorry for your loss, sir. I truly am."

"Do hurry, Anderson."

Or his self-reproach for having avoided Mrs. Munro, rather than dealing with her directly—his inability to convey his own remorse, to share something of his agony with her, to stand at her side when Anderson and his men entered the house. Instead, stupefied by Roger's death and the very idea of facing the boy's mother with the truth, he had climbed upstairs to his study, shutting and locking the door, forgetting to return to the apiary as planned. Then he had sat at his desk, jotting note after note, scarcely cognizant of the meanings of his hastily written sentences, paying some mind to the comings and goings outside, the impromptu sorrow of Mrs. Munro rising from down below (her guttural wails, the breathless sobs—a profound grief that coursed through the walls and floors, echoed along the corridors, and soon ended as abruptly as it had begun). Minutes later, Anderson had knocked on the study door, saying, "Mr. Holmes—Sherlock—" So Holmes had reluctantly allowed him entrance, though only for a short while. Nonetheless, the particulars of their discussion—the things Anderson had suggested, the things Holmes had agreed upon—were inevitably lost on him.

And in the silence thereafter—once Anderson and his men had left the house, taking Mrs. Munro in one vehicle and the boy in an ambulance—he went to the attic window, seeing nothing beyond except complete darkness. But still he perceived something, that disquieting image he couldn't shake completely from memory: Roger's blue eyes out there in the pasture, those wide pupils seemingly intent in their upward gaze, yet unbearably vacuous.

Going again to his desk, he rested for a while in his chair, hunched forward, with thumbs pressed against his shut eyelids. "No," he muttered, shaking his head. "Is that so?" he then said aloud, raising his head. "How can that be?" He opened his eyes, glancing about as if expecting to find someone else nearby. But, as always, he was alone in the attic, seated at his desk, a hand now reaching absently for his pen.

His stare fell on the work before him, the stacks of pages, the clutter of notes—and that unfinished manuscript bound by a single rubber band. In the subsequent hours preceding dawn, he wouldn't think much more of Roger, nor would he ever conceive of the boy sitting in the same chair, poring over the case of Mrs. Keller and wishing for the story's completion. And yet, on that night, he suddenly felt compelled to finish the story anyway—to reach for fresh sheets of writing paper, to begin fashioning a kind of closure for himself where previously none had existed.

Then it was as if the words were arriving well ahead of his own thoughts, filling the pages with ease. The words propelled his hand forward while also taking him back, back, back—past the summer months in Sussex, past his recent trip to Japan, past both great wars—to a world that thrived in the flux of one century's conclusion and another century's outset. He wouldn't cease his writing until sunrise. He wouldn't stop until the ink had almost been emptied.

16

III.

In the Gardens of the
Physics and Botanical Society

As documented in John's short sketches, I was often not above the unscrupulous when working on a case, nor was I always selfless in my actions; for, in that regard, to be honest about my intentions concerning the need for the photograph of Mrs. Keller is to confess that I had no real need of it whatsoever. Indeed, the case was finished before going from Portman's on that Thursday evening, and I might have revealed all to Mr. Keller then had the woman's face ceased to beguile me so. Yet by prolonging the outcome, I knew I could again witness her in person, but from a better vantage point. The photograph, too, was wanted for my own reasons, with some desire for it to remain among my possessions in lieu of payment. And later that night, sitting alone near the window, the woman continued to stroll effortlessly through my thoughts—her parasol held high against the sun as if to shield the alabaster whiteness of her skin—while her diffident image gazed up from my lap.

But several days passed before I was afforded the opportunity to consign my full attention to her. During the intervening time, my energies were spent on a matter of supreme importance which the French government had engaged me to settle—a sordid affair revolving around an onyx paperweight stolen from a diplomat's desk in Paris and, eventually, stashed beneath the floorboards of a West End stage. Even so, the woman persisted in my mind, manifesting in an increasingly fanciful manner, which, while being almost wholly of my invention, was as enticing as it was disconcerting. I did not, however, lack the insight of realising that my ruminations were based on fantasy and, therefore, were probably inaccurate; yet I cannot deny the complicated impulses which arose when I was preoccupied by such foolish reverie—for the tenderness I felt was, for once, extending beyond my sense of reason.

So it was to be on the subsequent Tuesday that I disguised myself accordingly, giving a fair amount of consideration towards the persona which might best suit the ineffable Mrs. Keller. I settled on Stefan Peterson, an unattached middle-aged bibliophile with a kind-natured, if not somewhat effeminate, disposition; a myopic, bespectacled character, attired in well-worn tweed, who had the habit of nervously running a hand across his unkempt hair while tugging absently at his blue ascot.

"Begging your pardon, miss," I said, squinting at my reflection in the mirror, assuming what I believed would be my persona's polite and shy first words to Mrs. Keller. "I'm sorry, miss—begging your pardon—"

Adjusting the ascot, I realised that his predisposition for flora was to rival her love of all things which bloomed. Tousling my hair, I was positive that his fascination for romance literature was unsurpassed. He was, after all, an avid reader, preferring the detached solace of a book above most human interaction. Yet at his core he was a lonely man, existing as someone who, as he had grown older, had begun to contemplate the value of steady companionship. To this end, he studied the subtle art of palmistry, more as a way to make contact with others than as a means for divulging future events; if the correct palm were to rest briefly within his hand, he imagined that the fleeting warmth of it could sustain him in the months thereafter.

And now it is here that I cannot envision myself concealed behind my own creation—rather, when recalling the moments of that afternoon, I am removed from the proceedings altogether. Instead, it was Stefan Peterson walking into the declining light of day, his head lowered and his shoulders drawn toward his chest, a floundering and pitiable figure gingerly ambling in the direction of Montague Street. The sight of him garnered no lingering glances, nor was his presence notable by any manner. He was, to those who brushed beside him, an imminently forgettable soul.

Yet he was resolute upon his mission, bringing himself to Portman's prior to Mrs. Keller's arrival. Entering the shop, he went silently past the counter, where, as before, the proprietor gazed at a book—magnifying glass in hand, face hovering near the text—and was unaware of Stefan's fleeting proximity; only then, as he roamed down an aisle, did the proprietor's hearing come into question, for the old fellow had not been stirred by the shop door squeaking on its hinges, or by the OPEN placard bumping against the glass after the door was shut. He wandered along the veiled corridors of bookcases, crossing through the dust motes which swirled amidst the scant rays of sunlight; the farther one went within the shop, he discerned, the darker it became ahead—until everything to the fore of him was blanketed by shadow.

Reaching the stairwell, he climbed seven steps and crouched there, then, so that he might clearly observe Mrs. Keller's entrance without being noticed. And, in due course, events would at last commence thusly: the armonica's mournful vibrations began from above—the boy's fingers sliding upon the glasses; moments later, the shop door swung back and, as she had done on previous Tuesdays and Thursdays, Mrs. Keller came in off the street with her parasol slipped under an arm and a book held in a gloved hand. Paying the proprietor no mind—nor he her—she drifted into the aisles, pausing at times to survey the shelves, occasionally touching the spines of various volumes as though her fingers were impelled to do so. For a while, she remained visible, yet her back was kept away from him; he watched her glide slowly towards the darker recesses, becoming less and less apparent. Finally, she moved from his view completely, but not before he saw her place the book she was carrying on a top shelf, trading it, then, for another volume, which she seemingly chose at random.

You are hardly a thief, he told himself. No, you are, in truth, a borrower.

Once she had passed from sight, he could only surmise her exact location—somewhere close, yes, as he caught the scent of her perfume; surely somewhere amidst the near pitch, if only for a few seconds. As it happened, what followed next was expected and offered little surprise, although his eyes were not quite prepared: a sudden bright white flash illuminated from the shop's rear, flooding the aisles momentarily with its brilliance, vanishing as swiftly as it had erupted. He promptly descended the steps, seeing still the afterglow upon his pupils of that light which had swept inside and, he knew, now enveloped Mrs. Keller.

He travelled along a narrow passage between the double row of bookcases, inhaling the powerful, guiding fumes of her fragrance, and stopped within the shadows by the far wall. As he stood facing the wall, his eyes began adjusting to the surroundings, and he whispered lowly, "Right here, and nowhere else." The muted sounds of the armonica continued falling quite distinctly upon his ear. He glanced to the left—precarious stacks of books; then to the right—more piles of books. And there, directly in front of him, was the portal of Mrs. Keller's departure—a back exit, a shut door framed by the same brightness which had stunned his vision. He took two steps forwards and pushed at the door. It took all his self-control to prevent himself from rushing after her. With the door swinging wide, the light again spilled into the shop. Yet he hesitated in going past the threshold, and cautiously, as he squinted outside at the trellis screens forming an enclosed walkway, gradually eased onwards with a shuffling, reserved gait.

Soon her perfume became obscured by the even richer odours of tulips and daffodils. Then he could compel himself no farther than the walkway's end, where he peered through the vine-covered lattice-work and beheld a tiny landscaped garden of the most elaborate design: Herb beds thrived beside a somewhat oblique topiary pruned from dense hedging plants, and perennials and roses cloaked the walled perimeter; such an ideal oasis the proprietor had fashioned in the heart of London, one which was barely glimpsed from Madame Schirmer's window. The old man had, likely in the years preceding his failing eyesight, tailored his garden to the differing microclimates of his backyard: Where the roof of the building kept sunlight from reaching long into places, the proprietor had planted variegated foliage in order to highlight the darkened areas; elsewhere, the perennial beds hosted foxglove, geraniums, and lilies.

A path of river stone curved towards the garden's centre and concluded at a square patch of turf which was encircled by a formal boxwood hedge. Upon the turf was a small bench, and near it was a large terra-cotta urn, painted with copper patina; and upon the bench— her parasol across her lap, the book she had taken gripped by both hands—sat Mrs. Keller within the building's shade, reading while the armonica's sound drifted from the window above and down into the garden like an enigmatic breeze.

Of course, he thought, of course—thinking this when she glanced up from the book, cocking her head to one side, listening intently as the playing slackened for a moment and, eventually, then swelled into a refined, less dissonant performance. Madame Schirmer, he was certain, had now taken Graham's place at the armonica, showing the boy how the glasses should be properly manipulated. And while those masterful fingers pulled exquisite tones from the instrument, transforming the very air with its lulling textures, he studied Mrs. Keller from afar, observing the subtle rapture in her expression—the gentle exhaling of her breath between parted lips, the loosening of her rigid posture, the slow closing of her eyes—and the hidden presence of something pacific about her which emerged, if but for a scant few minutes, in accord with the music.

It is difficult to remember how long he remained there, face at the trellis screen, watching her; for he, too, was captivated by all that had come to enrich the garden. Yet his concentration would at last be broken with the squeaking of the rear door, followed thereafter by the violent cough, which hastened the proprietor across the threshold. Wearing the soiled smock and brown gloves, the old man entered into the walkway, a hand clutching the handle of a watering can; soon enough, the proprietor would lumber past the figure pressed nervously against the trellis screen, stepping into the garden while never once giving heed to its trespassers, then reaching the flower beds just as the last strains of the armonica ebbed away, the watering can slipping from the hand and landing upon its side and emptying most of its contents.

At that instant it was over: The armonica had fallen silent; the proprietor was stooping by his rose beds, feeling upon the lawn for what had escaped his grasp. Mrs. Keller gathered her belongings and stood from the bench, going towards the old man with that by-now-familiar manner of leisure; her form cast over him as she bent in front of his outstretched hands, righting the watering can, and the proprietor, without having fathomed her ghostlike presence, promptly seized hold of its handle and coughed. Then like a cloud shadow passing easily upon the earth, she moved off in the direction of a little ironwork gate at the back of the garden; there, she turned the key which sat within the lock, allowing the gate to swing wide enough for her to leave—the gate opening and closing with the same mixture of rattles and scrapes. And then it seemed, to him, that she had never been in the garden or in the shop; she was, in a way, immediately nebulous to his mind, receding into nothingness like the final tones spun from Madame Schirmer's instrument.

Rather than hurrying after her, however, he found himself turning away, returning instead through the bookstore, and out upon the street; and, by dusk, he was mounting the steps leading to my flat. Yet while en route, he cursed the paralysis of his will, which had held him back, keeping him bound to the garden even as she ventured from sight. Only later—once the attributes of Stefan Peterson had been removed, folded neatly, and put within my chest of drawers—did I contemplate the very nature of one so deficient in resolve. How, I wondered, could a man as versed and knowledgeable as he become discomposed by such an unassuming wisp of a woman? For Mrs. Keller's passive countenance betrayed little that was unbridled or exceptional about her. So had the gap of isolation and detachment which surrounded his lifetime of study—the solitary hours spent absorbing all manner of human behaviour and thought—given him no amount of insight into what was required of him then?

You must be strong, I wished to impress upon him. You must think more as I do. She is real, yes, but she is also a figment, a longing formed out of your own need. In your loneliness, you have settled on the first face which has caught your eye. It might have been anyone, you know. You are, after all, a man, my dear fellow; she is only a woman, and there are thousands like her scattered throughout this great city.

I had a single day in which to plot Stefan Peterson's best course of action. On the forthcoming Thursday, I decided, he would keep himself outside of Portman's and watch from afar as she entered the shop—at which point, he would make his way into the alley behind the proprietor's garden and wait, out of range, for the back gate eventually to open. Without fail, my plan was realized on the next afternoon: At approximately five o'clock Mrs. Keller exited through the back gate with her parasol raised and a book in one hand. She began walking immediately, and he went after her, maintaining his distance. Even when he wished to draw closer, something kept him at bay. Still, his eyes discerned the hairpins in her thick black hair and the minute bustling of her hips. Every so often, she would pause and tilt her head to the sky, allowing him to catch sight of her profile—the outline of her lower jaw, the almost transparent smoothness of her skin. Then it would appear as if she was speaking beneath her breath, and her mouth mumbled without sound. Once her utterances were finished, she would stare ahead again and continue forwards. She moved through Russell Square, journeyed down Guilford Street, turned left upon Gray's Inn Road, headed across the intersection at King's Cross, and travelled for a short time on a side street, where, soon deviating from the footpath, she proceeded alongside railway tracks near St. Pancras Station. It was an undirected, circuitous route; yet from the deliberate movement of her steps, he understood that this was no mere stroll for Mrs. Keller. And when, finally, she passed through the large iron gates of the Physics and Botanical Society, the late afternoon had begun its transformation into early evening.

The park in which he found himself as he followed her beyond the high redbrick walls presented as great a contrast to the area as there could be: Outside, on a wide artery which conveyed the city's traffic, the roadway was packed with commerce streaming in either direction, while the footpaths were swarming with pedestrians; but past the iron gates, where olive trees stood amidst winding gravel pathways and beds of vegetables and herbs and flowers, was 6.4 acres of lush, pastoral terrain surrounding a manor house which, in 1772, had been bequeathed to the society by Sir Philip Sloane. There, in the shade of those trees, she went on ahead while lazily rotating the parasol; veering right from the main pathway, she took a slender trail, going past echium and *Atropa belladonna,* past horsetail and feverfew, stopping on occasion to touch the flowers lightly, whispering as she did. He, too, was there with her, but he was not yet willing to close the distance between them, even as he became aware that they were the only two people walking upon the trail.

They continued past irises, past chrysanthemums—one before the other—until, for a moment, he lost sight of her where the trail wound behind a tall hedgerow, seeing only the parasol, which floated above the foliage. Then her parasol dipped from view, and her footsteps on the gravel fell quiet. And when he rounded the corner, she was much closer than he expected her to be. Settling herself upon a bench which marked a fork in the trail, she placed the shut parasol across her lap and opened the book. Quite soon, he knew, the sun would angle below the park's walls, casting everything in darker hues. Now you must act, he told himself. Now, while light persists.

Tucking in his ascot, he nervously approached her, saying, "Pardon me." For he wanted to enquire about the volume she was holding, politely explaining that he was a collector of books, an avid reader, and was always interested to learn about what others were reading.

"I've only just begun it," she said, glancing at him warily when he sat down beside her.

"How wonderful," he said, speaking enthusiastically, as if to hide his own awkwardness. "It certainly is a pleasant location in which to enjoy something new, wouldn't you agree?"

"It is," she answered in a composed voice. Her eyebrows were very thick, almost bushy, giving her blue eyes a stern appearance. She seemed annoyed by something—was it the imposition of his presence, or simply the guarded reticence of a cautious, withdrawn woman?

"If I may—" he said, nodding at the book. A reluctant moment transpired before she offered it to him, and, marking her page with his index finger, he looked at its spine. "Ah, Menshov's *Autumn Vespers*. Very good. I, too, have a fondness for Russian writers."

"I see," said she.

There was a long silence, broken only by the measured tapping of his fingertips upon the book's cover. "A fine edition—the binding is well stitched." Her stare lingered on him as he gave her back the book, and he was struck by her odd, asymmetrical face—the cocked eyebrow, that forced half smile he had also seen in the photograph. Then she rose and reached for her parasol.

"You will excuse me, sir, but I must be going."

She had found him unappealing—how else to explain her need to depart after having just arrived at the bench?

"Forgive me. I have disturbed you."

"No, no," said she, "not at all. But it's getting rather late, and I'm expected at home."

"Of course," said he.

There was something otherworldly in her blue eyes, and her pale skin, and her overall demeanour—the slow, meandering movements of her limbs as she left him, the way she drifted like an apparition on the trail. Yes, something aimless and poised and unknowable, he was sure, as she went away from him and moved back around the hedgerow. Now with dusk creeping over the grounds, he felt at a loss. It was not meant to end so suddenly; to her, he was supposed to have been interesting, unique—a kindred spirit, perhaps. So what was that inability, that lacking in himself? Why, when it seemed every molecule within him pulled towards her, had she been quick to leave him? And what was it, just then, that made him go after her on the trail, even while it appeared that she regarded him as a nuisance? He could not say, nor could he fathom why it was that his mind and body were, at that moment, in disagreement: One knew better than the other did, yet the more rational of the two remained less determined.

Still, a chance of reprieval awaited him beyond the hedgerow, for she had not hurried on like he'd believed; instead, she was crouched beside the irises, the hem of her grey dress brushing against the gravel, and had set the book and parasol aside on the ground. Cupping one of the large showy flowers in her right hand, she was unaware of him coming near, nor, in the decreasing light, did she realise his shadow when it fell across her. And while standing over her, he watched intently as her fingers pressed gently against the linear leaves. Then as she withdrew her hand, he observed that a worker bee had strayed onto her glove. But she did not flinch, shaking the creature free, or crush it in her fist. A slight grin spread upon her face as she pondered the bee closely, doing so with apparent reverence, and for a while affectionate whispers were uttered. The worker bee, in turn, stayed upon her palm—not busying itself, or burying its stinger into her glove—as if regarding her the same. How unusual a communion, he thought, the likes of which he had never witnessed before. At last, she saw fit to release the creature, setting it loose on the very flower from whence it had come, and reached for the parasol and book.

"*Iris* means 'rainbow,' " he stammered, yet she was not startled to discover him there. As she rose up, assessing him with a dispassionate stare, he heard the waver of desperation in his voice but could not prevent himself from speaking. "It's easy to understand why, as they grow in so many colours—blues and purples, whites and yellows—like these—and pinks and oranges, browns and reds, even blacks. It is a resilient flower, you know. With enough light, they will grow in desert regions, or in the cold of the far north."

Her absent expression turned into one of permissiveness, and, going forth, she left space for him to stroll alongside her, listening as he told her everything he knew about the flower. Iris was the Greek goddess of the rainbow, the messenger of Zeus and Hera, whose duty it was to lead the souls of dead women to the Elysian fields. As a result, the Greeks planted purple irises on the graves of women; ancient Egyptians adorned sceptres with an iris, which represented faith, wisdom, and valour; the Romans honoured the Goddess Juno with the flower, and used it during purification ceremonies. "Perhaps you are already aware that the Iris Florentina—*Il Giaggiolo*—is the official flower of Florence. And if you have ever visited Tuscany, you have no doubt also inhaled the purple irises which are cultivated amongst the many olive trees there—a scent very much like that of violets."

Glancing at him, she was now attentive and fascinated, as if this sudden encounter had highlighted an uneventful afternoon. "It does sound rather pleasing, the way you describe it," said she. "But, no, I haven't visited Tuscany—or Italy, for that matter."

"Oh, you must, my dear, you really must. There is no place better than its Hill Country."

Then, in that instant, he could think of nothing else to say. The words, he feared, had all dried up, and there was little else for him to impart. She looked away, staring ahead. He hoped that she would offer something, yet he was sure that she would not. So it was as though, out of frustration or out of pure impatience with himself, he decided to dispense with the endless weighing of his own thoughts and, instead, speak without first considering the actual meaning of what would be said.

"I wonder—might I ask—what attracts you to such a thing as an iris?"

She drew a deep breath of temperate spring air and, for no clear reason, shook her head. "What attracts me to such a thing as an iris? It is something I have never really examined." She breathed deeply again and smiled to herself, finally saying, "I suppose a flower thrives during even the worst of times, does it not? And an iris endures: After it has withered, there comes another just like it to take its place. In that regard, flowers are short-lived yet persistent, so I suspect they are less affected by all which is great or awful around them. Does that answer your question?"

"Somewhat, yes."

They had reached the point where the trail verged with the main pathway. He slowed his steps, glancing at her, and when he stopped walking, she did, too. But what was it he wanted to tell her, then, as he searched her face? What was it, in the faint glow at dusk, which stirred his desperation once more? She gazed up into his unblinking eyes, waiting for him to continue.

"I possess a gift," he heard himself tell her. "I would like to share it with you, if you will allow me."

"A gift?"

"More of a hobby, really, although one which has proven rather beneficial for others. You see, I am somewhat of an amateur palmist."

"I don't understand."

He extended an arm towards her, showing her his palm: "From this, I can discern future events with a fair degree of accuracy." He could gaze upon any stranger's hand, he explained, and decipher the course of his or her life—the potential for true love, for a happy marriage, the ultimate number of offspring, various spiritual concerns, and whether one might expect a long life. "So if you can spare me a moment, I would very much like to give you a taste of my talent."

How despicable he felt, how manoeuvring he must have seemed to her. And the puzzled expression which she displayed made him confident that a polite rebuke was forthcoming; except—while the expression remained upon her—she knelt instead, depositing the parasol and book at her feet, then stood again to face him. Without a trace of hesitation, she tugged off the right glove and, fixing her eyes upon him, presented her bare hand, palm up.

"Show me," said she.

"Very well."

He took her hand into his hand, yet it was difficult to see anything in the evening light. Bending for a closer look, he could only make out the whiteness of her flesh—the pale skin muted by shadows, obscured at the day's end. Nothing distinguished its surface—no obvious lines, no deep-set grooves. It was nothing but a smooth, pure layer; all he could perceive about her palm, then, was its lack of depth. It was unblemished beyond measuring, and devoid of the telltale marks of existence, as if, in fact, she had not been born at all. A trick of the light, he reasoned. A trick of vision. But still came a voice from within himself which troubled his thoughts: This is someone who will never grow into an old woman, who will never become wrinkled or dodder from one room into the next.

Even so, there was another kind of clarity revealed upon her palm, and it contained both the past and the future. "Your parents are gone," said he. "Your father when you were but an infant, your mother rather recently." She did not move, nor did she reply. He spoke of her unborn, her husband's concerns for her. He told her that she was loved, that she would regain hope, and that, in time, she would find great happiness in her life. "You are correct to believe you are part of something larger," he said, "something benevolent, like God."

And there, in the shade of gardens and parks, was the affirmation she sought. There she was free, sheltered from the busy lanes where carriage after carriage rolled by, where the potential for death was always lurking, and where men swaggered about, throwing their long, dubious shadows behind them. Yes, he could see it upon her skin: She felt alive and intact when sequestered with nature.

"I cannot say any more, as it is getting too dark. But I would be more than willing to resume on some other day."

Her hand had begun trembling, and, shaking her head with consternation, she unexpectedly retracted it as if flames grazed her fingers. "No, I'm sorry" was her flustered reply, spoken while she knelt to collect her belongings. "I must be going, I really must. Thank you."

Then, as if he were not standing beside her, she promptly turned and hurried along the main pathway. Yet the warmth of her hand lingered; the fragrance she wore persevered. He did not attempt to call after her, or try to leave the grounds in her company. It was only right that she should go without him. It was foolish expecting anything else from her on that evening. Surely it is for the best, he thought, watching her drift onwards, her body receding from his. What happened next, however, was scarcely to be believed; he would, later on, insist that it had not occurred as it was remembered, and yet he would envision it so: For before his eyes, she vanished upon the pathway, dissolving within a cloud of whitest ether. But what remained—fluttering down at that instant like a leaf—was the glove which had held the bee. In astonishment, he ran to the spot where she had disappeared, stooping for the glove. Again, when returning to Baker Street, he questioned the accuracy of his memory, even while he was sure that the glove had moved farther away from him, like a mirage—until it, too, slipped beyond his grasp and was no more.

And soon, just like Mrs. Keller and the glove, Stefan Peterson would also swiftly dematerialise, forever lost with the shifting of limbs, the change of facial characteristics, the unbuttoning and folding of clothing. Once his removal was complete, an immense burden felt taken from my shoulders. Yet I was not fully satisfied, for there was much about the woman which continued to engage me. When a preoccupation stayed upon my mind, I would often go for days without sleep, mulling the evidence over and considering it from every angle. So with Mrs. Keller loitering in my thoughts, I realised that any kind of rest would elude me for a while.

That night, I wandered about in my large blue dressing gown, gathering pillows from my bed and cushions from the sofa and armchairs. In the drawing room, then, I fashioned a makeshift Eastern divan, upon which I placed myself, along with a fresh supply of cigarettes, a box of matches, and the woman's photograph. By the flickering of the lamp, I eventually saw her there; coming through the veil of blue smoke, her hands reached for me, her eyes locked upon mine, and I sat motionless, cigarette fuming between my lips, as the light shone over her softly defined features. Then it was as if her appearance resolved whatever intricacies were plaguing me; she had come, she had touched my skin, and, in her presence, I was lulled easily into a restful slumber. Sometime thereafter, I awoke, to discover the spring sun illuminating the room. The cigarettes were all consumed, and the tobacco haze still floated at the ceiling—but there was no lingering trace of her to be found, other than that remote, pensive face sealed behind a veneer of glass.

17

MORNING CAME.

His pen was nearly out of ink. The clean sheets of writing paper had been exhausted, and the desk was blanketed with Holmes's feverish nocturnal endeavor. Though as opposed to the mindless jotting of notes, it was a more focused undertaking that had spurred his hand until dawn—that continuation of the story regarding a woman he'd met once decades ago, and who, for some apart reason, had compelled herself into his thoughts during the nighttime, coming to him as a vivid, fully formed specter while he rested at his desk, thumbs pressed against his closed eyelids: "You haven't forgotten me, have you?" said the long-dead Mrs. Keller.

"No," he whispered.

"Nor I you."

"Is that so?" he asked, raising his head. "How can that be?"

She, too, like young Roger, had walked alongside him among flowers and on gravel pathways, often saying very little (her attention roving here and there, to the curious objects she encountered upon her way)—and, like the boy, her existence in his life was an ephemeral one, leaving him quietly distraught and senseless after their parting. Of course, she never knew anything factual regarding his true self, had no idea he was a renowned investigator following her in disguise; instead, she forever knew him as a timid book collector, a shy man sharing an equal love for flora and Russian literature—a stranger met in the park one day, but a kind soul all the same, nervously approaching her as she sat on a bench, inquiring politely about the novel she was reading: "Pardon me—I couldn't help noticing—is that Menshov's *Autumn Vespers* you've got there?"

"It is," she said in a composed voice.

"The writing is remarkable, wouldn't you agree?" he continued, speaking enthusiastically, as if to hide his own contrived awkwardness. "Not without its flaws—except in a translation, the mistakes are expected and, I suppose, somewhat forgivable."

"I haven't seen any. Actually, I've only just begun—"

"Still, you must have," he said. "Possibly you didn't realize it—they're easy to miss."

She glanced at him warily when he sat down beside her. Her dark eyebrows were very thick, almost bushy, giving her blue eyes a stern appearance. She seemed annoyed by something—was it the imposition of his presence, or simply the guarded reticence of a cautious, withdrawn woman?

"If I may—" he said, nodding at the book in her hands. After a silent moment, she gave it to him, and, marking the page with his index finger, he searched toward the front of the book, eventually saying, "See, here for example: Early in the story the gymnasium students were shirtless, for Menshov wrote: 'The imposing man stood the bare-chested boys in a line, and Vladimir, feeling exposed with Andrei and Sergei, hung his long arms at his side.' Later, however—on the next page—he writes: 'Upon hearing the man was a general, Vladimir discreetly fastened his cuffs behind his back, then straightened his narrow shoulders.' You can find many instances of this sort of thing in Menshov's writing—or at least in the translations of his writing."

Yet in his account of her, Holmes had failed to recall the exact conversation that had prompted their acquaintance, noting only that he'd asked about the book and that he had then been struck by the lingering stare she gave him (the odd, asymmetrical allure of her face—the one cocked eyebrow, that reluctant half smile he'd first studied in a photograph—was of the impassive-heroine type). There was something otherworldly in her blue eyes, and her pale skin, and her overall demeanor—the slow, meandering movements of her limbs, the way she drifted like a ghost on the garden pathways. Something aimless and poised and unknowable—something resigned and fatalistic, apparently.

Setting his pen aside, Holmes returned to the sharp reality of his study. Since dawn, he'd been ignoring his physical needs, but now he'd go from the attic (however much he dreaded the idea) and empty his bladder, and drink water, and, prior to stomaching a meal, investigate the apiary in the light of day. Carefully, he gathered up the pages on his desk, sorting them, organizing them into a stack. Afterward, he yawned, arching his spine. His skin and clothes smelled of cigar smoke, musty and pungent, and he felt light-headed from having worked through the night, his head and shoulders bent over the desktop. With canes in place, he pushed himself off the seat, gradually coming to his feet. Pivoting around, he began inching toward the door, oblivious to the popping of leg bones, the gentle cracking of joints put in motion.

Then as impressions of Roger and Mrs. Keller commingled in his mind, Holmes exited his smoke-filled workplace, reflexively checking for the supper tray usually left by the boy in the hallway, yet knowing even before crossing the threshold that it wouldn't be there. He proceeded along the hallway, tracing the route that had brought him miserably upstairs. However, his stupor of the previous evening was gone; the horrible black cloud that had stunned his senses and turned a pleasant afternoon to the darkest of nights had dissipated, and Holmes was ready for the task ahead: the descending into a house absent of any soul other than himself, the donning of suitable attire, the sluggish journey beyond the garden—where he'd approach the beeyard like a phantom concealed behind a veil, going forward in clothes of white.

But for a long time, Holmes stood at the top of the stairs, waiting as he did when Roger was coming to assist him downward. His tired eyes closed, and the boy moved swiftly up the stairs. Subsequently, the boy materialized elsewhere, too, appearing in places Holmes had seen him in the past: easing his slender form into the tide pool, the cool water producing goose pimples on his chest as it engulfed his body; running through high grass with his butterfly net outstretched, wearing an untucked cotton shirt, its sleeves rolled to his elbows; hanging a pollen feeder near the hives, positioning it in a sunny spot for the creatures he'd grown to love so. Curiously, each fleeting glimpse of the boy was in the spring or the summer. Still, Holmes could feel winter's cold, could suddenly imagine the boy underground, entombed beneath the frigid earth.

Mrs. Munro's words found him then: "He's a good boy," she'd said when taking the job of housekeeper. "Keeps to himself, rather shy—very quiet, more like his father was. He won't be a burden on you, I promise."

Except, Holmes knew now, the boy had become a burden, a most painful burden. All the same, he told himself, whether it was Roger or anyone else, every life had a finish. And every one of the dead he'd knelt beside had had a life. He set his sights on the stairs below, and while beginning his descent, he repeated within the questions he'd pondered to no avail since his youth: "What is the meaning of it? What object is served by this circle of misery? It must tend to some end, or else the universe is ruled by chance. But what end?"

Upon reaching the second floor—where he'd use the lavatory, and enliven his face and neck with cold water—Holmes heard, for a moment, the faint hum of what he imagined to be an insect or bird singing, and thought of the thick stems that likely guarded it. For neither stems nor insects took part in the misery of mankind.

Perhaps, he mused, this was why—as opposed to people—they could return again and again. Only later, when arriving on the ground floor of his house, would he realize that the humming was originating indoors—a soft drone, sporadic and human, brightening the kitchen; it was a woman's, or a child's voice, to be sure—although clearly not Mrs. Munro's, and, with certainty, not Roger's.

Taking half a dozen nimble steps, Holmes brought himself to the kitchen doorway, catching sight of steam rising from a boiling pot on the stove. Then moving inside, he spotted her at the cutting board, her backside to him as she sliced a potato and thoughtlessly hummed. But it was the long, waving black hair that at once unsettled him—the floating black hair, the pink-and-white skin of her arms, that diminutive form he associated with the unfortunate Mrs. Keller. How speechless he stood there, incapable of addressing such an apparition—until, finally, he parted his lips, desperately saying, "Why have you come here?"

With that, the humming ceased, and the head pivoting sharply to meet his stare revealed a plain-looking girl, a child no older than eighteen—large, mild eyes and a kind, possibly stupid, expression.

"Sir . . ."

Holmes ambled forward, looming in front of her.

"Who are you? What are you doing here?"

"It's me, sir" was her earnest answer. "I'm Em—I'm Tom Anderson's daughter—I thought you knew."

There was silence. The girl lowered her head, avoiding his glare.

"Constable Anderson's daughter?" asked Holmes quietly.

"Yes, sir. I didn't think you'd be taking your breakfast—I was getting your lunch ready."

"But what are you doing here? Where is Mrs. Munro?"

"She's asleep, poor dear." The girl didn't sound glum about this, but happy to have something to relate. She kept her head lowered, addressing the canes near her feet, and as she talked, she made a slight whistling noise, as if she were blowing the words between her lips. "Dr. Baker was with her through the night—except she's sleeping now. I don't know what he gave her."

"She is at the cottage?"

"Yes, sir."

"I see. And Anderson sent you here?"

She seemed bewildered. "Yes, sir," she said. "I thought you knew—I thought my father told you he'd send me."

Then Holmes recalled Anderson knocking on the study door the night before—the constable asking questions, saying some trivial things, placing a hand gently on his shoulder—but it was all a blur.

"Of course," he said, glancing at the window above the sink, the sunlight illuminating the countertop. He breathed rather hard, then looked again, with a hint of disarray, at the girl. "I am sorry—it's been a very trying few hours."

"No apologies, sir, really." Her head rose up. "Something to eat is what you need."

"Just a glass of water, I should think."

Listless from lack of sleep, Holmes scratched at his beard and yawned, watching as the girl promptly fetched his drink, frowning as she ran her hands on her hips upon filling the glass from the tap (the glass being delivered to him with a pleased, somewhat grateful smile).

"Anything else?"

"No," he said, hanging a cane on his wrist, freeing a hand so he could accept what she held for him.

"Got the pot boiling for your lunch," she told him, crossing back to the cutting board. "But if you change your mind about breakfast, you let me know."

The girl lifted a paring knife from the counter. She slouched carelessly forward, slicing at a potato piece, clearing her throat as the blade diced. And after Holmes emptied the glass, placing it in the sink, she resumed humming. So he left her, going from the kitchen without saying any more—along the corridor, out the front door—

listening to that wavering, tuneless hum, which stayed with him for a while—into the yard, toward the garden shed—even when it could no longer be heard.

But as he approached the shed, the girl's drone fluttered away like the butterflies around him, becoming replaced in his thoughts by the beauty of his own garden: the blooms aimed at the clear sky, the scent of lupine in the air, the birds twittering from the nearby pines—and the bees hovering here and there, alighting on petals, vanishing within the cups of flowers.

You wayward workers, he thought. You mercurial insects of habit.

Looking from the garden, facing the wooden shed directly before him, the centuries-old advice of a Roman writer on agriculture found Holmes at that moment (the name of the author eluding him, yet the man's antiquated message eased readily through his mind): *Thou must not come puffing or blowing unto them, neither hastily stir among them, nor resolutely defend thyself when they seem to threaten thee; but softly moving thy hand before thy face, gently put them by; and lastly, thou must be no stranger to them.*

He unlatched and pulled open the shed door fully so that sunshine could precede him into the shadowy, dust-rich hut—the rays irradiating the crowded shelves (bags of soil and seeds, gardening spades and claws, and empty pots, and the folded clothing of a once-novice beekeeper), those places where his hands now reached. On a rake standing upright in a corner, he'd hung his coat, leaving it there as he managed to slip on the white overalls, the light-colored gloves, the wide-brimmed hat, and the veil. Soon he emerged transformed, surveying his garden from behind the veil's gauze, shuffling onward—down the pathway, across the pasture, to the beeyard—with his canes as the only visible signatures of his identity.

Yet when Holmes wandered about his apiary, everything immediately appeared ordinary there, and suddenly he felt ill at ease in the confining clothing. Peering into the dark interior of one hive, then another, he saw the bees among their cities of wax—cleaning their antennae, rubbing forelegs vigorously around their compound eyes, readying themselves for departure into the air. On initial observation, all was customary in the bees' world—the machinelike life of such social creatures, that steady, harmonious murmur—with no clue of any rebellion brewing amid the ordered routine of their insect commonwealth. The third hive was the same, as were the fourth and fifth (whatever reservations he'd harbored quickly evaporated, replaced instead by more familiar feelings of humility and awe for the complex civilization of the hive). Taking his canes from where he'd propped them during an inspection, a sensation of invulnerability claimed him: You won't harm me, was his calming thought. There is nothing here for either of us to fear.

However—while hunched over, removing the cover of the sixth hive—an ominous shadow fell upon him, giving him a start. Glancing sideways through the veil, he first noticed black clothing (a woman's frock, fringed in lace), then a right hand, the thin fingers gripping a red gallon canister. But it was the stoic face gazing at him that provided the greatest vexation—those wide, sedated pupils, the grief conveyed only by the insensible absence of emotion—recalling the young woman who had come to his garden holding her dead infant, yet belonging now to Mrs. Munro.

"I am not sure it's safe, you know," he told her, becoming upright. "You probably should go back at once."

She didn't alter her gaze, or respond with as much as a blink.

"Did you hear me?" he said. "I cannot say for sure if you are at peril, but you might be."

Her eyes kept firmly on him, except her lips moved, imparting nothing for a moment, until asking in a whisper, "Will you kill them?"

"What's that?"

She spoke a little louder: "Will you destroy your bees?"

"Certainly not" came his emphatic reply, even as he felt sympathy for her, and suppressed a growing sense that she was intruding.

"I think you must," she said, "or I'll do it for you."

He already understood it was petrol she was carrying (for the canister belonged to him, its contents used on the dead wood in the nearby forest). In addition, he'd just seen the box of matches held in her other hand, although in her state he couldn't envision her mustering the vigor to ignite the hives. Still, there was something determined in the flatness of her voice, something resolute. The grief-stricken, he knew, were occasionally possessed by a powerful, ruthless indignation—and the Mrs. Munro before him (unflinching, cool, somehow impassive) was a far cry from that chatty, gregarious housekeeper he'd known for years; this Mrs. Munro, unlike the other, made him hesitant, and timid.

Holmes raised the veil, showing an expression as restrained as her own. He said, "You are upset, my child—and confused. Pray go to the cottage and I will have the girl send for Dr. Baker."

She didn't budge. She didn't take her stare from him. "I'm burying my son in two days," she told him plainly enough. "I'll be going tonight—he's going with me. He's going to London in a box—it isn't right."

A deep gloom settled on Holmes. "I am sorry, my dear. I am so sorry—"

And with the softening of his expression, her voice rose above his, saying, "You didn't have the decency to tell me, did you? You hid in your attic and refused seeing me."

"I am sorry—"

"I think you're a selfish old man, it's true. I think you are responsible for my son's death."

"Nonsense," he uttered, but all he felt was her anguish.

"I blame you as much as I blame these monsters you keep. If it weren't for you, he wouldn't have been here, would he? No, it'd be you that got stung dead, not my boy. It wasn't his job anyway, was it? He didn't have to be here alone—he shouldn't have been here, alone like that."

Holmes studied her austere face—the hollow cheeks, the blood-shot eyes—and searched for words, finally telling her, "But he wanted to be here. You must know that. Could I have foreseen the danger, do you imagine I would have let him tend the hives? Do you know how I ache from his loss? I ache for you, as well. Can't you see?"

A bee circled her head, landing briefly on her hair; yet, pinning Holmes with those glaring pupils, she paid the creature no mind. "Then you'll kill them," she said. "You'll destroy them all, if you care anything about us. You'll do what's right to do."

"I won't do that, my dear. It would serve no one to do so, not even the boy."

"Then I'll do it now. You can't stop me."

"You will do nothing of the sort."

She remained motionless, and for several seconds, Holmes con-templated his course of action. If she toppled him, he could do little to prevent her havoc. She was younger; he was frail. But if the attack was his, if he could swing a cane into her chin or neck, she might fall to the ground—and if she fell to the ground, he could strike her again, repeatedly. He glanced at his canes, both propped against the hive. His stare returned to her. Moments passed in silence, neither shifting an inch. At last she relented, shaking her head, saying with a trembling voice, "I wish I'd never met you, sir. I wish I'd never made your acquaintance in this world—and I'll shed no tears on your passing."

"Please," he implored her, reaching for his canes, "it isn't safe for you. Go back to the cottage."

But already Mrs. Munro had turned, going sluggishly away, as if walking in her sleep. By the time she reached the edge of the bee-yard, the canister had been dropped, followed shortly thereafter by the box of matches. Then as she traveled across the pasture, where presently she went from view, Holmes heard her weeping, her sobs becoming more severe, yet fainter and fainter along the cottage pathway.

Stepping in front of the hive, he continued looking at the pasture, at the high grass swaying in Mrs. Munro's wake. She had disrupted the equanimity of the beeyard, now the tranquil grass. There's important work to be done, he wanted to shout out, but stopped himself, for the woman was ravaged by sadness, and he could think only of the business at hand (inspecting the hives, finding a degree of peace within the apiary). You are right, he thought. I am a selfish man. The reality of this notion produced a frown on his troubled face. Propping his canes once more, he sank to the ground, sitting there as a feeling of emptiness swelled up inside. His ears registered the low, concentrated murmur of the hive—the sound of which, in that moment, refused to summon his isolated, content years cultivating the beeyard, but, rather, conveyed the undeniable and deepening loneliness of his existence.

How thoroughly the emptiness could have consumed him then, how easily he might have begun sobbing like Mrs. Munro—if not for the lone yellow-and-black-winged stranger landing on the side of the hive, drawing Holmes's attention, pausing long enough for him to speak its name *"Vespula vulgaris"*—before taking flight again, zigzagging overhead and off in the direction of Roger's death place. Absently, he went for his canes, his brow creasing with puzzlement: What of the stingers? Were there stingers on the boy's clothing, on his skin?

But try as he did—conjuring Roger's body, seeing just the boy's eyes—he couldn't say for sure. Even so, he had probably warned Roger about wasps, mentioning the danger they posed to the apiary. He would, most certainly, have explained that the wasp was the natural enemy of the bee, capable of crushing honeybee after honeybee with its mandibles (some species killing as many as forty bees per minute), wiping out an entire hive, and robbing the larvae. Surely, he would have told the boy the differences between a bee's stinger and a wasp's stinger—the heavily barbed organ of the bee fixing into skin, disemboweling the creature; the wasp's lightly barbed needle barely penetrating flesh, getting withdrawn and used many times.

Holmes climbed to his feet. Hastily, he crossed the beeyard, and as his legs brushed through high grass, he began trampling down a parallel trail alongside the one that Roger had previously created, hoping to chart the boy's journey from the beeyard to his death place. (No, you weren't fleeing the bees, he reasoned. You weren't running from anything, not yet.) Roger's trail curved sharply at its halfway point and veered toward the spot that had obscured the corpse, dead-ending where the boy had fallen—a small clearing of limestone encircled by the grass. There, Holmes saw two more man-made trails, stretching from the distant garden pathway, circumventing the beeyard altogether, each leading to or from the clearing (one fashioned by Anderson and his men, the other by Holmes after finding the body). Then he wondered if he should simply continue forging his own trail farther into the pasture, pursuing what he knew he would likely find. But when turning and staring at the flattened grass, noting the curve that had sent the boy to the clearing, he began retracing his own steps.

Stopping near the curved area, he looked ahead at Roger's trail. The grass was crushed deliberately and evenly, suggesting the boy, like himself, had walked slowly from the beeyard. He glanced to the clearing. The grass was flattened only intermittently, telling him that the boy had been running there. He set his sights on the curve, that changing of course, that abrupt departure. To this point you walked, he thought, and from here you ran.

He moved forward, bringing himself to stand on the boy's trail, where he peered into the grass just beyond the curve. Several yards away, he saw a glint of silver among the thick stems. "What's this?" he said to himself, searching for the glint again. No, he was not mistaken: Something was gleaming dully there in the high grass. He pushed onward for an improved view, departing the boy's trail but soon discovering he had entered another, less obvious path—a detour that had taken the boy step by gradual step into the pasture's densest overgrowth. Pressed with impatience, Holmes quickened his pace, crushing the spots the boy had been careful to tread upon, unaware of the wasp riding on his shoulder—or the other wasps skimming above his hat. Half-crouching, he took a few more steps and found the source of the strange gleaming. It was a watering can, one belonging to his garden, resting on its side, the spout still wet and dripping and obliging the thirst of three wasps (the black-and-yellow workers bustling around the sprinkler, scurrying about for a fuller drop).

"A grave decision, my boy," he said, nudging the watering can with a cane, watching as the startled wasps gave flight. "A terrible miscalculation—"

He lowered the veil before proceeding, feeling little concern about the wasp who then roamed along the beekeeper's gauze like a sentinel. For he knew he was close to their nest, and, he knew, they could do nothing to defend themselves. He was, after all, better suited for their destruction than the boy had ever been, so he would finish what Roger had attempted but ultimately failed to do. Yet as he scanned the ground below, minding every step he took, he was filled with regret. In teaching the boy much, he had apparently not taught him a most vital fact: that pouring water into a wasps' nest only hastened the insects' wrath; it was—Holmes wished he had told him—like using petrol to quell a fire.

"Poor boy," he said, spying a hole in the ground formed curiously like a gaping, filthy mouth. "My poor boy," he said, dipping a cane just past the lips of the hole, extracting it then, bringing the inserted end in front of the veil and studying the wasps that were now clinging to it (seven or eight of the creatures, agitated by the cane's violation, angrily probing the offender's circumference). He shook the cane, scattering the wasps. Then he gazed into the hole, its lips muddy from where the water had spilled, and saw the darkness inside taking shape, writhing upward as wasp after wasp began scrambling from the opening—a good many going straight into the air, some landing on the veil, others swarming around the hole. So this was how it happened, he thought. This, my boy, was how you were taken.

Without panic, Holmes retreated, heading woefully to the beeyard. In time, he would phone Anderson, uttering exactly what the local coroner was in the process of recording, something Mrs. Munro would hear related at the afternoon's inquest: There were no stingers protruding from the boy's skin or clothing, indicating that Roger was the victim of wasps, not bees. Moreover, Holmes would make clear, the boy was trying to protect the hives. Roger had no doubt observed wasps in the apiary, had then found their nest, and, attempting to eradicate the creatures by drowning them, provoked the brood into a full-scale attack.

There was more Holmes would share with Anderson, various minor details (the boy fleeing in the opposite direction of the beeyard while getting stung, perhaps intending to steer the wasps away from the hives). Before calling the constable, however, he would retrieve the dropped petrol canister and find the matches Mrs. Munro had discarded. Leaving one cane at the apiary, his fingers grasping the canister's handle, he'd journey again to the pasture, eventually pouring petrol into the hole as doused wasps struggled helplessly outward. A single match would complete his task, the flame cutting like a fuse across the ground, igniting the gaping mouth with a hiss, producing a slight eruption, which momentarily belched fire past the earthen lips (nothing escaping from within afterward save a single twisting ribbon of smoke that dissipated above the undisturbed grass), eliminating in an instant the queen and the fertile eggs and the throng of workers trapped inside their colony: a vast and intricate empire encased by the yellowish paper of the nest, gone in a flash, like young Roger.

Good riddance, mused Holmes while weaving through the high grass. "Good riddance," he said aloud, his head arched to the cloudless sky, his vision disoriented by the expanse of blue ether. And upon speaking those words, he was overcome by an immense melancholy for all enduring life, everything that had and did and would someday rove beneath such perfect, ever-present stillness. "Good riddance," he repeated, and began weeping noiselessly behind the veil.

18

W<small>HY HAD</small> the tears come? Why—while resting in bed, then pacing the study, then going to the beeyard the next morning, and the morning after that—did Holmes find his head touched by his own hands and his fingertips wetted from brushing his whiskers, even as no crippling sob or mighty lament or paralysis transfigured him? Somewhere else—he imagined a small cemetery on the outskirts of London—stood Mrs. Munro and her relatives, everyone dressed in clothes as bleak as the gray clouds brooding over the sea and land. Was she crying, too? Or had Mrs. Munro shed all her tears during the lonely trip to London, sustaining herself in the city with the strength of family, the comfort of friends?

It's unimportant, he told himself. She is elsewhere, and I am here—and I can do nothing for her.

Still, he had made some effort toward helping her. Prior to her departure, he'd sent Anderson's daughter to the cottage twice, the girl carrying an envelope with more than enough money for travel and funeral expenses; both times, the girl returned, her features demure yet pleasant, informing him that the envelope had been refused.

"She won't take it, sir—won't talk to me, either."

"It is all right, Em."

"Should I try again?"

"Best not—I don't think it will accomplish much."

Now facing the apiary alone, his expression was abstracted and strict and frozen in dismay, as if he were also standing with the mourners at Roger's graveside. Even the hives—the white rows of boxes, the unadorned rectangular shapes rising from the grass—seemed like burial monuments to him. A small cemetery not dissimilar to the beeyard, he hoped was the case. A simple place—well tended and green, no weeds, no buildings or roadways visible nearby, no motorcars or human bustle disrupting the dead. A peaceful place aligned with nature, a good location for the boy to rest and for the mother to say good-bye.

But why was he weeping so effortlessly, yet without emotion, the tears impelled by their own accord? Why couldn't he cry out loud, sobbing into his palms? And why—on the occasion of other deaths, when the pain was equal to what he felt now—had he shunned the funerals of loved ones and never once spilled a single tear, as if sorrow itself was something to be frowned upon?

"No matter," he muttered. "It's pointless."

He wouldn't strive for any answers (at least not on this day), nor would he ever believe that his tearfulness might be the concentrated sum-total result of everything he had seen, known, cared for, lost, and kept stifled throughout the decades—the fragments of his youth, the destruction of great cities and empires—those vast, geography-changing wars—then the slow atrophy of fond companions and one's own health, memory, personal history; all of life's implicit complexities, each profound and altering moment, condensed to a welling salty substance in his tired eyes. Instead, he sank downward without dwelling any more, lowering himself to the ground, sitting there like some stone figure that had inexplicably been set in the shorn grass.

He'd sat there previously, on the very same spot—near the apiary, the location marked off by four rocks carried up from the beach eighteen years earlier (black-gray stones made smooth and flat by the tide, fitting perfectly into his palm), placed exactly apart—one in front of him, one behind, one to the left, one to the right—forming a discreet, unassuming patch, which had, in the past, contained and muted his despair. It was a slight trick of the mind, a game of sorts, though often beneficial: Within the rocks' domain, he could meditate, thinking warmly of those who were gone—and later, when stepping beyond the patch, whatever grief he'd brought into the space was kept there, if only for a short while. *"Mens sana in corpore sano"* was his incantation, spoken once inside the patch, repeated afterward when stepping from it. "Everything comes in circles, even the poet Juvenal."

First in 1929, and then again in 1946, he'd regularly used the spot to commune with the dead, subduing his woes in the unanimity of the beeyard. But 1929 was almost his undoing, producing a far more grievous period than the current upset, for elderly Mrs. Hudson—his housekeeper and cook since his London days, the only person who had accompanied him to the Sussex farmhouse upon his retirement—fell to the kitchen floor with a broken hip, cracking her jaw, losing teeth and consciousness (the hip, it was learned, had likely fractured just prior to the lethal fall, her bones having become too brittle to support her overweight body); in hospital, she eventually succumbed from pneumonia. (*A mild enough ending,* Dr. Watson wrote to Holmes, after being notified of her passing. *Pneumonia is, as you well know, a blessing to the feeble, a light touch for the aged.*)

But no sooner had Dr. Watson's letter been filed away—and Mrs. Hudson's belongings collected by her nephew, and an inexperienced housekeeper hired for the farmhouse chores—than that companion of many seasons, the good doctor himself, died unexpectedly of natural causes late one night (he'd enjoyed a nice supper with his visiting children and grandchildren, drunk three glasses of red wine, laughed at a joke his eldest grandson whispered in his ear, wished everyone good night before ten, and was dead before midnight). The heartbreaking news came in a telegram sent from Dr. Watson's third wife, delivered unceremoniously into Holmes's hands by the young housekeeper (the first of many women who would pass wretchedly through the farmhouse, quietly tolerating their irascible employer, usually quitting inside a year's time).

In the days thereafter, Holmes wandered the beach for hours, from dawn till dusk, contemplating the sea and, for long periods, the many rocks beneath his feet. He hadn't seen or spoken directly to Dr. Watson since the summer of 1920, when the doctor and his wife spent a weekend with him. Yet it had been an awkward visit, more so for Holmes than for his guests; he wasn't particularly friendly toward the third wife (finding her rather dull and overbearing), and, aside from rehashing some of their earlier adventures together, he realized he shared little in common with Dr. Watson anymore; their evening conversations inevitably faded into uncomfortable silences, broken only by the wife's inane need to mention her children, or her love of French cuisine—as if silence was somehow her ultimate foe.

All the same, Holmes regarded Dr. Watson as someone who had passed beyond his kin, so the man's sudden death, coupled with the recent loss of Mrs. Hudson, felt like a door slamming abruptly shut on everything that had previously shaped him. And while strolling along the beach, pausing to watch the waves curl in on themselves, he understood how adrift he'd become: Within that month, the purest connections to his former self had dwindled to almost no one, but he remained. Then on his fourth day of walking the shore, he began considering rocks—holding them to his face, discarding one in favor of another, finally settling on the four that pleased him the most. The tiniest of pebbles, he knew, held the secrets of the entire universe. Moreover, the rocks he soon carried up the cliff in his pockets had preceded his lifetime; they had—as he was conceived, as he was born and educated and made old—waited on the shore, unchanged. Those four common rocks, like the others he had tread upon, were infused with all the elements that then formed the great sweep of humanity, every possible creature and imaginable thing; without question, they possessed rudimentary traces of both Dr. Watson and Mrs. Hudson, and, obviously, much of himself as well.

So Holmes gave the rocks a specific area, sitting among them with legs crossed, clearing his mind of what troubled him—the muddle caused by the permanent absence of two people he cared deeply about. Yet, he had determined, to feel someone's absence was, in a way, also to feel his or her presence. Breathing the beeyard's autumn air, exhaling his remorse (*tranquillity of thought* was his unspoken mantra—*tranquillity of the psyche,* just as he'd been taught by the Lamaists of Tibet), he sensed the beginnings of closure for himself and the dead, as if they were ebbing away gradually, attempting to depart from him in peace, finally allowing him to rise and go forward, his transient sorrow bridled between the venerable rocks. *"Mens sana in corpore sano."*

During the latter half of 1929, he occupied the spot on six different occasions, each subsequent meditation growing shorter in duration (three hours and eighteen minutes, one hour and two minutes, forty-seven minutes, twenty-three minutes, nine minutes, four minutes). By the new year, his need to sit among the rocks had abated, and whatever attention he then afforded the spot was for its tending (the removal of weeds, the trimming of grass, the rocks pressed firmly into the earth like the stones lining the garden pathway). Almost two hundred and one months would transpire before he lowered himself there again, doing so several hours after being informed of his brother Mycroft's passing—his breath streaming outward in puffs on a frigid November afternoon, dissipating beyond like some half-glimpsed, ethereal vision.

But it was an inward vision that engaged him, already taking shape within his mind, welcoming him into the Strangers' Room of the Diogenes Club four months earlier—where Holmes had a final meeting with his only surviving sibling (the two enjoying cigars while sipping brandy). Mycroft looked well, too—clear-eyed, with a hint of color in his plump cheeks—although his health was failing and he was prone to exhibiting a loss of mental faculties; yet on that day, he was incredibly lucid, reliving stories of his wartime glories, seemingly delighted with his younger brother's company. And while Holmes had just recently begun sending jars of royal jelly to the Diogenes Club, he believed the substance was already bettering Mycroft's condition.

"Even with your imagination, Sherlock," Mycroft had said, his massive body verging on laughter, "I do not think you could picture me clambering ashore from a landing barge with my old friend Winston. 'I'm Mr. Bullfinch,' Winston said—for that was the code name agreed upon—'and I've come to see for myself how things are going in North Africa.' "

However, Holmes suspected that the two great wars had, in fact, been a terrible strain on his brilliant sibling (Mycroft having continued in service well past the retirement age, rarely leaving his Diogenes Club armchair, yet indispensable to the government nonetheless). As the most mysterious of men, an individual poised at the very top of the British Secret Service, his elderly brother had often functioned for weeks without proper sleep—fueling his energy by eating voraciously—while single-handedly overseeing a multitude of intrigues, both domestically and abroad. It came as no surprise to him that—at the conclusion of the Second World War—Mycroft's health was declining rapidly; nor was Holmes astounded to observe an improvement in his brother's vigor, brought about, he was sure, by the sustained use of royal jelly.

"It's good to see you, Mycroft," said Holmes when standing to go. "You have become the antithesis of lethargy once more."

"A tramcar coming down a country lane?" said Mycroft, smiling.

"Something like that, yes," said Holmes, reaching for his brother's hand. "It has been too long between meetings, I fear. When shall we do it again?"

"We won't, I'm sorry to say."

Holmes bent forward at his brother's chair, clutching Mycroft's heavy, soft hand. He would have laughed at that moment, except he saw those eyes contrasting his brother's smile. Irresolute and precarious with resignation, they suddenly fixed and held his stare, communicating as best they could: Like you, they seemed to say, I have dipped my toes into two centuries, and my race is about run.

"Now, Mycroft," said Holmes, lightly tapping a cane against his brother's shin, "I wager you are mistaken on that count."

But as had always been the case, Mycroft was never wrong. And soon the last thread to Holmes's past was severed by an unsigned letter sent from the Diogenes Club (the contents offering no condolences, stating simply that his brother had died quietly on Tuesday, November 19, and—in keeping with the final wishes—the body had been interred anonymously and unceremoniously). How very Mycroft, he thought, folding the letter, putting it among the other papers on his desk. How right you were, he considered later when sitting among the rocks—staying there into the chilly night, unaware of Roger spying on him from the garden pathway at dusk, or Mrs. Munro finding the boy, speaking with an admonishing tone: "You leave him be, son. He's in a queer mood today—Lord knows why."

Of course, Holmes said nothing of Mycroft's death to anyone, nor did he openly acknowledge that second delivery from the Diogenes Club: a small package following the letter by exactly a week, discovered on the front doorsteps and nearly crushed underfoot as he went outside for a morning walk. Beneath the brown wrapping, he found a worn edition of Winwood Reade's *The Martyrdom of Man* (the same copy his father, Siger, had given him while he was a convalescent boy, languishing for months in the attic bedroom of his parents' Yorkshire country house), with a short note from Mycroft attached. What a depressing book it was, but one that had made a great impression on Holmes as a youngster. And in reading the note, in holding the volume once again, a memory he'd long since suppressed revealed itself—for he had loaned the book to his older brother in 1867, insisting Mycroft read it: "When finished, you must share your impressions—I wish to know what you think." *Many interesting ruminations,* was Mycroft's brief assessment some seventy-eight years later, *although a bit too meandering for my tastes. Took me ages to get through it.*

It wasn't the only time that the departed offered their words to him. There were the notes Mrs. Hudson had apparently written for herself, possible reminders jotted on scraps of torn paper and tucked away—in kitchen counters, in the broom closet, scattered throughout the housekeeper's cottage—only to be chanced upon by her initial replacement, who gave them to Holmes with always the same perplexed expression. For a while, he kept the notes, contemplating each one as if it might piece together what seemed a nonsensical puzzle. But in the end, he could gather no definitive meaning from Mrs. Hudson's messages, all of which consisted of two nouns: *Hatbox Slippers; Barley Soapstone; Girandole Marzipan; Hound Cheapjack; Ordo Planchet; Carrot Housecoat; Fruitlet Prelibation; Tracheid Dish; Pepper Scone.* The library fireplace, he concluded without sentiment, was where the notes belonged (Mrs. Hudson's cryptic scraps igniting on a winter's day, smoldering into nothing, along with various letters sent to him by complete strangers).

A similar fate had previously befallen three of Dr. Watson's unpublished journals, and for good reason. From 1874 until 1929, the doctor had recorded the minutiae of his daily life, producing countless volumes, which lined his study bookshelves. But the three journals he bequeathed to Holmes—covering Thursday, May 16, 1901, through late October 1903—were more sensitive in nature. For the most part, however, the journals chronicled hundreds of minor cases, a few notable exploits, as well as a particularly humorous anecdote concerning stolen racehorses ("A Case of the Trots"); yet mixed with the trivial and the noteworthy were a handful of sordid, potentially damaging affairs: various indiscretions by relatives of the royal family, a foreign dignitary with a palate for small Negro boys, and a prostitution scandal that had threatened to expose fourteen parliamentary members.

So it was prudent of Dr. Watson to bestow the three journals to him, lest they fall into the wrong hands. Moreover, Holmes had decided, it was important for the volumes to be destroyed; otherwise, after his own passing, the doctor's texts might become public. What would get lost, he figured, was either already published as fictional accounts, likely inconsequential, or worthy of perishing to maintain the secrets of those who had sought his confidentiality. And with that—avoiding even a flip through the pages, resisting even a brief glimpse at all that Dr. Watson had written down—the volumes ended up in the library fireplace, the paper and binding smoking profusely, suddenly bursting into orange-blue flames.

But many years later, while traveling across Japan, Holmes recalled the destruction of the journals with some misgivings. According to Mr. Umezaki's story, he had supposedly advised the man's father in 1903, which meant—if the story had any truth value—the details of that encounter had surely been reduced to ashes. Then resting at an inn in Shimonoseki, he again envisioned Dr. Watson's journals blazing on the hearth—those glowing cinders once etched with days gone by, breaking apart gradually and soaring up the chimney like ascending souls and becoming irretrievable as they floated off into the sky. The remembrance blunted his mind; stretched on a futon, eyes closed, he experienced a sensation of emptiness, of inexplicable loss. Such an acute, hopeless sensation returned to him months thereafter, finding him while he sat among the rocks on that overcast, gray morning.

And as Roger was being buried elsewhere, Holmes could neither perceive nor understand a single thing, nor could he push aside the suffocating feeling of his self somehow stripped bare (his diminished faculties now navigating an uninhabited region, exiled from the familiar, bit by bit, without a way back into the world). Yet it was a lone tear that revived him—sliding into his whiskers, coursing toward his jawline—a tear then dangling on a chin hair, hastening fingers. "All right," he said with a sigh, opening his inflamed eyes to the beeyard, his fingers lifting from the grass, rising to catch a tear before it fell.

19

THERE, near the apiary—then there, somewhere else: The sunlight increased; the overcast summer morning shifted backward to a windy spring day—to another shore, to that far-off land. Yamaguchi-ken, the extreme western tip of Honshu, the island of Kyushu visible across the narrow strait. *"Ohayo gozaimasu,"* said the round-faced hostess as Holmes and Mr. Umezaki sat on tatami mats (both wearing gray kimonos, seated at a table with a garden view). They were staying at the Shimonoseki Ryokan, a traditional inn where every guest was loaned a kimono and given an opportunity to sample, upon request, regional famine food with each meal (a variety of soups, rice balls, and dishes using carp as the main ingredient).

The hostess went from the morning room to the kitchen, from the kitchen to the morning room, carrying trays. She was a heavy woman. Her stomach bulged against the sash around her waist; the tatamis vibrated on her approach. Mr. Umezaki wondered aloud how she stayed so fat, with the country's shortage of food. But she continually bowed at her guests without ever understanding Mr. Umezaki's English, coming and going from the morning room like a well-fed, obedient dog. Then as bowls, plates, and steaming dishes were set on the table, Mr. Umezaki wiped his glasses, replacing them while reaching for chopsticks. And Holmes—studying their break-fast, gingerly taking up chopsticks—yawned away what had been a fitful sleep (a vagrant wind having shaken the walls until dawn, its frightful whine keeping him half-awake).

"If you don't mind, what is it you dream in the night?" Mr. Umezaki abruptly asked, picking at a rice ball.

"What do I dream in the night? I am sure I dream nothing whatsoever."

"How is it possible? You must dream sometimes—doesn't everyone?"

"As a boy I did—I am fairly certain of that. I cannot say when it stopped—possibly after adolescence, or later on. In any case, I don't recall the details of whatever dreams I may have once had. Such hal-lucinations are infinitely more useful to artists and theistic minds, wouldn't you agree? For men like me, however, they are rather an un-reliable nuisance."

"I've read about people who claim they are dreamless, but I've never believed it. I just assumed they felt the need to suppress them for some reason."

"Well, if indeed the dreams do come, then I have grown accus-tomed to ignoring them. But now I ask you, my friend: what is it that plays in your head at night?"

"Any number of things. It can be very specific, you see—places I've been, everyday faces, often mundane situations—other times it's remote, disconcerting scenes that are seen—my childhood, dead friends, people whom I know well but who look nothing like them-selves. Sometimes I awake confused, unsure of where I am or what I've glimpsed—it's like I'm caught somewhere between the real and the imagined, though only for a short moment."

"I know the feeling." Holmes smiled, glancing to the window. Beyond the morning room, in the garden outside, a breeze swayed the red and yellow chrysanthemums.

"I regard my dreams as frayed pieces of my memory," Mr. Umezaki said. "Memory itself is like the fiber of one's existence. Dreams, I think, are like broken strands of the past, little ragged edges that veer from the fiber but remain a part of it. Maybe that's a fanciful notion—I don't know. Still, don't you think dreams are a kind of memory, an abstraction of what was?"

For a while, Holmes continued gazing out the window. Then he said, "Yes, it is a fanciful notion. As for me, I have shed my skin and regenerated for ninety-three years now, so those ragged strands you speak of must be many—yet I am positive I dream nothing. Or maybe it is that the fibers of my memory are extremely durable; otherwise—judging from your metaphor—I would likely be lost in time. Anyway, I don't believe dreams are an abstraction of the past— they could easily be symbols for our fears and desires, like the Austrian doctor was so fond of suggesting." With chopsticks, Holmes took a pickled cucumber slice from a bowl and Mr. Umezaki watched as he moved it carefully toward his mouth.

"Fears and desires," Mr. Umezaki said, "are products of the past as well. We simply carry them with us. But there's a lot more to dreaming than that, isn't there? Don't we seem to occupy another region in sleep, a world built on the experiences we've had in this one?"

"I haven't the foggiest."

"What are your fears and desires, then? I myself have plenty."

Holmes did not reply, even as Mr. Umezaki paused and waited for a response. Keeping his eyes fixed on the bowl of pickled cucumbers, a deeply troubled expression appeared on his face. No, he would not answer the question, nor would he say that his fears and desires were, at some point, one and the same: the forgetfulness increasingly plaguing him, startling him awake, gasping, a sense of the familiar and safe turning against him, leaving him helpless and exposed and struggling for air; the forgetfulness also subduing the despairing thoughts, muting the absence of those he could never see again, grounding him in the present, where all he might want or need was at hand.

"Forgive me," Mr. Umezaki said. "I didn't mean to pry. We should've spoken last night, after I came to you—but it seemed the wrong moment."

Holmes lowered his chopsticks. Using his fingers, he picked two slices from the bowl, eating them. When finished, he rubbed his fingers on his kimono. "My dear Tamiki, do you suspect I dreamt something about your father last night? Is this why you are asking me these questions?"

"Not exactly."

"Or were you dreaming of him, and now you wish to relate the experience to me over breakfast, in a somewhat roundabout fashion."

"I have dreamt of him, yes—although it's been a long while."

"I see," said Holmes. "So pray tell me: What is the pertinence of this?"

"I'm sorry." Mr. Umezaki bowed his head. "I apologize."

Holmes realized he was being needlessly short, but then it was irksome to be pressed repeatedly for answers he didn't possess. Besides, he was already annoyed that Mr. Umezaki had entered his room during the previous night, kneeling near the futon while he slept restlessly; when he was stirred by the wind—a plaintive, mournful whir at the windows—the shadowy presence of the man must have taken his breath away (hovering just above him like a black cloud, asking with a hushed voice, "Are you all right? Tell me. What is it?"), because he couldn't utter anything, couldn't move his arms, his legs. How difficult it was at that moment to remember where exactly he was, or to comprehend the voice addressing him through the darkness: "Sherlock, what is it? You can tell me."

Only as Mr. Umezaki left him, silently crossing the floor, opening and shutting the sliding wall panel between their rooms, did

Holmes regain himself. Turning on his side, he listened to the wind's melancholy din. He touched the tatami beneath the futon, pushing his fingertips against the mat. Then closing his eyes, he pondered what Mr. Umezaki had asked, the words at last registering: *Tell me. What is it? You can tell me.* For, in truth, despite all the man had said earlier about enjoying their trip together, Holmes knew that Mr. Umezaki was determined to learn something of his lost father, even if it meant holding a vigil at his bedside (why else would Mr. Umezaki enter his room—what other explanation could bring him there?). Holmes, too, had questioned sleepers—thieves, opium addicts, suspected murderers—in a similar manner (whispering into their ears, gathering information from the breathless mumbles of dreamers, those drowsy confessions, which later surprised the perpetrators with their accuracy). So he didn't begrudge the method, yet he wished Mr. Umezaki would let the mystery of his father rest, at least until their trip was finished.

Such concerns are long in the past, Holmes wanted to tell him, and little will be gained by fretting over them now. Matsuda's motives for fleeing Japan were possibly justifiable, and maybe the family's better interests were very much a factor. Even so, without a father ever really present for Mr. Umezaki, he understood how the man could feel like an incomplete person. And whatever else Holmes convinced himself of during that night, he never pretended Mr. Umezaki's search was irrelevant. On the contrary, he'd always believed that the conundrums of one's own life were worthy of tireless investigation, but in the case of Matsuda, Holmes knew that any clues he might offer—if indeed they existed—had been destroyed on the hearth ages ago; the recollection of Dr. Watson's incinerated journals then preoccupied him, eventually dulling his mind, and soon he could envision nothing. Nor could he hear the wind anymore—while awake upon the futon—rampaging along the streets, tearing slits in latticed paper-covered windows.

"It is I who should apologize," said Holmes at breakfast, reaching across the table to pat Mr. Umezaki's hand. "I had a rather rough night, what with the weather and all, and feel worse for it today."

Mr. Umezaki, his head kept bowed, nodded. "It's just that I'm worried. I thought you cried out in your sleep—it was a horrible sound."

"Of course," said Holmes, humoring him. "You know, I have wandered moors where the wind gave the distinct impression of someone yelling, a distant shout or wail, almost like a cry for help. A tempest can easily fool your ears; I have been fooled myself, I assure you." Grinning, he retracted his hand, moving his fingers into the bowl of cucumbers.

"You believe I was mistaken, then?"

"It is possible, isn't it?"

"Yes," said Mr. Umezaki, bringing his head up with a gesture of relief. "It is possible, I suppose."

"Very good," said Holmes, holding a slice before his lips. "That puts an end to it. Shall we begin the day anew? And what is on the agenda this morning—another stroll along the beach? Or should we pursue our purpose for coming here—the quest for the elusive prickly ash?"

But Mr. Umezaki looked perplexed. How often had they discussed Holmes's reasons for visiting Japan (the desire to taste prickly-ash cuisine, and also witness the shrub growing in the wild), and their destination, which would lead them, later that day, into the rustic *izakaya* by the sea (a Japanese version of a pub, Holmes would realize when stepping past the doorway)?

When they entered the *izakaya*, there was a cauldron boiling inside and fresh prickly-ash leaves being cut by the proprietor's wife, and the local faces looked up, some with mistrust, from glasses of beer or sake. Yet since Holmes's arrival, how often had Mr. Umezaki spoken of the special cake sold at the *izakaya*, created with the roasted ground fruits and seeds of prickly ash, the ingredients kneaded into flour as a flavoring? And how often had they mentioned the letters sent back and forth over the years, the contents always touching on their interest in the slow-growing, mounding, perhaps life-enhancing shrub (nourished by salt-spray exposure, full sun, and drying winds)? Not once, it seemed.

The *izakaya* smelled of peppercorns and fish, and they sat at a table, sipping tea and listening to the boisterous conversations around them. "Those two are fishermen," said Mr. Umezaki. "They are arguing about a woman."

Presently, the proprietor passed through a back-room curtain, revealing his toothless grin as he did so, addressing each patron in an overbearing, comical voice, laughing with those he knew, then eventually making his way to their table. The man appeared amused at the sight of the elderly Englishman and his refined companion, happily patting Mr. Umezaki on the shoulder, winking at Holmes as if they were all close friends. Sitting down at the table, the proprietor glanced at Holmes while saying something to Mr. Umezaki in Japanese—a remark that made everyone in the *izakaya* laugh, except Holmes. "What did he say?"

"It's rather funny," Mr. Umezaki told him. "He thanked me for bringing my father here—he said we're the spitting image—but he thinks you're more pleasing on the eye."

"I would agree with the latter statement," said Holmes.

Mr. Umezaki translated the message to the proprietor, who then burst out laughing, nodding his head in agreement.

Then upon finishing his tea, Holmes said to Mr. Umezaki, "I should like a look at that cauldron. Will you ask our new friend if I may? Will you tell him that I would very much like to see how the prickly ash is stewed?"

When the request was conveyed, the proprietor promptly stood. "He'll gladly let you," said Mr. Umezaki. "But his wife does the cooking. She alone can show you the process."

"Delightful," said Holmes, rising. "Are you coming?"

"In a moment—I still have my tea."

"It is a rare chance, you know. I hope you won't mind if I don't wait for you."

"No, not at all," said Mr. Umezaki, even though he stared sharply at Holmes, as if he were somehow being deserted.

Soon, however, they would both be at the cauldron, holding the shrub's leaves in their hands and watching as the wife stirred the broth. Afterward, they were directed to where the prickly ash thrived—farther along the beach, somewhere among the dunes.

"Should we go tomorrow morning?" asked Mr. Umezaki.

"It isn't too late in the day to go now."

"It's a good distance, Sherlock-san."

"Shall we go part of the way—at least until dusk?"

"If you wish."

They took a last, curious look around the *izakaya*—at the cauldron, the soup, the men with their glasses—before stepping outside, hiking across the sand, moving gradually into the dunes. By dusk, they had found no sign of the shrub and so decided to head back for supper at the inn, both feeling exhausted from the hike, each retiring early, instead of taking the usual evening drinks. But that night—the second evening of their stay in Shimonoseki—Holmes awoke around midnight, stirring from another fitful sleep. What struck him initially was that he could no longer hear the wind as on the previous night. Then he remembered what had preoccupied him in the minutes prior to sleep: the run-down *izakaya* by the sea, the prickly-ash leaves boiling in a cauldron of carp soup. He lay under the covers, staring at the ceiling in the dim light. After a while, he felt sleepy once more and closed his eyes. Except he didn't drift off; instead, he thought of the toothless proprietor—Wakui was his name—and how his humorous comments had delighted Mr. Umezaki, among them a rather tasteless joke at the emperor's expense: "Why is General MacArthur the belly button of Japan? Because he is above the prick."

Yet no comment had pleased Mr. Umezaki more than Wakui's playful remark about Holmes being his father. In the late afternoon, as they had walked the beach together, Mr. Umezaki had brought up the remark again, saying, "It's strange to think of it—if my father was living, he would be just a bit older than you are."

"I suppose so," Holmes had said, peering ahead at the dunes, surveying the sandy soil for signs of the prickly, sprawling shrub.

"You're my English father—how's that?" Mr. Umezaki had unexpectedly taken hold of Holmes's arm, his hand remaining firmly on him as they went forward. "Wakui is a funny fellow. I'd like to visit him tomorrow."

Only then had Holmes perceived of himself as having been chosen—perhaps not consciously—as Matsuda's surrogate. It was already obvious that behind Mr. Umezaki's mature, circumspect demeanor lurked the psychic wounds of childhood. The rest did not become apparent until Wakui's remark had been repeated and Mr. Umezaki's needful fingers had grabbed him on the beach. Then how clear it had suddenly become: The last time you heard word from your father, Holmes had thought, was the first time you heard of me. Matsuda vanishes from your life, and I arrive in the form of a book—one replaces the other, as it were.

So there were the letters postmarked in Asia, the subsequent invitation following months of genial correspondence, the eventual trip through the Japanese countryside, the days spent together—like father and son making quiet amends after living many years estranged. And if Holmes could provide no concrete answers, then maybe—by traveling a vast distance to join Mr. Umezaki, in sleeping at the family's Kobe house, finally embarking on the journey westward and visiting the Hiroshima garden where Matsuda had taken Mr. Umezaki as a boy—his very nearness might provide some resolution. What had also become clear was that Mr. Umezaki really cared little for prickly ash, or royal jelly, or anything else that those intelligent letters had discussed in detail. A simple ruse, Holmes had

realized, yet effective—each topic well researched, articulated on sta-
tionery, and likely forgotten.

These children with missing fathers, Holmes had mused, imagining Mr. Umezaki and young Roger when trekking into the dunes.
This age of lonely, searching souls, he'd thought as the fingers tight-
ened on his arm.

But as opposed to Mr. Umezaki, Roger understood his own
father's fate and harbored a belief that the man's death—while tragic
on a personal level—was truly heroic in the grand scheme. Mr.
Umezaki, however, could claim nothing of the sort, relying instead
on the frail old Englishman he had accompanied into the sandy hills
by the beach, clutching at his bony elbow, clinging to him, in reality, rather than guiding him along: "Should we turn back?"

"Have you tired of the search?"

"No, I was more concerned for you."

"I believe we are too close to turn back now."

"It's getting dark."

Holmes opened his eyes now and looked again at the ceiling,
weighing the problem's solution; for to appease Mr. Umezaki was to
reveal something that must be conceived of as the truth beforehand
(like Dr. Watson working out the plot of a story, he reasoned—the
mixing of what was and what never had been into a single, undeniable creation). Yes, his association with Matsuda wasn't an impos-
sibility—and, yes, the man's disappearance could be explained,
though not without careful elaboration. And where had they first
been introduced? Perhaps in the Strangers' Room of the Diogenes
Club, at Mycroft's urging. But why?

"If the art of the detective began and ended in the reasoning from
this room, Mycroft, you would be the greatest criminal agent who
ever lived. Yet you are absolutely incapable of working out the practical points that must be gone into before a matter can be decided
upon. I gather that is why you have called me here once again."

He pictured Mycroft in his armchair. Nearby sat T. R. Lamont (or was it R. T. Lanner?)—a dour, ambitious man of Polynesian descent, a London Missionary Society member who had lived on the Pacific island of Mangaia and, as a spy for the British Secret Service, kept rigid police supervision over the indigenous population in the name of morality. Hoping to aid New Zealand's expansionist ambitions, Lamont, or Lanner, was under consideration for a more important role, that of British resident—a position which included negotiations with the Cook Islands' chiefs to pave the way for New Zealand's annexation of the islands.

Or was he known as J. R. Lambeth? No, no, recalled Holmes, he was a Lamont, surely a Lamont. In any case, it was 1898—or 1899, or was it 1897?—and Holmes had been summoned by Mycroft to give an opinion on Lamont's character (*As you know, I can return an excellent expert opinion,* his brother had written in a telegram, *but gathering the details of someone's true value is not my métier*).

"We must have our cards in the game," explained Mycroft, well aware of France's influence on Tahiti and the Society Islands. "Naturally, Queen Makea Takau wants her islands annexed to us, but our government remains a reluctant administrator. New Zealand's prime minister, on the other hand, has his sights set—so we are obligated to be as helpful as we can—and seeing how Mr. Lamont is acquainted with the natives—and shares more than a few common physical traits—we believe he will be quite useful toward that end."

Holmes eyed the short, uncommunicative fellow seated at his brother's right (looking down through his spectacles, hat in his lap, dwarfed by the huge form to his left). "Aside from you, Mycroft, who are the *we* you speak of?"

"That, my dear Sherlock—like everything else mentioned in my company—is of the utmost secrecy and is of no issue at present. What is required, however, is your counsel on our colleague here."

"I see. . . ."

Except it wasn't Lamont, or Lanner, or Lambeth, that Holmes now saw beside Mycroft, but, rather, the tall stature, the long face, the goatee of Matsuda Umezaki. In that private room, they had been introduced, and almost immediately Holmes could tell he matched the position's proviso; from the dossier Mycroft had given him, it was evident that Matsuda was an intelligent man (the author of several notable books, one of which dealt with covert diplomacy), capable as an agent (his background in the Japanese Foreign Ministry attesting to that fact), an Anglophile disenchanted by his own country (willing to travel, whenever needed, from Japan to the Cook Islands, then to Europe, and then back to Japan).

"You think he's our man for the job?" asked Mycroft.

"Indeed," said Holmes, grinning. "*We* think he is the perfect man."

Because like Lamont, Matsuda would be discreet in all maneuvering and politicking—mediating the Cook Islands' annexation even as his own family imagined him researching constitutional law in London.

"Best of luck to you, sir," said Holmes, shaking Matsuda's hand when the interrogation was finished. "I am sure your mission will go smoothly."

As it happened, they would meet once more—in the winter of 1902—or, better still, in early 1903 (some two years after New Zealand's formal occupation of the islands began)—when Matsuda would seek Holmes's advice about the troubles in Niue, an island previously associated with Samoa and Tonga but seized a year following the annexation. Again, Matsuda was being sought for another influential position, although now on behalf of New Zealand and not England: "It's a most lucrative opportunity, Sherlock, I'll admit it—staying among the Cook Islands indefinitely, quelling Niue's protests and working to place the rebellious island under separate administration, while also managing the upgrading of the other islands' public facilities."

They were sitting in Holmes's Baker Street drawing room, talking over a bottle of claret.

"Yet you fear your doing so will be viewed as a betrayal of White-hall?" asked Holmes.

"Somewhat, yes."

"I shouldn't worry, my good fellow. You have fulfilled what has been asked of you, and you have done your job admirably. I suspect you are now free to apply your talents elsewhere, and why shouldn't you?"

"Do you really think so?"

"I do, I do."

And just like Lamont, Matsuda would thank Holmes, asking thereafter that their conversation stay between them. Then he'd finish his glass before departing, bowing as he stepped out the front door and into the street. He would return to the Cook Islands forthwith, traveling routinely from island to island, meeting the five head chiefs and the seven lesser ones, outlining his ideas for a future Legislative Council, then eventually extending himself to Erromango in the New Hebrides, where he was last seen journeying into its deepest region (a locale rarely visited by outsiders, an isolated, densely overgrown realm known for its large totems erected from skulls and its necklaces fashioned from human bone).

Of course, it was hardly an airtight story. If pressed by Mr. Umezaki, Holmes feared he might confuse details, names, dates, various historical specifics. Furthermore, he could give no proper explanation as to why Matsuda had abandoned his family to live on the Cook Islands. Yet as desperate for answers as Mr. Umezaki was, Holmes felt certain the story would suffice. Whatever other unknown reasons had impelled Matsuda into a new life, he figured, were of no concern to him (such reasons were, without doubt, based on personal or private considerations, ones that resided beyond his knowledge). Still, what Mr. Umezaki would learn about his father was not insignificant: Matsuda had played a pivotal role in preventing a French invasion of the Cook Islands, as well as suppressing Niue's revolt, and,

prior to his vanishing within the jungle, had sought to rally the is-
landers into someday forming their own government. "Your father,"
he would tell Mr. Umezaki, "was highly respected by the British
government, but for the elders of Rarotonga—and those on the surrounding islands old enough to remember—his name is legendary."

Finally, aided by the soft glow of a lantern burning by the futon,
Holmes gripped at his canes and rose. After donning his kimono, he
made his way across the room, taking care not to trip over his own
feet as he went. When he came to the wall panel, he remained standing before it for a while. Beyond, in Mr. Umezaki's room, he could
hear snoring. As he continued staring at the panel, he tapped the
floor lightly with a cane. Then he heard what sounded like a cough
from within, followed by slight movements (Mr. Umezaki's body
shifting, the ruffling of sheets). He listened for some time but heard
nothing else. Eventually, he found himself feeling for a handle, finding instead a hollowed groove, which helped him slide the panel
open.

The adjoining room was a duplicate of where Holmes had
slept—cast in the dim yellowish light of a lantern, a single futon
centered on the floor, the built-in desk, and, leaning against a wall,
the floor cushions used for sitting or kneeling. He approached the futon. The sheets had been kicked away and he could barely see Mr.
Umezaki sleeping half-naked on his back, motionless and now silent,
not appearing to breathe. To the left of the mattress—by the
lantern—a pair of slippers had been placed, one aligned evenly with
the other. And as Holmes lowered himself to the floor, Mr. Umezaki
suddenly awoke, speaking apprehensively in Japanese, peering at the
shadowed figure looming beside him.

"I must talk," said Holmes, setting the canes lengthwise upon
his lap.

Mr. Umezaki, still peering forward, sat up. Reaching for the
lantern, he raised it, illuminating Holmes's stern face. "Sherlock-
san? Are you all right?"

Holmes squinted in the lantern's glare. He rested a palm on Mr. Umezaki's raised hand, gently pushing the lantern downward. Then, from the shadows, he spoke: "I ask that you only listen—and when I am finished, I ask that you press me no further on the subject." Mr. Umezaki gave no reply, so Holmes continued. "Over the years, I have made it a rule never—under any circumstances—to discuss those cases that were of the strictest confidence or involved national affairs. I hope you understand—making exceptions to the rule could risk lives and jeopardize my good standing. But I realize now that I am an old man, and think it's fair to say that my standing is beyond reproach. I think it's also fair to say that the people whose confidences I have kept for decades are no longer of this world. In other words, I have outlived everything that has defined me."

"That isn't true," Mr. Umezaki remarked.

"Please, you mustn't speak. If you just say nothing, I will be forthcoming about your father. You see, I wish to explain what I know of him before I forget—and I want you to simply listen. And when I am finished and have left you here, I ask that it never be discussed with me again—because tonight, my friend, you receive the first exception to the rule of a lifetime. Now please let me attempt to put both our minds at rest, as best as I possibly can."

With that, Holmes began relating his story, doing so in a low, whispering tone, which had a vaguely dreamlike quality. Once his whispering concluded, they remained facing each other for a while, neither moving or saying a word—two indistinct forms sitting there like each other's obscure reflection, their heads hidden by shadow, the floor glowing beneath them—until Holmes stood without a sound, shuffling then toward his room, heading wearily for bed as his canes thumped along the mats.

20

SINCE HIS return to Sussex, Holmes had never dwelled much on what he had told Mr. Umezaki that night in Shimonoseki, nor had he reflected on his trip as having been hampered by the enigma of Matsuda. Instead—when locked inside the attic study, his mind suddenly carrying him there—he pictured the far-off dunes where he and Mr. Umezaki had strolled; more specifically, he saw himself heading to them again, walking the beach with Mr. Umezaki, both pausing along the way to survey the ocean or the few white clouds hanging above the horizon.

"Such beautiful weather, isn't it?"

"Oh, yes," agreed Holmes.

It was their last day visiting Shimonoseki, and while neither had slept very well (Holmes slipping in and out of sleep before going to Mr. Umezaki's bedside, Mr. Umezaki then staying awake long after Holmes had gone from him), they proceeded in good spirits, resuming the search for prickly ash. That morning, the wind had ceased altogether and a perfect spring sky presented itself. The city, too, was vivified as they departed the inn following a late breakfast: People emerged from their homes or shops and swept the ground of what the wind had scattered; at the bright vermilion shrine of Akamajingu, an elderly couple chanted sutras in the sunshine. Then moving along the seaside, they spotted beachcombers farther down the shore—a dozen or so women and old people rummaging through the flotsam, collecting shellfish or whatever useful items had drifted in with the currents (some lugging bundles of driftwood on their backs, others wearing thick strands of wet seaweed about their necks like ragged, filthy boas). Soon they had wandered beyond the beachcombers, stepping onto the slender trail that led into the dunes and then gradually widened, until becoming just the radiant, pliable terrain all around them.

The dunes' wind-rippled surface, dotted by wild grass, flecks of seashells or stones, obscured any view of the ocean. The sloping hills seemed to stretch endlessly from the coastline, ascending and falling toward a distant mountain range to the east, or toward the sky to the north. Even on such a windless day, the sand shifted as they trudged onward, swirling in their wake, dusting their cuffs with a salty powder. Behind them, the impressions of their footsteps slowly vanished, as if covered over by an invisible hand. Ahead, where the dunes met the sky, a mirage shimmered like vapors rising from the earth. Yet they could still hear the waves breaking against the shore, the beachcombers shouting to one another, the gulls crying above the sea.

To Mr. Umezaki's surprise, Holmes pointed to where they had searched on the previous evening, and to where he believed they should look now—north, near those dunes that sloped closest to the water. "You will see that the sand is damp there, creating an ideal breeding place for our shrub."

They continued without stopping—screwing up their eyes from the glare, blowing sand from their lips—their shoes occasionally swallowed by deeper pockets within the dunes; at times, Holmes struggled to maintain his balance, only to be rescued by Mr. Umezaki's steadying grip. Finally, the sand hardened underfoot, the ocean appeared several yards away, and they came to an open area comprised of wild grass, various mounds of foliage, and a single bulky piece of driftwood, likely having belonged to a fishing vessel's hull. For a while, they stood together, catching their breath, brushing sand off their trouser legs. Then Mr. Umezaki took a seat on the driftwood—dabbing himself with a handkerchief, wiping the sweat that dripped from his brow and down his face and chin—while Holmes, having stuck an unlit Jamaican between his lips, began exploring the wild grass in earnest, studying the surrounding foliage, stooping at last beside an expansive shrub set upon by flies (the pests swarming the plant, gathering in large numbers on the blooms).

"So here you are, my lovely," Holmes half-exclaimed, setting his canes aside. He gently touched the twigs, which were armed with short paired spines at the base of the leaves. He noted the male and female flowers on separate plants (inflorescent axillary clusters; flowers unisexual, greenish, minute—a tenth of an inch long, petals five-seven, white)—the male flowers with about five stamens, the female ones with four or five free carpels (each containing two ovules). He peered at the seeds, round and shiny black. "Exquisite," he said, addressing the prickly ash as if it were a confidant.

Presently, Mr. Umezaki crouched beside the shrub, dragging on a cigarette, blowing smoke at the flies and scattering them. But it wasn't the prickly ash that held his attention; rather, it was Holmes's enchantment with the plant—those nimble fingertips stroking the leaves, the mumbled words uttered like a mantra ("Odd-pinnately compound, one to two inches long—the main axis narrowly winged, prickly, leaflets three-seven pairs, plus a terminal leaflet, glossy—"), the pure contentment and wonder made evident by the old man's slight grin and beaming eyes.

And when Holmes glanced at Mr. Umezaki, he, too, observed a like expression, one he hadn't seen on his companion's face during their whole trip—a heartfelt look of ease and acceptance. "We have found what we wanted to find," he said, spotting his reflection in Mr. Umezaki's glasses.

"Yes, I believe we have."

"It is a truly simple thing, really—yet it affects me so, and I am at a loss to explain why."

"I share your feeling."

Mr. Umezaki bowed, righting himself almost immediately. Just then, it was as if he had something urgent to express, but Holmes shook his head, dissuading him. "Let us savor the remainder of this moment in silence, shall we? Our elaborations might do an injustice to such a rare opportunity—and we don't want that, do we?"

"No."

"Good," said Holmes.

After that, neither spoke for a time. Mr. Umezaki finished the cigarette and lit another watching as Holmes stared into and felt and probed the prickly ash while chewing relentlessly at the end of his Jamaican. Nearby, the waves curled in on themselves, and the beach-combers could be heard drawing closer. Still, it was their agreement of silence that, later on, formed a vivid impression within Holmes's mind (the two men there by the ocean, by the prickly ash, in the dunes, on an ideal spring day). Had he attempted imagining the inn where they'd stayed—or the streets they'd walked together, the buildings passed along the way—very little of substance would have materialized. Even so, he retained images of the sandy hills, the sea, the shrub, and the companion who had lured him to Japan. He remembered their brief speechlessness, and, as well, he remembered the strange sound wafting from the beach—faint at first, then growing louder, an attenuated voice and droning, sharply played chords—ending their mutual silence.

"It's a *shamisen* performer," said Mr. Umezaki, standing to peek over the wild grass, his chin tickled by stems.

"A performer of what?" Holmes grabbed his canes.

"A *shamisen*—it's like a lute."

With Mr. Umezaki's aid, Holmes rose alongside him, gazing past the wild grass. They spied a long, thin procession of children up the shore, moving slowly southward in the direction of the beach-combers; at its head walked a wild-haired man in a black kimono, plucking a three-stringed instrument with a large pick (the middle and index fingers of one hand pressing against the strings).

"I've known his sort before," said Mr. Umezaki after the procession had streamed by. "They're beggars who play for food or money. Most are accomplished—they actually do quite well in the bigger cities."

Like those entranced with the Pied Piper, the children trailed the man closely, listening while he sang and played for them. When the procession reached the beachcombers, it stopped, as did the singing and playing. The procession disbanded, and the children encircled the musician, finding places to sit in the sand. Joining the children, the beachcombers untied the ropes around their bundles, shrugging off their loads, and came to kneel or stand behind the youngsters. Once everyone was settled, the *shamisen* performer began—singing in a lyrical yet narrative style, his high-toned voice interspersed with chords that gave a kind of electric vibration.

Mr. Umezaki lazily tilted his head to one side, looking at the beach, and then, almost as an afterthought, said, "Should we go hear him?"

"I believe we must," replied Holmes as he stared at the gathering.

But they didn't hurry from the dunes, for Holmes had to gaze upon the shrub a final time, yanking several leaves and depositing them into a pocket (the samples eventually getting misplaced some-where en route to Kobe). Before crossing the beach, his eyes required a few lingering seconds on the prickly ash. "Haven't met the likes of you," he told the plant, "and I won't ever again, I fear—no—"

Then Holmes could depart, pushing through the wild grass with Mr. Umezaki, making his way onto the beach, where soon he sat among the beachcombers and the children, listening as the *shamisen* performer sang his stories and tugged strings (a partially blind man, he would learn, who had traveled Japan mostly by foot). Gulls dipped and glided overhead, seemingly buoyed by the music, while a ship grazed the horizon, sailing for port; all of it—the perfect sky, the engrossed audience, the stoic performer, the alien music, and the subdued ocean—Holmes could see with total clarity, fixing on that scene as the pleasant apex of his journey. What remained thereafter, however, flashed through his mind like glimpses of a dream: the procession re-forming in the late afternoon, the half-blind musician leading the entire group along the beach, guiding his followers between burning pyres of driftwood; the procession finally entering the thatched-roofed *izakaya* near the sea, greeted inside by Wakui and his wife.

Sunshine radiated the paper-covered windows; the shadows of tree branches were fuzzy and black. *Shimonoseki, last day, 1947,* Holmes had written on a napkin, which he then tucked away as a reminder of that afternoon. Like Mr. Umezaki, he was on his second beer. Sold out already, Wakui had informed them, of the special cake created with prickly ash. He'd make do anyway, cooling himself within the *izakaya.* He'd enjoy some drinks for a while, and the knowledge of what had been found. There, in the late day, as he drank with Mr. Umezaki, he saw the solitary shrub, thriving beyond the city, insect-pestered, a spiky thing, lacking beauty but still unique and useful—somehow not too different from himself, he was amused to think.

Patrons were filing into the *izakaya,* summoned by the shamisen music played at the end of the bar. The children were going home, faces sunburned, clothes sandy, waving bye to the performer and thanking him. "His name is Chikuzan Takahashi—he walks here yearly, Wakui says—and the children stick to him like flies." But the special cakes were sold out, so it was beer and soup for the wander-

ing musician, and Holmes, and Mr. Umezaki. The boats were un-
loading their haul. Fishermen were shuffling down the streets, arriving at the open doors of the establishment, breathing the inviting
aroma of alcohol, which hit them like a calming breeze. Even now
the setting sun was beckoning the evening, and Holmes felt—was it
in the second or third or fourth drink, in the finding of the prickly
ash, in the music of a spring day?—a sense of something complete,
ineffable yet replete, as in the gradual waking from a full night's
sleep.

Mr. Umezaki lowered his cigarette, leaned forward across the
table, and said as softly as he could, "If you'll allow me, I wish to
thank you."

Holmes looked at Mr. Umezaki as if he were a nuisance. "What
on earth for? It should be I thanking you. It has been a splendid experience."

"But if you'll only allow me . . . You've shed light on one
quandary of my life—perhaps I haven't received every answer I've
sought, but you've given me more than enough—and I thank you for
assisting me."

"My friend, I assure you I have no idea what you're speaking of,"
Holmes said stubbornly.

"It's important I say it, that's all. I promise not to speak of it
again."

Holmes toyed with his glass, at last saying, "Well, if you are so
grateful, you might better display it by replenishing my cup, for it
appears I'm running low."

Then Mr. Umezaki's gratefulness overtook him—in more ways
than one—and he promptly ordered another round, and soon
another, and another—smiling throughout the evening for no obvious reason, asking questions about the prickly ash as if he was suddenly interested, conveying his cheer to patrons who glanced at him
(bowing and nodding and hoisting his glass). Even intoxicated, he
was quick on his feet, helping Holmes stand up once they had fin-

ished their drinks. And the next morning, while riding the train destined for Kobe, Mr. Umezaki maintained his gregarious, mindful bearing—grinning and relaxed in his seat, apparently untroubled by the same hangover that plagued Holmes—indicating sights along the route (a temple concealed behind trees, a village where a famous feudal battle had occurred), periodically asking, "Are you feeling okay? Do you need anything? Should I open the window?"

"I am quite all right, really" was Holmes's grumbled answer; how, in those moments, he missed the hours of reserve that had previously marked their travels. Still, he was aware of return trips being always more tedious than a voyage's beginning (the initial departure, in which everything then encountered was wonderfully singular, and each subsequent destination offering a multitude of discoveries); so whenever heading back, it was better to nap as much as possible, slumbering while miles subtracted and his oblivious body raced toward home. But stirring repeatedly in his seat, cracking his eyelids and yawning into his hand, he became conscious of that overly attentive face, of that unending smile hovering nearby.

"Are you feeling okay?"

"I am quite all right."

Never before had Holmes imagined he'd welcome the sight of Maya's unforgiving expression, or that, upon arriving in Kobe, the normally affable Hensuiro might convey less enthusiasm than the overreaching Mr. Umezaki. Yet for all the annoying grins and disingenuous vigor, Holmes suspected Mr. Umezaki's intentions were, at the very least, honorable: In order to create a favorable impression during his guest's final days there, to eliminate the aura of his own erratic moods and unhappiness, he wanted himself recognized as a changed man—as someone who had benefited from Holmes's confidence, and as someone who would be forever appreciative for what he now believed was the truth.

This change, however, wouldn't transform Maya. (Had Mr. Umezaki even told his mother what he'd learned, Holmes wondered, or did she even care?) She avoided Holmes if possible, hardly acknowledging his presence, grunting her disdain as he sat down at her table. Ultimately, it made no difference whether Holmes's tale of Matsuda was shared with the woman or not, for the knowing would be no more comforting than the unknowing. Either way, she'd continue blaming him (the reality of the situation having little consequence, naturally). Moreover, the latest revelations would only suggest that Holmes had inadvertently sent Matsuda off to be cannibalized and, as a result, her surviving son lost his father (a devastating blow to the boy, which, in her mind, had deprived him of a sufficient male role model and turned him away from any woman's love other than her own). Regardless of which lie she chose—the contents of a letter sent ages ago by Matsuda, or the story told to Mr. Umezaki late one night—Holmes knew she'd despise him nonetheless; it was pointless expecting otherwise.

Even so, his last days in Kobe were pleasurable, although surely uneventful (several tiring walks around the city with Mr. Umezaki and Hensuiro, drinks after supper, early to bed). The details of what had been said or done or exchanged was beyond his memory's retrieval, and instead it was the beach and the dunes that filled the gap. And yet, having grown wary of Mr. Umezaki's attentiveness, he took from Kobe a feeling of true affection for Hensuiro—the young artist gripping at his elbow without any ulterior motives, graciously inviting Holmes into his studio room, showing his paintings (the red skies, the black landscapes, the contorted blue-gray bodies) while modestly casting his stare down to the paint-spattered floor.

"It's quite—I don't know—modern, Hensuiro."

"Thank you, *sensei,* thank you—"

Holmes studied an unfinished canvas—ravaged, bony fingers clawing desperately outward from beneath rubble, in the foreground an orange tabby cat gnawing apart its own hind paw—then he studied Hensuiro: the sensitive, almost shy brown eyes, the kind, boyish face.

"Such a gentle soul, I think, with such a harsh outlook—it is difficult reconciling the two."

"Yes—I thank you—yes—"

But among the finished pieces leaning against the walls, Holmes came to stand before a work that was different from Hensuiro's other paintings: a formal portrait of a handsome young man in his early to mid-thirties, posing against a backdrop of dark green leaves, and wearing a kimono, with *hakama* trousers, *haori* coat, *tabi* socks, and geta clogs.

"Now who is this?" asked Holmes, unsure at first if it was a self-portrait he was seeing, or perhaps even Mr. Umezaki in his younger days.

"This my bro-ther," Hensuiro said, and as best he could, he explained that his brother was dead—but not because of the war or some great tragedy. No, he indicated by moving an index finger across his wrist, his brother had killed himself. "This woman he loves—you know—like this, too." He slashed at his wrists again. "My only bro-ther—"

"A double suicide?"

"Yes, I think so."

"I see," said Holmes, bending for a closer look at the subject's oil-colored face. "It is a lovely painting. I like this one very much."

"Honto ni arigato gozaimas, sensei—thank you—"

Later, in the minutes prior to his departure from Kobe, Holmes felt an unusual desire to hug Hensuiro good-bye, except he resisted doing so, offering only a nod and the tap of a cane against the man's shin. It was Mr. Umezaki, however, who stepped forward on the train station platform, bringing his hands to Holmes's shoulders, bowing before him at the same time, saying, "It's our hope to see you again someday—perhaps in England. Perhaps we can visit you."

"Perhaps," said Holmes.

Afterward, he boarded the train, claiming a window seat. Outside, Mr. Umezaki and Hensuiro remained on the platform, looking upward at him, but Holmes—disliking sentimental departures, that often overwrought need to make the most of a parting—avoided their stares, busying himself with situating his canes, stretching out his legs. Then, as the train began pulling from the station, he glanced briefly to where the two had been standing, and frowning, he saw that they had already gone. Not until approaching Tokyo would he find those gifts that had been secreted into his coat pockets: a small glass vial containing a pair of Japanese honeybees; an envelope with Holmes's name written on it, containing haiku from Mr. Umezaki.

> *My insomnia—*
> *someone cries out while asleep,*
> *the wind answers him.*

> *Searching in the sand,*
> *twisting and turning, the dunes*
> *hide the prickly ash.*

> *A shamisen plays*
> *as dusk ushers forth shadows—*
> *trees embraced by night.*

> *The train and my friend*
> *have gone—summer beginning,*
> *springs' query fulfilled.*

While the origins of the haiku were certain, Holmes was perplexed by the vial when holding it near his face, contemplating the two dead honeybees sealed within—one mingling upon the other, their legs intertwined. Where had it come from? Tokyo's urban apiary? Somewhere along his travels with Mr. Umezaki? He couldn't say for sure (any more than he could explain most of the oddments that ended up in his pockets), nor could he envision Hensuiro collecting the bees, placing them carefully into the vial before slipping them inside his coat, where they lurked among scraps of paper and tobacco shreds, a blue seashell and grains of sand, the turquoise-colored pebble from Shukkei-en Garden, and a single prickly-ash seed. "Where did I find you? Think. . . . " No matter how he tried, he couldn't remember the vial coming into his possession. Still, he'd obviously gathered the dead bees for a reason—likely as research, maybe as a memento, or, possibly, as young Roger's present (a gift for tending the beeyard during his absence, of course).

And again, two days following Roger's funeral, Holmes saw himself read over the handwritten haiku, the page discovered under stacks of paper on his desk; fingertips at the creased edges, his body slumped forward in the chair, a Jamaican between his lips and smoke twisting toward the ceiling; saw himself set the page down sometime later, inhale the fumes, exhale through his nostrils, look at the window, look at the hazy ceiling. Saw the risen smoke float like wisps of ether. Then saw himself riding on that train, coat and canes in his lap, past diminishing countryside, past the outskirts of Tokyo, beneath bridges erected above the railroad tracks. Saw himself on a Royal Navy ship, amid enlisted men as they watched him, sitting or eating by himself, a relic from an age that had dismantled itself. Avoiding most conversation, the seafaring meals and the monotony of travel being a strain on retention. Returning to Sussex—Mrs. Munro had found him napping within the library. Going afterward to the beeyard, giving Roger the vial of honeybees. "This was meant for you. *Apis cerana japonica*—or perhaps we'll simply call them Japanese honeybees. How's that?" "Thank you, sir." He saw himself awaken in darkness, listening to his own gasps, feeling his mind had at last deserted him, but finding it still intact by daylight and cranking to life like some outmoded apparatus. And as Anderson's daugh-

ter brought him his breakfast of royal jelly spread upon fried bread
and asked him, "Has Mrs. Munro sent any word yet?" he saw himself shake his head, saying, "She has sent nothing."

But what of the Japanese honeybees? he deliberated now, reaching for his canes. Where did the boy keep them? he wondered, standing while glancing at the window—seeing the overcast, gray
morning that had proceeded from the night, stifling the dawn as he
had worked at his desk.

Where exactly has he put you? he thought when finally exiting
the farmhouse, the spare key to the cottage pressing against his
palm, enclosed in a hand wrapped about a cane's handle.

21

As storm clouds spread above the sea and his property, Holmes unlocked Mrs. Munro's living quarters, shuffling inside to where the drapes had been drawn, and the lights were kept off, and the woodsy barklike smell of mothballs obscured whatever else he inhaled. Each three or four steps, he paused, peering ahead into the darkness, and readjusted his grip on the canes, as if anticipating some vague, unimaginable form to spring out at him from the shadows. He continued forward—the taps of his canes falling less heavily, less wearily than his footsteps—until trudging past Roger's open doorway, entering the only cottage room that wasn't sealed wholly from daylight. Then, for the first and last time, he found himself among the boy's few possessions.

He took a seat at the edge of Roger's neatly made bed, looking over the general surroundings. The schoolbag hanging from the closet doorknob. The butterfly net standing in a corner. Eventually, he stood, wandering slowly about the room. The books. The *National Geographic* magazines. The rocks and seashells on the chest of drawers, the photographs and colorful drawings on the walls. The objects covering a student's writing desk: six textbooks, five sharpened pencils, drawing pens, blank paper—and the vial containing the two honeybees.

"I see," he said, lifting the vial, briefly staring at the contents (the creatures being undisturbed within, remaining as they had when he discovered them on the Tokyo-bound train). He lowered the vial to the desktop, making sure its placement was in no way changed. How methodical the boy had been, how precise—everything arranged, everything aligned; the items occupying the nightstand were also ordered: scissors, a bottle of rubber cement, a large scrapbook with an unadorned black cover.

And soon it was the scrapbook that Holmes took into his hands. Sitting again upon the bed, leisurely turning the pages, he examined the intricate collages depicting wildlife and forests, soldiers and war, ultimately bringing his gaze to the desolate image of the former prefectural government building in Hiroshima. When at last finishing with the scrapbook, the weariness he had carried since dawn seized him completely.

Outside, the diffusive sunlight grew suddenly dimmer.

Slender branches scraped against the windowpanes, almost noiselessly.

"I don't know," he uttered incomprehensibly, there on Roger's bed. "I don't know," he said again, lowering himself to the boy's pillow and shutting his eyes, the scrapbook pressed against his chest. "I haven't a clue."

He drifted away after that, though not into the sort of sleep that came from total exhaustion, or even a restless slumber in which dreams and reality were interlaced, but, rather, a torpid state submerging him into a vast stillness. Presently, that expansive, downreaching sleep delivered him elsewhere, tugging him from the bedroom where his body rested. For more than six hours, he was gone—his breathing steady and low, his limbs neither altering positions or flinching. The midday thunder cracks were inaudible to his ears, and he didn't perceive the storm blowing across his land, the tall grass bending wildly toward the ground, the stinging, hard drops of rain wetting the soil; with the storm's passing, he didn't sense the front door swinging back, sending a gust of cool rain-fresh air through the main room, along the corridor, into Roger's bedroom.

But Holmes felt the chill touch his face and neck, urging him awake like cold palms pushing gently upon his skin. "Who's there?" he mumbled when stirring. Cracking his eyelids, he stared at the nightstand (scissors, rubber cement). His gaze shifted minutely, fixing on the corridor beyond: that murky passage between the brightness of the boy's bedroom and the open front door, where, after several ascertaining seconds, he realized someone now waited in its shadows, motionless and facing him, silhouetted by the light coming from behind. The rushing air faintly ruffled clothing, flapping the hem of a dress. "Who is it?" he asked, not yet capable of sitting up. And only when the figure receded—gliding backwards, it seemed, stepping to the entryway—did she become visible. He watched while she brought a suitcase inside before closing the front door—once again steeping the cottage with darkness, vanishing as quickly as she had appeared. "Mrs. Munro—"

She materialized, gravitating toward the boy's bedroom, her head floating like a formless white sphere amid a pitch background; yet the darkness itself was not of one shade, and looked as if it were fluctuating and swaying beneath her: the fabric of her dress, Holmes suspected, the attire of mourning. Indeed, it was a black dress she wore, fringed with lace and austere in design; her skin was pallid, and bluish circles were visible under her eyes (the grief had diminished her youthfulness—her face was haggard, her movements sluggish). Stepping across the threshold, she nodded without expression when approaching him, showing none of the agony he'd heard the day Roger died or the festering anger she'd displayed at the beeyard. Instead, it was something benign he sensed about her, something yielding and likely tranquilized. You cannot blame me anymore, he thought, or my bees—you've judged us wrongly, my child, and you've realized your mistake. Her pale hands reached down to him,

gingerly extracting the scrapbook from his fingers. She avoided his
stare, but he glimpsed her wide pupils at an angle, recognizing in
them the same vacuous quality he had seen on Roger's corpse. Saying nothing, she returned the scrapbook to the nightstand, positioning it uniformly as the boy might have done.

"Why are you here?" asked Holmes after lowering his feet to the
floor, pushing himself upright on the mattress, and sitting there.
The moment he spoke, his face flushed with embarrassment, for she
had found him resting inside her quarters, embracing her dead son's
scrapbook; if anything, he knew the question should have been hers.
Even so, Mrs. Munro didn't seem terribly disturbed by his presence,
a factor that made him more uncomfortable. He glanced around,
spotting his canes propped against the nightstand. "Wasn't expecting you home this soon," he heard himself say, absently fumbling to
grasp the cane handles. "I trust your trip wasn't too taxing." Shamed
with the superficiality of his own words, his face turned redder.

Mrs. Munro now stood in front of the writing desk, keeping her
back to him (just as he sat on the bed, his back to her). She'd decided
it was better for her at the cottage, she explained, and once Holmes
heard the calm voice in which she addressed him, his uneasiness
waned. "I've plenty here that needs dealing with," she said. "I've affairs that need settling—Roger's and mine."

"You must be famished," he said, readying his canes. "I will have
the girl bring you something—or perhaps you would rather dine at
my table?"

He wondered if Anderson's daughter had already finished the
grocery shopping in town, and as he stood, Mrs. Munro answered
from behind him: "I'm not hungry."

Holmes turned toward her, meeting her sidelong glare (those reluctant, empty eyes never quite focusing on him, allocating him to
the periphery). "Is there anything you might want?" was all he could
think to ask. "Can I do anything?"

"I'll take care of myself, thank you," she said, averting her eyes completely.

Then Holmes understood her true reason for returning so soon, and—as she began considering the objects on the desk, her arms unfolding beneath her breasts—he observed the profile of a woman who was debating how best to conclude another chapter of her life. "You will be leaving me, won't you?" he said abruptly, the words escaping his mouth in midthought.

Her fingertips roamed the desktop, brushing over drawing pens, touching the blank paper, pausing for a while on the polished woodgrain surface (the spot where Roger had completed homework, fashioned his elaborate drawings for the walls, and surely pondered his magazines and books). Even in death, she saw the boy sitting there, while she cooked and cleaned and busied herself off in the main house. And Holmes, too, had conceived of Roger at the desk— slumped forward, like himself, as the day shifted into night, the night into dawn. He wanted to share the vision with Mrs. Munro, telling her what he believed they'd both imagined, but instead he remained silent, anticipating the answer that finally passed confidently between her lips: "Yes, sir—I'll be going from you."

Of course you will, thought Holmes, as if sympathetic with her decision. Yet he felt so wounded by the assuredness of her answer that he stammered like someone pleading for a second chance: "Please, you needn't make such a rash choice—really—especially at this time."

"But it wasn't rash, you see. I've spent hours thinking about it— and it's impossible seeing it differently. There's little here of value anymore—just these things and nothing else." She picked up a red drawing pen, rolling it thoughtfully with her fingers and thumb. "No, it wasn't rash."

A breeze suddenly hummed at the window above Roger's desk, scraping branches on the glass. The breeze increased momentarily, rustling the tree outside, tapping the branches harder against the panes. Dejected by Mrs. Munro's response, Holmes sighed with resignation, then asked, "And where will you go, to London? What will become of you?"

"I honestly don't know. I don't feel my life matters one way or the other."

Her son was dead. Her husband was dead. She was speaking as one who had buried those she cherished the most, and, in doing so, had placed herself within their graves. Holmes recalled a poem he'd read during his youth, that single line which had haunted his childhood: *I shall go beyond alone, so you may seek me there.* Overwhelmed by her complacent desperation, he stepped toward her, saying, "Of course it matters. To relinquish all hope is to relinquish everything—and you mustn't do that, my dear. In any case, you have an obligation to persevere, if you don't, your love for the boy won't endure."

Love: It was a word Mrs. Munro had never heard him utter. She gave him a sidelong glance, stopping him with the coldness of her stare. Then, as if to avoid the issue, she gazed again at the desktop, saying, "I've learned quite a lot about these."

Holmes saw that she was reaching for the vial of honeybees. "Have you indeed?" he remarked.

"These are Japanese—gentle and shy insects, right? Not like them ones of yours, ain't that so?" She set the vial in the palm of her hand.

"You are correct. You have done your research." He was surprised by the small amount of knowledge Mrs. Munro possessed, but he frowned when she had nothing further to say (her eyes remaining on the vial, fixed on the dead bees inside). Unable to bear the silence, he continued: "They are rather remarkable creatures—timid, as you say—although industrious in killing off a foe." He told her that the Japanese giant hornet hunted various species of bees and wasps. Once a hornet had discovered a nest, it left a secretion to mark the location; the secretion then signaled other hornets in the area to congregate and attack the colony. Japanese honeybees, however, could detect the hornet's secretion, allowing them to prepare for the imminent assault. As the hornets entered the nest, the honeybees would surround each attacker, enveloping it with their bodies and subjecting it to a temperature of forty-seven degrees Celsius (too hot for a hornet, perfect for a honeybee). "They really are fascinating, aren't they?" he concluded. "I chanced upon an apiary in Tokyo, you know—was fortunate enough to witness the creatures firsthand."

Sunlight broke through the clouds, illuminating the curtains. Just then, Holmes felt wretched for having launched into a speech at such an inappropriate moment (Mrs. Munro's son was in a grave, but all he could offer her was a lecture on Japanese honeybees). Burdened by helplessness, he shook his head at his own stupidity. And as he contemplated an apology, she placed the vial on the desktop, her voice trembling with emotion. "It's meaningless—it ain't human, the way you talk—none of it is human, just science and books—things stuck in bottles and boxes. What have you ever known about loving anyone?"

Holmes bristled at the caustic, hateful tone—the pointed, contemptuous emphasis in her hushed voice—and struggled to compose himself before replying. Then he realized his hands were clutching the canes, and that his knuckles had become white: You have no idea, he thought. Releasing an exasperated sigh, he loosened his grip on the canes and shuffled back to Roger's mattress. "I am surely not as rigid as that," he said, taking a seat at the bed's foot. "At least I don't wish to think I am—but how could I convince you otherwise? And what if I told you my passion for the bees didn't evolve from any branch of science or from the pages of books—would you find me less inhuman?"

Keeping her stare on the vial, she didn't respond, nor did she move.

"Mrs. Munro, I fear my advanced age has produced some diminishment of retention, as you are, no doubt, completely aware. I often misplace things—my cigars, my canes, sometimes my own shoes—and I find things in my pockets that mystify me; it's rather amusing and horrifying at the same instant. There are also periods when I cannot remember why I have gone from one room into another—or even fathom the sentences I have just written at my desk. Yet many other things are indelibly etched within my paradoxical mind. For example, I can recall being eighteen with the utmost clarity—very tall, lonely, an unhandsome Oxford undergraduate—spending evenings in the company of the don who lectured on mathematics and logic—a prim, fussy, disagreeable man, a resident of Christ Church like myself—someone you might know well as Lewis Carroll—but whom I knew as the Reverend C. L. Dodgson, an inventor of fantastic mathematical and word puzzles—and ciphers, to my infinite interest—his sleight-of-hand and paper-folding tricks are as vivid to me now as they were then. As well, I can see the pony I kept as a boy—and myself riding it on the Yorkshire moorland, getting gladly lost in an ocean of heather-covered waves. There are many such scenes in my head, and all are easily accessible. Why they remain and others flit away, I cannot say.

"But let me share something further about myself, for I feel it is relevant. When you look upon me, I believe you find a man incapable of feeling. I am more at fault for that perception than you are, my child. You have only known me in my declining years, sequestered out here and within my apiary. If I choose to speak at any length, I usually talk of the creatures. So I won't blame you for thinking too ill of me. In any case, until the age of forty-eight, I had scarcely a passing interest for bees and the world of the hive; however, by my forty-ninth year, I could think of nothing else. How do I explain it?" He inhaled, shutting his eyes for a second, then he continued: "You see, there was a woman under my investigation—she was younger, rather strange to me, but alluring—and I found myself preoccupied with her—it is not something I have ever fully understood. Our time together was fleeting—less than an hour, really—and she knew nothing about me—and I knew very little about her, except that she enjoyed reading books, and strolling and loitering around flowers—so I strolled with her, you see, among flowers. The details of the case are unimportant, aside from the fact that eventually she was gone from my life—and, as inexplicable as it was, I felt something essential had been lost, creating a void inside me. And yet—and yet—she began manifesting in my thoughts—existing in a lucid moment, which was as insignificant as when it had originally occurred, but which, soon thereafter, presented itself once again to me and hasn't left me." He fell silent, his eyes squinting, as if he were conjuring the past.

Mrs. Munro glanced back at him, grimacing slightly. "Why are you telling me this? What does this have to do with anything?" When she spoke, her unblemished face showed creases on her forehead, the deep-set lines being the most expressive thing about her. But Holmes wasn't looking toward her; his gaze had drifted to the floor, transfixed by something only he could envision.

It was of minor consequence, he told her—even as Mrs. Keller revealed herself to him, stretching her gloved hand outward through time. There in the Physics and Botanical Society park, she had brought her fingers to the echium and the *atropa belladonna*—the horsetail and the feverfew—and now she cupped an iris in her palm. Withdrawing her hand, she noticed that a worker bee had strayed onto her glove. But she didn't flinch, shaking the creature away, or crush it in her fist; instead, she pondered it closely, doing so with apparent reverence (a curious grin, affectionate whispers uttered beneath her breath). The worker bee, in turn, stayed upon her palm—not busying itself, or burying its stinger into her glove—as if regarding her the same.

"It is impossible to give an accurate view of such an intimate communion, the likes of which I haven't witnessed since," Holmes said, raising his head. "In all, the episode lasted perhaps ten seconds, certainly no more than that; then she saw fit to release the creature, setting it loose on the very flower from where it had come. Yet this brief and simple transaction—the woman and her hand and the creature she held without distrust—propelled me headfirst into what has become my greatest preoccupation. You see, it wasn't exacting, calculating science, my dear—it isn't as meaningless as you suggest."

Mrs. Munro kept her eyes on him: "But that's hardly true love, is it?"

"I have no understanding of love," he said miserably. "I have never made claim that I do." And regardless of who or what had ignited the fascination, he knew his solitary life's pursuit relied completely on scientific methods, that his ideas and writings weren't intended for the sentiments of the layman. Still, there was the golden throng. The gold of flowers. The gold of pollen dust. The miracle of a culture that had sustained its way of living—century after century, age after age, aeon after aeon—proving how adept its insect commonwealth was in overcoming the problems of existence. The self-reliant community of the hive, in which not a single dispirited worker relied upon human dispensation. The partnership of man and bees, relished solely by those who tended the fringes of the bees' world and safeguarded the evolution of their complex realms. The measure of peace discovered in the harmony of the insects' murmuring, soothing the mind and providing assurance against the confusion of a changing planet. The mystery and the astonishment and the deference, and accentuating that, the late-afternoon sunlight permeating the beeyard with colors of yellow and orange: all of it experienced and valued by Roger, he had no doubt. More than once, while at the apiary together, Holmes had recognized wonder on the boy's face, the sight of it consuming him with a sensation he couldn't readily express. "Some might call it a kind of love—if they so choose." His expression shifted to one of sorrow and dejection.

Mrs. Munro realized he was weeping almost imperceptibly (the tears welling in his eyes, dripping down his cheeks and into his

beard). However, the tears ended as quickly as they'd begun, and
Holmes brushed the wetness from his skin, sighing. Finally, he heard
himself say, "I wish you would reconsider—it would mean a great
deal to me if you'd stay on," but Mrs. Munro refused to speak and,
instead, glanced around at the drawings on the wall, as if he weren't
there. Holmes lowered his head again. I deserve as much, he
thought. The tears started welling—then stopped.

"Do you miss him?" she asked plainly enough, at last breaking
her silence.

"Of course I do" was his immediate answer.

Her gaze had traveled over the drawings, pausing on a sepia-
tinted photograph (Roger cradled as an infant in her arms while her
young husband stood proudly beside them). "He admired you, he
did. Did you know that?" Holmes raised his head, nodding with a
gesture of relief as she turned toward him. "It was Roger who told
me about them bees in the jar. He mentioned everything you'd told
him about them; he told me everything you said."

The hushed, caustic tone had vanished, and Mrs. Munro's sudden
need to address him directly—the softness in her melancholy voice,
her stare meeting his stare—made Holmes feel that she had somehow absolved him. Yet he could only listen and nod, looking narrowly at her.

With her anguish becoming evident, she searched his morose,
withered face. "What am I supposed to do now, sir? What am I without my boy? Why'd he have to die like that?"

But Holmes could think of nothing affirming to tell her. Yet her
eyes implored him, as if they wanted one thing: to be given something of value, something resolute and beneficial. In that moment,
he doubted if there could be any mental state more relentlessly cruel
than the desiring of real meaning from circumstances that lacked
useful or definitive answers. Moreover, he knew he couldn't fabricate
an appeasing falsehood to ease her suffering, as he'd done for Mr.
Umezaki; nor could he fill in the blanks and create a satisfactory

conclusion, like Dr. Watson had often done when writing his stories.
No, the truth itself was too clear and undeniable: Roger was dead, a
victim of misfortune.

"Why'd it have to happen, sir? I must know why—"

She spoke like so many before her had—those who had sought
him out in London, and the ones who years later had intruded on his
retirement in Sussex—requesting his help, beseeching him to allevi-
ate their troubles and restore order to their lives. If only it were that
easy, he thought. If only every problem was guaranteed a solution.

Then the perplexity that signified periods when his mind
couldn't grasp its own ruminations cast its shadow over him, but he
managed to articulate himself as best he could, solemnly saying, "It
seems—or rather—it's that sometimes—sometimes things occur beyond our own understanding, my dear, and the unjust reality is that
these events—being so illogical to us, devoid of whatever reason we
might attach to them—are exactly what they are and, regrettably,
nothing else—and I believe—I truly believe that that is the hardest
notion for any of us to live with."

Mrs. Munro stared at him for a while, as if she had no intention
of responding; then, smiling bitterly, she said, "Yes—it is." In the silence that followed, she faced the desk again—the pens, the paper,
the books, the vial—and straightened all she had previously touched.
When finished, she turned to him, saying, "Excuse me, but I'm
needing my sleep—it's been an exhausting few days."

"Would you stay with me tonight?" Holmes asked, concerned for
her and prompted by a feeling that told him she shouldn't be alone.
"Anderson's girl is doing the cooking, although you will find her
meals are far from appetizing. And I am sure there're clean sheets in
the guest room."

"I'm comfortable here, thank you," she said.

Holmes considered insisting she accompany him, but already
Mrs. Munro was gazing past him, peering into the darkened corri-

dor. Her hunched, determined body and head, her wide pupils—full
and black, ringed by faint circles of green—had now disregarded his
presence, pushing him aside. She had entered Roger's room without
speaking, so he imagined that she would exit in the same way. Yet
when she started for the door, he intercepted her, seizing her hand,
stopping her from going forward.

"My child—"

But she didn't pull herself away, nor did he attempt to inhibit her
further; he simply held her hand as she gripped his, neither saying
more or looking upon the other—his palm against her palm, their
regards communicated in the gentle mutual pressure of fingers—until, nodding once, she slipped free and proceeded on through the
doorway, soon fading down the corridor, leaving him to navigate the
darkness by himself.

After a while, he rose to his feet and, not looking back, went from
Roger's bedroom. In the corridor, his canes tapped in front of him as
if guiding a blind man (behind was the brightness of the boy's room,
ahead was the dimness of the cottage, and somewhere beyond him
was Mrs. Munro). Coming into the entryway, he fumbled for the
doorknob, clasped it, and, with some effort, opened the door. But the
outside light stunned his vision, preventing him from advancing for
a moment; and it was as he stood there, squinting his eyes, inhaling
the rain-saturated air, that the sanctuary of the beeyard—the peace-
fulness of his apiary, the tranquillity he felt while sitting among
those four rocks—beckoned him. He took a steadfast breath before
starting, still squinting when he stepped to the path. Along the way,
he paused, searching his pockets for a Jamaican, but he found only a
box of matches. That's all right, he thought, resuming his walk, his
shoes squishing in mud, the high grass on either side of the path
glistening with moisture. Nearing the beeyard, a reddish butterfly
fluttered by him. Another butterfly followed, as if in pursuit—and
another. Once the last butterfly had passed, his eyes surveyed the

beeyard, settling on the rows of hives and then the grassy spot that concealed the four rocks (everything now dampened, sodden and subdued by raindrops).

So he continued onward instead, heading for where his property met the sky, and the sheer white earth fell perpendicularly beneath the farmhouse and flower gardens and Mrs. Munro's cottage—its strata showing the evolution of time and jagging beside the meager trail that wound to the beach, while each layer indicated history's uneven progress, gradually transforming, persistent nonetheless, with fossils and tendril-like roots pressed between them.

As he began his descent upon the trail (legs coaxing him forward, the marks of his canes dotting the wet, chalky ground), he listened to the waves breaking against the shore, that distant rumble and hiss and brief silence afterward, like the initial dialect of creation before human life had been conceived. The afternoon breeze and the coursing of the ocean meshed in accord, as he observed—there beyond the shore, miles away—the sun reflected on the water and rippled among the currents. With every passing minute, the ocean grew increasingly radiant, the sun seemingly rising from its depths, the waves curling in expanding hues of orange and red.

But it all appeared so remote, so abstract and foreign to him. The more he watched the sea and sky, the more removed it felt from humanity; and this was why, he reasoned, mankind was at such odds with itself—this detachment being the inevitable by-product of a species accelerating way ahead of its own innate qualities, and that fact consumed him with an immense ruefulness he could hardly contain. Still, the waves broke, the cliffs loomed high, the breeze carried the smell of salt water, and the storm's aftermath tempered the summer's warmth. Proceeding down the trail, the desire to be a part of the original, natural order stirred inside him, the wish to escape the trappings of people and the meaningless clamor that heralded its self-importance; this need was set in him, surpassing everything he treasured or believed was true (his many writings and theories, his observations on a vast number of things). Already the heavens were wavering as the sun declined; the moon, too, occupied the sky while reflecting the sun's light, and hung there obscurely like a transparent half circle in the blue-black firmament. Briefly, he considered the sun and the moon—that hot, blinding star and that frigid, lifeless crescent—finding himself made content by how each one traveled in an orbit with its own motion, yet both were somehow essential to the other. The words sprang to his mind even as the source was forgotten: *The sun must not catch up the moon, nor does the night outstrip the day.* And at last—just as it had happened again and again for him while going along that winding trail—dusk approached.

When he reached the trail's midpoint, the sun had dipped toward the horizon, spilling its rays across the tide pools and scree below, mixing its light with deep-edged shadows. After easing himself to the overlook bench, he set his canes aside, peering downward at the shore—then the ocean, then the shifting, endless sky. A few lingering storm clouds remained in the distance, sporadically flashing within like lightning bugs, and several seagulls, which seemed to cry out at him, swam around one another, swaying deftly upon the breeze; underneath them, the waves were orangish and murky and also shimmering. Where the trail crooked, angling for the beach, he noticed clusters of new grass and riots of bramble, but they were like outcasts banished from the fertile land up above. Then he thought he heard the sound of his own breathing—a sustained low rhythm, not unlike the droning of wind—or was it something else, something emanating from nearby? Perhaps, he mused, it was the faint murmuring of the cliffs, the vibrations of those immeasurable seams of earth, of the stones and roots and soil stating its permanence over man as it had done throughout the ages; and it was addressing him now like time itself.

He closed his eyes.

His body slackened: Weariness was running through his limbs, keeping him on the bench. Don't move, he told himself, and envision the things that are durable. The wild daffodils and the herb beds. The breeze rustling in the pines, as it had since before his birth. A tingling sensation began on his neck, a vague tickling among the hairs of his beard. He lifted a hand, raising it slowly from his lap. The giant thistles snaked upward. The purple buddleias were in bloom. Today it had rained, wetting his property, soaking the ground; tomorrow the rain would return. The soil was made more fragrant after the downpour. The profusion of azaleas and laurel and rhododendrons shuddered in the pastures. And what's this? His hand captured the sensation, the tickling going from his neck into his fist. His breathing had grown shallow, but his eyes opened anyway. There, revealed in the unfurling of his fingers, it flitted about with the skittish movements of a common housefly: a lone worker bee, its pollen baskets full; a straggler far from the hives and foraging on its own. Remarkable creature, he thought, watching as it danced upon his palm. Then he shook his hand, sending it into the air—envious of its speed and how effortlessly it took flight into such a mutable, inconsistent world.

22

An Epilogue

Even after all this time, I am overcome with a heavy heart while taking up my pen to write these last paragraphs regarding the circumstances in which Mrs. Keller's life was cut short. In a disconnected and, as I now feel certain, a thoroughly unreliable manner, I have attempted to present some record of my rare connection to the woman, from the first glimpse of her face in a photograph, up to the afternoon which, at last, offered some fleeting insight into her mien. It was always my intention to have concluded there, at the Physics and Botanical Society, and to relate nothing of that event which has since fashioned a strange void in my mind—

which the gradual passing of forty-five years has yet to fully appease or displace.

However, my pen has been compelled on this dark night by my desire to report as much as possible, lest my rapidly faltering retention chooses, without my acquiescence, to soon banish her elsewhere. Fearing that inevitability, I feel I have no choice but to present the details just as they occurred. As I recall, there was a single brief account in the public press on the Friday following her departure from the Physics and Botanical Society park, appearing in an early edition of the *Evening Standard*; it seemed from its placement in the paper to have been judged an event of minor importance, and the account of it ran as follows:

> *A tragic railway accident occurred this afternoon on the tracks near St. Pancras Station, which involved a locomotive engine and culminated in the death of one woman. Engineer Ian Lomax, of the London & North Western Railway line, was surprised to see a woman with a parasol walking towards the oncoming engine at half past two. Unable to stop the locomotive before it could reach her, the engineer signalled with the engine's whistle, but the woman remained on the tracks and, making no noticeable attempt to save herself, was struck down. The force of the engine's impact shattered her body, and she was thrown a good distance from the tracks. Examination of the unfortunate woman's belongings later identified her as Ann Keller of Fortis Grove. Her hus-*

band, who is said to be inconsolable, has made no official state-
ment yet as to why she may have strayed onto the tracks, although
the police are making private enquiries in an attempt to determine
the reasons.

Such are the only facts known concerning the violent end of Mrs.
Ann Keller. Even so, while it has already stretched into too great a
length, I shall prolong this narrative by mentioning how—on the
morning after learning of her death—I donned my facade of eyeglasses and false moustache with unsettled hands, how I regained my
composure while going by foot from Baker Street to the house on
Fortis Grove, of how the front door was slowly opened for me and all
I could see beyond was Thomas R. Keller's listless visage framed by
the darkness which loomed behind him. He appeared neither dismayed nor heartened by my arrival, nor did my disguise register any
questioning look from him. I immediately detected a harsh whiff
of brandy de Jerez—La Marque Speciale, to be precise—reeking
strongly from him when he uttered flatly, "Yes, please come in." But
the little which I wished to share with the man was left unspoken
for the moment—as I then followed him silently through rooms
where the curtains remained drawn, past a staircase, and into a study
which was illuminated by a single lamp; its glow was cast over two
chairs and, between them, a side table holding two bottles of the very
spirit I had smelled upon his breath.

And here it is that I miss John more than ever. With clever details and hyperbole verging on grandeur, he could transfigure a mundane story, which is the measure of a writer's true talent, into a thing of interest. Yet when I forge my own story, I have no real ability to paint in such lavish but refined strokes. I will, however, do my utmost to draw as vivid a portrait as is possible of that pallor of grief which had descended upon my client: For even while I sat near Mr. Keller, conveying to him my deepest expressions of sympathy, he said almost nothing in reply, but kept motionless, his stubbled chin upon his breast, sunk in the gravest stupor. His vacant, inanimate stare was fixed on the floor; with one hand clutching an arm of the chair, he kept the other wrapped tightly around the neck of a brandy bottle—yet in his debilitated state he was incapable of lifting the bottle from the side table to his mouth.

Nor did Mr. Keller behave as I imagined he would; he assigned no blame for her death, and when I absolved his wife of any wrongdoing, my words sounded hollow and unimportant. What did it matter, then, if she had not been taking covert armonica lessons, or that Madame Schirmer had been unfairly judged, or that his wife had, for the most part, been honest with him? Still, I imparted the few bits of information that she had withheld, explaining about Portman's tiny garden oasis, the books borrowed from the shelves, the music lessons which played to her as she read. I mentioned the back gate which led her into the alley behind the shop. I mentioned the aimlessness of her strolling—along footpaths, down narrow avenues, beside railway tracks—and how she managed to guide herself to the Physics and

Botanical Society. All the same, there was no reason to bring up Stefan Peterson, or to point out that my client's wife had spent a late afternoon in the company of one whose pursuit of her was less than noble.

"But I don't understand it," said he, stirring in the chair and turning his miserable gaze towards me. "What made her do it, Mr. Holmes? I don't understand."

I had repeatedly asked myself the same question, yet found myself at a loss to hit upon an easy answer. I patted him kindly on the leg; then I looked into his bloodshot eyes, which, as if wounded by my stare, moved wearily again to focus on the floor.

"I cannot say with any degree of certainty. I really cannot say."

It might well have been that several explanations existed, but I had already tried test after test in my mind and nothing convincing presented itself. There was the possible explanation of the pain of losing her unborn children being too much of a burden to bear. There was the explanation that the supposed power of the armonica's tones had exerted some control over her fragile psyche, or that she was driven mad by the injustices of life, or that she had some unknown disease which caused her madness. I could find no other solutions which were as adequate, so these became the explanations which I had spent hours sifting through and balancing against one another—without a satisfactory end.

For a time, I settled on madness as the more plausible conclusion. The restless, obsessive preoccupation with the armonica suggested something psychoneurotic about her nature. The fact that she had once locked herself in an attic for hours and created music to summon her unborn only gave strength to the idea of insanity. On the other hand, this woman who read romance literature on park benches, who showed great empathy for the flowers and creatures of gardens, seemed at peace with herself and the world around her. It is not impossible, however, for the mentally disturbed to betray any number of behavioural contradictions. Yet she showed no outward signs of being deranged. Indeed, there was hardly anything about her which hinted at a woman capable of walking headlong toward an approaching train; for if that had been the case, why, then, had she displayed such an infatuation for all that lived, flourished, and thrived in the spring? Again, I could not reach a conclusion which made sense of the facts.

There remained, however, a final theory, which seemed rather likely. Plumbism was, in those days, barely an uncommon ailment, especially since lead could be found in dinnerware and utensils, candles, water pipes, the leading of windows, paint, and pewter drinking vessels. Without question, lead would also be found in the armonica's glass stemware and the paint applied to each bowl as a means to differentiate the notes. I have long suspected that chronic lead poisoning was the cause of Beethoven's illnesses, deafness, and ultimate death, for he, too, devoted hours to the mastering of the armonica's glasses. Therefore, the theory was a strong one—so strong that I had determined to prove its validity. But what soon became apparent was that Mrs. Keller carried none of the symptoms of acute or chronic plumbism; she had no staggering gait, or seizures, or colic, or decreased intellectual functioning. And while she could have acquired lead poisoning by never having touched an armonica, I understood that the general malaise she experienced early on had been eased somewhat by the instrument and not compounded by it. Furthermore, her very hands dismissed that initial suspicion; they were lacking of blemishes or the blue-black discolourment which would have been seen nearest the fingertips.

No, I had finally concluded, she was never mad or ill, nor was she despairing to the point of insanity. She had, for reasons unknown, simply extracted herself from the human equation and ceased to be; doing so, perhaps, as some contrary means of survival. And even now I wonder if creation is both too beautiful and too horrible for a handful of perceptive souls, and if the realisation of this opposing duality can offer them few options but to take leave of their own accord. Beyond that, I can give no other explanation which may strike closer to the truth of the matter. Still, it has never been a conclusion I have wanted to live comfortably with.

As it happened, I was finishing this analysis of his wife when Mr. Keller eased forwards in the chair, his hand sliding limply down the bottle's length to rest palm upwards on a corner of the side table. But for once, his grim, haggard features had softened and there was a gentle breathing which rose from his chest. Too much grief and too little sleep, I was sure. Too much brandy. So I remained for a while, indulging myself with a glass of La Marque Speciale—then another—rising to go only when the liqueur flushed my cheeks and blunted the melancholy which had saturated my entire being. Soon I would cross the rooms of the house, seeking the sunlight which was seen faintly along the edges of those pulled curtains—although not until I retrieved Mrs. Keller's photograph from an overcoat pocket and, with some reluctance to do so, placed it in the lax palm of my client's outstretched hand. After that, I made my exit without looking back, traversing the space between darkness and light as swiftly as possible, jettisoning myself into an afternoon which persists in my memory just as bright and blue and cloudless as it was on that long-ago day.

But I was not yet willing to return to Baker Street; rather, on that sunny spring afternoon, I set off towards Montague Street, savouring the experience of strolling along the thoroughfares Mrs. Keller had known so well. And all the while, I imagined what might await me when I stepped into Portman's garden. In time, I found myself there—having passed through the empty shop, along the shadowy aisles, out the back—at the garden's centre where the small bench was encircled by the boxwood hedge. I paused to admire the view, surveying the perennial beds and the roses along the perimeter wall. There was a slight breeze, and looking beyond the hedge, I observed the foxglove and geraniums and lilies swaying. Presently, I seated myself upon the bench and waited for the armonica to play. I had brought with me several of John's Bradley cigarettes, and removing one from my waistcoat,

I began to smoke while listening for the music. And it was as I stayed there, peering at the hedge, relishing the scents of the garden, which mixed not unfavourably with the tobacco, that a tangible feeling of longing and isolation began to stir within me.

The breeze increased in strength, but only for a moment. The hedge shuddered wildly; the perennials wavered this way and that. The breeze settled, and in the ensuing quiet, I realised that the music would not, while the day dimmed, play for the likes of me. How regrettable that that alluring instrument, whose strains were so possessing, so richly emblematic, would fail to arouse me as before. How could it ever be the same? She had taken her life; she had gone. And what did it matter if, eventually, everything was to be lost, vanquished, or if there existed no ultimate reason, or pattern, or logic to all which was done on the earth? For she was not there, and yet I remained. Never had I felt such incomprehensible emptiness within myself, and just then, as my body moved from the bench, did I begin to understand how utterly alone I was in the world. So with dusk's fast approach, I would take nothing away from the garden, except that impossible vacancy, that absence inside which still had the weight of another person—a gap which formed the contour of a singular, curious woman who never once beheld my true self.

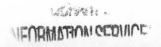

SOURCES OF ILLUSTRATIONS

The three illustrations in *A Slight Trick of the Mind* were origi-
nally printed in *New Observations on the Natural History of
Bees,* by Francis Huber (London: W. & C. Tait, and Longman,
Hurst, Rees, Orme, and Brown, 1821).

A NOTE ABOUT THE TYPE

The text of this book was set in Garamond 3, the Linotype version of Garamond from 1936, which is based on the American Type Founders design by Morris Fuller Benton and Thomas Maitland Cleland. They based their work on the types of the sixteenth-century printer, publisher, and type designer Claude Garamond, whose sixteenth-century types were modeled on those of Venetian printers from the end of the previous century.